ICE QUEEN

AN ACCIDENTAL PREGNANCY ROMANCE

LILIAN MONROE

Editing by Lawrence Editing

ISBN-13: 978-1-922457-19-6

PROLOGUE

A QUEEN DOESN'T MOURN the same way a woman does.

Wife.

Widow.

She doesn't curl up and soak her pillowcase in tears. She doesn't stare at the wall and lose long stretches of time, even when her grief is so heavy it becomes hard to think or breathe or move.

No, a queen must be a queen before anything else. She wears black and looks mournful—but not so much that the kingdom worries for her mental state. She dabs her eyes with a monogrammed handkerchief, but she doesn't wail. Her tears are restrained. Her voice doesn't tremble when she gives a speech to the kingdom, telling its citizens that the man she meant to grow old with is dead.

A queen's back remains straight, her shoulders always thrown back. Her hair is perfectly styled. She knows her clothing will be the subject of scrutiny, so it must remain flawless. She accepts condolences with grace, but doesn't share her own suffering. There's no one to share it with.

She takes her own broken, malfunctioning body—one

that refused to give her an heir—and she accepts that pain with the rest of the agony in her spirit. Gulps it down like a bitter potion, wondering if her failures somehow caused this tragedy to happen. If in some twisted version of reality, she might deserve to walk through life alone.

A queen doesn't buckle or bend or break.

She takes her suffering and buries it under a thousand miles of ice. As she stares out at the cold, snowy kingdom over which she rules, she sees the next decades of her life laid out at her feet.

She'll walk through the snow and embrace the numb coldness in her heart. She'll leave behind the wife she used to be. The mother she never was. The girl who smiled and laughed.

She'll give her kingdom what it needs.

A monarch.

A leader.

A queen.

1

PENELOPE

A BEAD of sweat starts a long journey at the nape of my neck and travels down my spine. Another adventurous droplet gets a head start from right between my boobs. They both trickle in unison down my body, and I wonder which will reach my panties first. Surprisingly, the sweat race currently taking place on my overheated skin is not the worst thing about today. At least if I focus on how uncomfortable I feel physically, I don't need to think about the emotional riot currently taking place inside my chest.

It's been nearly seven years since my husband died in a skiing accident, but going to weddings still makes my gut twist. Time, it seems, doesn't heal this wound.

Seeing other people's happiness—remembering how full of love and hope I used to be—makes me realize just how frigid I've become.

I guess the names I'm called in the kingdom's newspapers are accurate.

Ice Queen. Heartless Witch. Cold. Bitter. The Worst Thing to Happen to the Arctic Since Climate Change.

Okay, okay. I made that last one up, but I wouldn't be surprised if I saw it splashed across the front page of a tabloid.

A waiter hands me a flute of champagne. He bows his head with trembling reverence, making sure to never make eye contact. I take the glass without a word and relish the cool feeling of the glass beneath my fingertips. The waiter lifts his eyes up to stare at my face and immediately reddens and drops his head.

I know people call me a bitch. I suppose I probably am one. How else am I supposed to act? I have a kingdom to run, and pleasantries aren't high on my list of priorities.

The waiter scurries away as I sip my drink, my lipstick leaving a dusty pink mark on the rim. It tastes terrible—but maybe that's just my own discomfort at having to be here. The champagne is probably lovely and expensive. Fit for royalty.

A warm breeze ruffles my hair. My armpits are soaked. Who the heck decided an outdoor wedding is ever a good idea? And an outdoor *royal* wedding? Somewhere as warm as this?

Please.

That's just asking for soggy paparazzi photos.

Sure, the series of tents they've set up beside the rose garden at Westhill Palace are immaculately decorated. The sun is shining and a string quartet plays delicate melodies that accompany the birds in the trees. It's...gorgeous. I guess.

Farcliff Kingdom is beautiful. It's located between the United States and Canada, to the east of the Great Lakes. The summertime is warm and sunny. Picture-perfect. In the countryside, where we are, the air tastes sweet and flowers are in full bloom.

I just...prefer the cold. I like being wrapped up in a warm

jacket, staring out at a vast, white expanse of tundra. I like sitting on the edge of the Arctic, feeling alone in the wilderness with my people. I like staring into a fire, watching the flames dance and knowing my frail, human body is no match for the elements. My kingdom is called Nord, and I love every jagged coastline, every frozen lake, every explosion of life that happens during the short summer months.

Muggy heat? Happiness? Birds singing in trees and flowers bursting to life all around me while I feel altogether too *damp*?

Stifling.

My brother Silas nudges me with his elbow. "Lighten up, Pen. You're supposed to be happy for Prince Gabriel and his bride."

"It's too warm in Farcliff," I grumble.

"For your cold, dead heart?"

"Don't you have some poor woman to swindle into sleeping with you?" I arch a brow at him.

"I've never swindled anyone." Silas grins, mirth dancing in his deep blue eyes. A curl of rich, chocolate-brown hair falls over his forehead. Somehow, Silas' brow isn't damp with sweat like mine. He looks roguish and happy, not a bit bothered by the sticky heat.

I turn away from him, casting an eye over the wedding guests and all their finery. "No, you just leave a trail of heartbreak wherever you go."

"I leave a trail of something." Silas laughs, gulping down champagne as he scans the room—presumably for a woman who will serve as his next conquest.

I wrinkle my nose. "You're disgusting."

"Come on, Penelope. You haven't left Nord in months, and you haven't seen Prince Gabriel in, what, ten years?"

I nod. "Since my own wedding."

"At least try to pretend to be happy for him."

"I am happy for him. He's marrying the love of his life, which means he'll forever be exposed to having his heart wrenched out of his chest if anything goes wrong. Hooray for him."

Silas lets out a sigh, wrapping an arm around my shoulder in an awkward half-hug. "I know this is hard for you," he says quietly. "I'm proud of you for being here."

Shaking my brother off, I pinch my lips together. "It's fine. It's no harder than the dozens of state dinners I need to attend every month."

"It's a bit different." Brown eyebrows arch as he stares at me, waiting for an answer I won't give.

He's right, of course. This isn't just a state dinner. This is the wedding of an old friend—and seven years after the death of my own husband, it's the first wedding I've had the guts to attend.

Gabriel and I went to the same boarding school. I've known him since I was a child, but we've had vastly different lives. His wife-to-be, Jolie, came to work at the castle as a gardener. She and Gabriel fell desperately in love, and the whole kingdom of Farcliff has embraced their beautiful romance.

How wonderful for them.

Oh—and she's heavily pregnant, which feels like another dagger in my heart. That's one thing I never got to experience before the love of *my* life was taken away from me. Xavier and I didn't have a whirlwind romance. We didn't meet in dark rooms and steal kisses from each other. It was all arranged, approved by the people who needed to approve—but it was far from loveless. Our marriage blossomed into something that felt deep and real and everlasting.

'Til death.

Being here, on what must be the happiest day of Prince Gabriel's life, makes me feel hot and uncomfortable. I readjust the neckline of my dress, bringing my glass of champagne to my lips with a shaky hand. "Where are these mining moguls I'm supposed to scope out?" I ask my brother, scanning the room just like he is.

"Donovan Enterprise's CEO is supposed to be here. Reginald Donovan. He has two large mines in Farcliff, and there have been mentions of his desire to expand into Nord." My brother grunts, jerking his head across the tent. "There."

An old, graying man gives a big belly laugh, looking a young waitress up and down with lecherous eyes. I pinch my lips together. "He wants to mine land in Nord?"

"Hundreds of acres in the north of the kingdom, near Roston. They've found vast diamond fields. He has a bad track record with environmental breaches, and they say his company is in financial trouble." My brother's gaze shifts from the old mining tycoon to the group of ladies again, and I know I don't have much time before he leaves my side.

"Tell me again why it's a bad idea for him to expand to Nord?"

"He's notorious for having little or no regard for the environment, for one," my brother says, shifting his gaze back to Donovan. "And there are rumors he's shorted the Farcliff government out of millions of unpaid royalties. He's bad news, Pen."

"And the Nord Resources Group is in enough debt that they need the Crown to bail them out every year. We can't develop those mines as a public project without external investment." I sigh, shaking my head.

"NRG would be the first option, but the CEO says until

they've finished restructuring, they can't take on any more work. If unemployment weren't so bad in Nord, Donovan would be laughed out of the country, but things are getting dire. We might actually need to entertain his offer."

"I've seen the protests." Thousands of people in the streets, demanding employment. Telling me I've failed them as their Queen.

Silas grunts. "We need to provide jobs for people, and soon. We can't wait for NRG to get their act together."

I let out a sigh. Just another day as Queen, really. There have been dozens of prospectors trying to exploit my country's natural resources. Politics are a delicate tightrope, and I'm growing weary of walking it every day.

Maybe I should just try to enjoy Prince Gabriel's wedding and worry about Mr. Donovan tomorrow.

Weddings are tougher than politics, though. I had what Gabriel has. I had a loving spouse and a bright future. I didn't have a child, but I hoped for one. A decade ago, when I married Xavier, I thought it would be less than a year before I was a mother.

I suppose, in a way, it was a small mercy that I didn't know of my infertility on my wedding day. There was nothing to dampen my spirits that day. Nothing to make me feel the icy chill of my own barrenness.

I have polycystic ovary syndrome. PCOS. It went undiagnosed for years because I was largely asymptomatic. Sure, I had irregular periods, sometimes not menstruating for months at a time—but the doctors said it was normal. I was young. I was a healthy weight, and I didn't have excessive unwanted hair growth. I had a bit of acne, but nothing that caused huge concern. My periods would even out as I got older, the medical team assured me. It wouldn't be a problem for childbearing.

They were wrong.

Nothing became normal. Even when I was twenty-three and getting married, way past the end of puberty. Even as I tried and tried and tried to get pregnant, the doctors assured me it was still possible. My body would cooperate. I just had to keep trying.

And try I did. Every method. Fertility treatments. IVF. Every invasive, heartbreaking procedure that wore me down, month after month after month.

My body betrayed me.

No baby grew in my womb, and I became desperate. I wasn't thinking of the kingdom, of my duty, of my people. I wasn't thinking of politics, or the hundreds of tightropes that were being snipped while I was distracted.

I was only thinking of my own failures as a woman and a wife.

That's when the doctors finally diagnosed me with infertility and PCOS. Three months later, Xavier went skiing, crashed into a tree, and I lost him, too.

I'm a barren, childless, husbandless queen. I've been drifting through life on my own, wondering what I did to deserve this. Was I a naughty child and somehow brought this on myself? Is it because I didn't exercise enough? Because I snuck too much alcohol at parties in my teens? Is it because of the stress of becoming a monarch when I was ten years old? I skipped class too many times at boarding school?

What did I *do*? Why me?

Putting my champagne flute down on a table, I clasp my hands together to stop them from trembling.

Stop thinking of the past, Penelope.

What use is it dwelling on my own failures? I'm still a queen. The reigning monarch of the arctic kingdom of Nord. I successfully led my kingdom out of one recession and made sure my people were happy and safe; now I'm staring down the barrel of another economic downturn. After Xavier died, politics became my sole priority. The wealth and happiness of my people became my only duty.

I've done truly good things for the people of Nord, even though I was the youngest female monarch in the kingdom's history, and I had plenty of detractors. I've silenced most of the criticism, except the ones that call me nasty names.

Straightening my shoulders, I lift my chin.

Silas makes an approving noise. "There she is." He smirks.

"What are you talking about?"

"The Ice Queen."

Turning my head, I give my brother the iciest Ice Queen glare I can manage. Bitter satisfaction gurgles in my heart when his smile slips.

Silas throws his hands up, dipping his chin. "Fine. Be miserable. I'm going to go over there." My brother waves an arm at a group of young women on the other side of the tent. One of them glances at him, hiding her coy smile behind a hand.

I roll my eyes. "You're going to get yourself in trouble one day, Silas."

Flashing an impish grin at me, my brother pushes his silky, perfectly tousled hair off his forehead and sets off in the direction of the women.

My heart pangs, but I shut down the feeling as soon as it appears.

The only thing that's kept me sane for the past seven years has been my strength. My frigid demeanor. My ability to lock up all my feelings into a tiny metal chest and bury it at the bottom of the Arctic Sea.

Even if I pretend to hate the title, I *am* the Ice Queen, who rules over a land of snow and wind. The Queen who listens to the howling of the storm outside and lets a smile tug at the corners of her lips.

Cold loneliness is my home, and I can't wait to go back.

2

ASHER

"Donovan is already here." My assistant, Nico, looks up from the seat beside me. "Just got word."

I grunt in approval as our limousine enters the Westhill Palace gates. There are flower baskets hanging off every lamp post with flags flapping in the wind to celebrate Prince Gabriel's wedding.

I'm not here to celebrate, though. I'm here for business.

I adjust the collar of my shirt. "We need to find out what he's planning. He's been too smug lately, and I have a feeling he'll drop out of this acquisition before we can finalize it."

"He doesn't want to merge with us," Nico says.

"I know." I stare out the window, buzzing with the familiar thrill of the hunt. It seeps into my blood, making every muscle tighten inside me. My eyes narrow as we drive up to the castle and I know this is where I'm meant to be. I'll bring Donovan to his knees whether he wants it or not.

Some men chase sex. Some men appease their inner beast by finding unsuspecting women to pursue, fuck, and leave behind.

Not me.

Women are easy targets. Even with scars covering a third of my body, with burn marks crawling up my neck onto my jaw. Even with danger in my eyes, women still fall down at my feet and offer their warm orifices to me. Yawn.

No, sex doesn't thrill me.

Companies are what I hunt. Businesses with an arrow in their flank that leave a trail of blood dripping behind them in the forest. I sniff them out and deliver the final blow, carrying them back on my shoulders with a triumphant grin on my face.

My father may have hated what the fire did to my body and face when I was twelve years old. He may think I'm a grotesque beast, an ugly son, a disfigured monster—but he can't deny that I've been the person who's caused his business to expand beyond his wildest dreams. I am the hunter. I've acquired more businesses for our corporation than any other person in its history.

I made my father a billionaire—but his lips still drip with disgust when he looks at my scars.

No matter.

Reginald Donovan is my next target, and any bitterness within me will pour out into this merger. It doesn't matter what Donovan is planning, because I'll find out. I'll ruin his plans, acquire his company, and destroy his dreams.

It's what I do.

The car pulls up to the front of the palace. My blood runs hot at the thought of meeting Donovan in there. Sniffing out his weaknesses. Crushing any hope he has of wriggling out of this deal. I'll wipe that smug smirk off his ugly face.

A staff member in a crisp black uniform opens the door and leads me up the steps and through the palace entrance. On the other side, a kind, old woman looks at me, her eyes brightening. "Mr. Gerhard!" She gives me a low curtsy, and two other staff members stiffen, spinning their heads to stare at me.

My reputation precedes me—but then again, it always does. I wonder if they've heard of me as a ruthless businessman, or as the man with scars marring a third of his body?

The old lady straightens, and a vague memory filters through my hazy mind. I remember her from summers at Westhill Palace—Mrs. Grey, maybe? Her face radiates joy and warmth as she gestures for me to enter. "Welcome."

I nod in thanks, wrestling my lips into a thin smile.

Mrs. Grey sweeps her hand down the wide hallway, indicating I should follow her. There's a buzz in the air as everyone readies for the wedding. Staff scurry from one door to the other. A few of them flash furtive glances my way, then tuck their chins into their chests and duck into the nearest door.

I see eyes drop to my jaw and my neck, where the scarred skin from my accident pokes out from above my shirt. I should be used to it by now—it's been twenty years. I've had to endure the stares since I was twelve years old.

Still, I throw my shoulders back and mash my lips together. This is why I've become the ruthless businessman I am—because anything less than brute strength opens me up to their pity. I'd rather be hated than pitied. It's only skin, charred and melted and ugly. Let them stare.

I haven't seen Gabriel in twenty years. Not since the fire. We went to boarding school together as children. He was one of my good friends, but we lost touch, as kids do. After the fire, I was in and out of hospitals for years. I didn't go back to boarding school at all.

The last day I saw him, the dorms were engulfed in flames. He was running away with all the other kids, ushered across the lawn by the teachers, and I was watching them from the window of my room on the top floor.

Across the flat roof that separated the boys' dorms from the girls' dorms, there was no movement. My best friend had lived across the little strip of roof, but she'd been whisked away just the day before.

I was stranded and alone in a burning building.

Gulping, I push the memories down. That was another time. Another life.

I'm not that weak little boy anymore. I'm not vulnerable and even if I'm alone, it's by choice. I've recovered from the burns and built a name for myself. For this business of my father's.

A cushy wedding at a royal palace doesn't exactly tickle me in all the right places, but I do feel a sick sort of curiosity at seeing Gabriel and his bride.

Mrs. Grey leads me through the corridors. The carpet is soft beneath my shoes, and the whole place is bright with sunlight and twinkling chandeliers. "This way," Mrs. Grey says. "There's a cocktail hour happening in the garden." She gives me a warm smile, but I don't quite have the energy—or the desire—to return it.

My steps feel heavy as I walk, like my limbs are too long and gangly to move gracefully. I should be happy for Gabriel, but there's a piece of me missing. Empathy has never been easy for me. I'd much rather be the enemy.

Even now, I hate the stares. The quick flick of the eyes down to my neck, followed by the rearranging of features and the awkward smile. Or the people who pointedly ignore my scars and struggle to hold eye contact for far too long. *Just look*, I want to scream at them. *Stare. Grimace. I already know I'm ugly as sin.*

Mostly, I hate that it still bothers me. My scars have been

a part of my life for as long as I can remember. The burns covering a third of my body shaped me into who I am. Why do I care if someone looks at the skin on my neck with disgust?

...But I *do* care. Every time I see the wrinkling of a nose, or the pity-filled stare, anger comes over me like a red wave.

"Last time I saw you, you were eleven years old," Mrs. Grey says. I have a feeling she likes to fill comfortable silences with pointless conversation.

I grunt in response.

She lets out a happy sigh, shaking her head. "You and Gabriel were thick as thieves. So much has happened since then. Gabriel changed, but now, with Lady Jolie, I see the happy little boy inside him again."

My chest constricts. I know Gabriel went through dark times. I know he came to Westhill to be alone, and I understand the urge to do so. I, too, crave isolation.

But now, he's magically healed? The touch of a woman changed him?

Please.

I wouldn't be so foolish as to hope for the same thing. There hasn't been a woman in my life who has pierced through the thick scar tissue that shelters me from the outside world.

When we walk back outside, my hand lifts to shield my eyes from the sun. I squint, hating the feeling of being exposed out here. Mrs. Grey leads me down a flagstone path and around a low wall. To the left, a huge tent is set up with tables, chairs, waiters, and a fully stocked bar. Gauzy material twists around tent poles, gathered into rosettes every few feet. Flowers bloom over every surface, from the tent to the chairs to the tables. Uniformed staff walk around the guests with silver platters laden with bite-sized appetizers and tall crystal flutes bubbling with champagne.

Mrs. Grey leads me to the edge of the tent, curtsies, and takes her leave.

I should get a drink and try to mingle. I should find someone I recognize amongst the silk gowns and perfectly tailored tuxedos and pretend to be happy to be here. I take a step toward the bar, but my eyes are drawn across the lawn. An aroma floats along the summer breeze, faintly sweet and familiar. It reaches deep into my memories and stirs something in the cold, dark depths of my chest.

Roses.

Thousands of them in full bloom, bursting over every wall and trellis, fanning their petals out and showing their beauty to the world. Westhill is famous for them. The rose garden here is legendary, but I'd...forgotten. It's not these particular roses that call out to my childhood, though. My feet carry me to the rose garden as my heart starts to thump.

An aisle is set up in the center of the garden, with chairs lined up on either side. More gossamer covers every piece of furniture, with roses woven into garlands that line the aisle. Romantic. Beautiful. Fit for a prince and his princess.

That's where Gabriel will be married—but something else tugs at me. A memory. A whisper of the past.

It's the smell that carries me away. The sweet scent of the roses stops me in my tracks, and I remember the rooftop of the boarding school dorms. My room was the only one with a window that overlooked the flat roof connecting the boys' and girls' dorms. Across the narrow, flat strip, a single other window faced mine.

Penelope Stone's room.

The little girl with the sunshine smile and hair like spun gold.

The first time I saw her, she was climbing out of her dorm room window onto the roof, hauling a potted plant after her. I leaned on the windowsill, fascinated. Her cheeks had grown red and her hair fell out of its bun. Those wiry little arms strained with effort, but she managed to drag the miniature shrub up onto the roof, wiping her brow and letting out a sigh when she was done.

I'd pushed my window up, the scrape of the window against its frame drawing her gaze. She'd smiled at me, then, and it was like a bolt of lightning straight to my chest. She told me her name, and I told her mine. I helped her drag three more little shrubs up onto the roof, fascinated. She told me they were roses, and they'd bloom this summer, if we were lucky.

I reached out to touch one, pricking my finger and wincing.

"Careful," she said, grabbing my hand. "Roses have thorns."

I watched in fascination as she pulled a clean, white handkerchief out of her dress pocket and wrapped it around my finger. I didn't want it to end. At twelve years old, my heart had never beat so hard. I wanted her to hold my hand forever.

"Do you grow roses at home?"

Penelope shook her head. "It's too cold where I'm from." There was sadness in her eyes. "So this is my only chance."

"Where are you from?" I asked, staring at her mouth and marveling at the softness of her skin. She was so delicate. So small. So, so perfect. I thought she was an angel.

"Nord," she told me with a smile.

And we were friends.

That rooftop became our sanctuary. We'd steal moments there, staring at the stars, watching miniature rose bushes bud and bloom. We'd skip class together and run to the roof or climb over the schoolyard walls to explore the forest beyond. Gabriel was my friend, but Penelope was my everything.

As I stare at the Westhill Palace rose garden, it feels like all the blood has drained out of my heart. Like I'm so empty it hurts, but there's nothing I can do to change it.

I thought business filled that void? I thought hostile takeovers made me feel alive?

Right now, it doesn't seem so true.

Penelope left the day before the fire. Before my whole life changed. Before loneliness and scar tissue became my only companions. Reaching out, I brush my fingers over a rose petal. In the deep recesses of my mind, I remember how it felt to have Penelope's fingers brush my palm. How her skin was as silken as this rose, how sweet she smelled when she rested her golden head on my shoulder.

"Careful," a voice says behind me. Smooth and honeyed, but with a sharp edge that sounds unfamiliar. "Roses have thorns."

Startled, I jump. My hand drops, snagging on a thorn. I wince as it pierces my skin, a drop of blood beading on my fingertip.

Spinning around, I see her.

Penelope, Queen of Nord.

Older. Colder—but *here*.

My lips part as my eyes widen. I let a drop of blood drip off my finger and fall into the earth. I don't have the energy to worry about my bleeding finger, though, because all that matters is Penelope. Pen.

My first true friend. The girl I thought I loved. The girl who left.

Her hair is still blond, but it's lost some of the whiteness it had during childhood. Now, it's a true golden color, gleaming under the sun like a million gilded strands. Her lips are still soft and pink, but her eyes look different.

Haunted. Icy.

Curious.

My gaze drifts down her body, where a blue lace gown hugs every curve. She looks demure and regal and...delicious. Heat snakes through my stomach—a heat I haven't felt in a long, long time.

"Pen," I whisper, unable to say anything else.

She takes a step toward me, every movement measured. Every hair in place. Everything about her completely and utterly in control, when I feel like I'm falling apart at the sight of her. She lets her gaze drift down my body, taking in the slacks and white shirt that have become my uniform for the hunt. When her eyes climb back up to meet mine, there's a new light shining in them. She dips her head. "Hello, Asher."

3

___

PENELOPE

I haven't seen Asher Gerhard in decades.

The last time I saw him, we were lying on the rooftop of the boarding school dormitories, staring at the clouds as they passed through the sky. He made me laugh, and every time his eyes would meet mine, a blade of excitement would pierce my belly.

I thought I was in love with him. A little ten-year-old girl with stars in her eyes and a boy she thought she'd never leave.

Then the headmistress came to my room and told me my parents had died in a car accident. In an instant, I became the Queen of Nord. The youngest in history.

I left boarding school. I left Asher. Life swept me up in its current, carrying me far, far away from those happy memories.

Cold distance is my constant companion now. There's been so much tragedy and death in my life. So much grief. I hardly even feel the pain of it. I hardly feel anything anymore.

Except...now.

Asher's grown into a man. A perfect male specimen, broad chested with carved angular features. He stares at me, mouth open, letting his gaze sweep down my body and back up again. Heat follows wherever his eyes fall, my body reacting to nothing more than the way he stares. *Heat.* It's… unfamiliar. It almost hurts to feel the warmth wash over me, because I've felt so cold for so long.

Asher's tall, with big, strong shoulders. More muscular than most courtiers I've met, but with a leanness that reminds me of a warrior.

He could snap me in half, I find myself thinking, but it's not an unpleasant thought. Excitement trills through me as his deep brown eyes finally meet mine again.

"Pen," he whispers, his voice full of gravel and longing.

A tremor passes through my stomach. I *feel* the need in his voice, echoing my own. I see the loneliness in his eyes. The hunger. Has he spent the past few decades battling a hostile world? Has he been beat down by life the way I have? Does he feel like a shell of who he used to be, with his heart frozen in a block of ice?

He doesn't call me *Your Majesty*, which I like. I'm still Pen to him. I'm still the little girl who convinced him to haul rose bushes onto the roof. The girl who dragged him across the boarding school lawn to catch fireflies in the evening. The girl who got him in trouble for climbing over the school walls on a moonless night.

I want to get in trouble with him again.

I want to *feel*.

But I'm a queen now, not a little girl with mischief in her eyes. Still, when Asher looks at me with those hungry eyes, I want to be the girl I was before. My body riots under its layer of ice, and it takes every bit of self-control to keep myself together.

My feet take a step toward him, as if unable to resist the pull of his presence. I stop myself, throwing my shoulders back as I dip my chin down. "Hello, Asher."

He sucks in a breath, as if the sound of his name makes his heart skip a beat. Saying his name feels familiar and foreign all at once. Like my tongue enjoys the movement of his name as it rolls over it, but my body hasn't quite caught up to the feeling of speaking it out loud. My heart tries to thump harder, but it's been dead for so long it hurts. My ribs creak and bend under the pressure of my pulse. I gulp, trying to regain control over my body.

I'm a monarch now. The Queen of Nord. I'm not a little girl who can thread my fingers with Asher's and wonder what it would be like to press my lips against his.

Asher looks down at his finger, where a small trail of blood is still flowing. He brings the finger to his lips and I watch in fascination as his tongue swipes over its bloodied tip. Perfect male lips, wrapped around the tip of his finger. I want to kiss him. Desperately. The thought crashes into me without warning and the need to feel those lips against mine overwhelms me, as if nothing else ever existed.

My heart hammers, like it's trying to burst free of a cage I built years ago. I lift a hand to my chest, watching how Asher follows the movement. His eyes are dark brown, almost black. Whenever his gaze meets mine, I feel like I'm on the boarding school roof once more.

Blinking, I look away. His gaze is an assault. Why do his eyes make my body burn up like that? Why do I care about the little boy I left behind?

"You're a queen now," Asher says, his unreadable eyes dropping to my lips. He shouldn't be looking at me like that. *No one* should look at me like that.

He says the word queen, but what he means is *woman*. His

gaze shifts down to my shoulders, my clavicle, my breasts. Everything is sensitive beneath his gaze. Every stitch of fabric feels rough. My heart thumps as I watch him take in my waist and the fluttery fabric of my gown. He shouldn't be staring. I shouldn't allow it.

I'm not a woman. I'm not a widow. I'm not a wife.

I'm a *queen*.

Nothing more, nothing less. I gave up my life to serve my kingdom. Seven years ago, I gave up my future when my husband died. I gave up my desire for an heir. I gave up everything except my duty.

Asher has no right to make me feel anything again. He has no right to look at me like I'm anything more than a monarch. He has no right to want me, or to awaken this hungry desire.

Clearing my throat, I nod. "I've been a queen for a long time."

My feet won't cooperate. They should be walking away from him. I shouldn't allow him to remind me of all the things I've lost or left behind—but I find myself taking another step closer. As if watching someone else, I notice my hand rising and my fingers brushing his jaw.

The bumpy yet smooth skin of his scarred cheek feels warm to the touch. The edge of the burn mark crawls up the side of his cheek, covering one entire side of his neck. Asher closes his eyes for a moment, letting out a sigh as my fingertips brush the marred skin. It's so...imperfectly *perfect*. He wears his scars on his body, while I keep mine hidden away. He's brave—much braver than me. My eyes roam over every feature, feeling the edge of the smooth scar tissue where his stubble starts to prickle my finger. The boy I remember has grown to be a man I barely recognize, but somehow I feel like I've known him forever.

And this scar—that's new to me, too.

"I heard about the fire at the dorms," I say softly. "I'm sorry."

Asher's eyes open again, and he pulls his face away. My cheeks burn. I drop my hand, turning away from him. I shouldn't have touched him like that.

He clears his throat and shakes his head. "It was a long time ago."

When his eyes meet mine again, the pain inside them calls out to the agony I've pushed down. His suffering is so raw it makes me want to spill my heart open and show him, *Look, I've suffered, too.*

I've worked too hard to bury my own pain—I can't let those rich brown eyes carve new wounds in my flesh.

"Roses have always reminded me of you," Asher says in a gravelly voice.

I close my eyes, trying to ignore the thrill his words elicit. I shake my head. "I haven't seen roses in a long time."

Then, Asher surprises me. He extends an arm to me, letting his lips tug into a smile. "Walk with me," he says. "Tell me how you've been."

Every thought in my mind screams at me to turn away. I try to will myself to shake my head, to take my leave, to turn my back on this beautiful man and retreat into my castle made of ice.

But a delicious kind of warmth tugs deep in my core, and I find myself slipping my fingers into the crook of his elbow. When I fall in beside him, I inhale his scent.

Rugged. Spicy. *Male.*

It makes my head spin. For just a second, I close my eyes and let all my senses revel in the beauty that is Asher Gerhard. The strength that radiates from him. The need that pulses through me.

"I wasn't expecting to see you here," he rasps, his voice sending shivers tumbling through my veins.

"Me neither." When I glance up at him, his eyes are on me. Drinking me in. Staring at me like nothing else in the world exists, and he's perfectly happy to let it fall away.

"You look good, Pen." His lips tug.

No one has said anything like that to me in years. So casual. Easy. No *Your Majesty*, or *as you wish*, or *this dress will be appropriate in the eyes of the press.*

A casual compliment layered with complicated desires. Blinking, I glance at Asher to try to see if he feels this fire, too. Have I been so cut off, so cold, that a simple compliment makes me feel like my world is spinning?

Asher's smile widens. "You don't believe me?"

"I'm getting new wrinkles every day," I say. "I found two gray hairs last week. I don't think I look that good."

Asher laughs, as if I'm joking. He puts his palm over my hand in the crook of his arm, as if making sure that I'm actually real. His fingers are calloused, but their roughness sends another shiver tripping down my spine. As we let our feet carry us into the rose garden, I inhale the sweet scent of the flowers, mixed with the smell of him.

For a moment, I'm that happy little girl. I'm there, on the roof, showing Asher a pretty leaf I found in the school yard. I'm sharing the box of cookies I received from my parents in the mail. I'm laughing at the funny faces he's making.

I'm happy.

We walk around the perimeter of the rose garden in silence, stopping at the arch near the pulpit where Gabriel and Jolie's wedding will take place. My heart clenches at the sight of the chairs, the flowers, the flowing gauzy material.

Seeing me waver, Asher squeezes my hand. "It's hard to

pretend to be happy when the world you know is bleak, isn't it?"

Meeting his gaze, I know he understands me. He must have heard about my husband dying. He must see that I have no children. He understands my suffering like no one's understood it before, and I haven't had to say a word.

Somehow, standing here with Asher, I feel like I've found someone who knows me.

And that is dangerous. That makes politics fall away. It makes me not care about mines in Roston or rich businessmen wanting to exploit my kingdom. It makes me not care about anything except the danger in Asher's eyes and the warmth of his skin against mine.

I should walk away, but I already know I won't.

4

ASHER

PRINCE GABRIEL'S wedding is beautiful, I guess, if you're into that kind of thing. I spend most of it staring at the back of Penelope's head. The complicated twists of her blond hair capture my attention for minutes at a time. The sun catches the strands as she moves, gleaming when she gracefully bows her head and reveals the column of her neck, the pearl of every vertebrae straight all the way down her spine. Every inch of her is enchanting. I want to run my fingers up her back and sweep them over the nape of her neck. How does her hair look when she lets it down? When it cascades over her shoulders and frames her beautiful face?

She's sitting near the front—a place fit for a queen.

My seat, on the other hand, is in the back row. Childhood friend and rich businessman I may be, but I'm no noble. Just like in boarding school. My family was wealthy enough to send me there, but my father's fortune was self-made. I was always half a rung below the rest of the kids. I saw it in the way they sneered at my last name. How they made fun of me when I didn't know someone's proper title or family history. How they laughed when I said I never played polo.

Except Penelope. The little queen who treated me as her equal.

When the bride and groom walk back down the aisle, Gabriel puts his hand on Lady Jolie's stomach and looks like the happiest man alive. His daughter, Flora, slips her hand into Jolie's, and the overjoyed family walks back toward the castle together. My gaze shifts to Penelope, whose face is completely still. I'm the only one who notices the flash of pain that crosses her features, and how quickly it disappears behind a smooth mask. I can tell it's a mask she's honed to perfection over the years. One she wears often.

It doesn't take me long to walk through the crowd and stand beside her. Another cocktail hour is beginning while Gabriel and Jolie greet their guests. Gabriel comes straight over to the two of us, wrapping me in a big bear hug.

"Gerhard," he grunts, pulling away. His hands are on my shoulders, pure joy blazing in his eyes.

"Highness."

"Oh, shut up." He laughs. "You refused to call me anything but Gabe when we were kids, and I don't expect that to stop now. Here, meet my wife." His beaming bride nods to me, extending a hand. She glances at Gabriel, one hand on her stomach, unable to stop herself from smiling.

It's sickening—their love. Beside me, Penelope tenses. She paints a forced smile on her face and congratulates the couple, speaking in platitudes that sound appropriate for a queen and not an old friend.

Within seconds, Gabe is whisked away to another guest, and Pen and I are left alone. My brows climb up my forehead. "You okay?"

Gulping, Penelope nods. "Fine. Just...weddings, you know? All that...happiness." She pinches a smile and shakes her head. "Sorry. Debbie Downer."

"Never apologize. I happen to think weddings are torture, and I'm planning on leaving as soon as I can."

Penelope's shoulders soften, and she flicks those ice-blue eyes my way. A jolt of heat pierces my stomach and I lean in Penelope's ear, inhaling the sweetness of her perfume. "Let's get out of here," I whisper.

Her eyes widen. "And go where?"

"See how this palace compares to yours."

Penelope rolls her eyes, but her lips twitch into a smile.

"Come on, Pen," I whisper. "Just like old times."

A flash crosses her pale blue eyes, and warmth knots in my stomach. She rests her hand on my arm and lets me lead her around the perimeter of the tent. My heart hammers as we walk, but I gather every scrap of composure and use it to keep my breath steady and my steps measured.

Out of the corner of my eye, I see Reginald Donovan downing a glass of champagne in one gulp. Now would be the perfect time to try to pull information out of him. He's tipsy and distracted by all the beautiful women around, which means he's vulnerable.

Any other day, I'd be beside him, asking him just the right questions to find out what he's planning, and why he doesn't seem scared of the Gerhard Corporation acquiring his sorry excuse for a company. I'd be in his ear, intimidating him and letting him know that this merger *will* go ahead, whether he likes it or not. Whatever he's planning is irrelevant.

Now, though? With the Queen of Nord hanging off my arm and a new kind of warmth flowing through my body?

Donovan can wait.

Pen and I walk around the side of the castle behind the rose garden. She glances over our shoulder.

"Anyone notice us leaving?" Not that I care.

"Probably." She laughs, the sound making my heart

thump. Glancing at her, I catch the tail end of the laughter on her face. Bright, open, and so fucking beautiful it makes my chest ache. I want to make her laugh again, all the time, every day.

Intertwining my fingers with hers, I pick up the pace. She giggles, jogging alongside me before telling me to stop. I watch her lean over to slip off her heels, flashing a smile at me. Mischief gleams in her eyes, and another tug jostles my heart.

"Torture devices," she huffs. "Heels are my least favorite part of being a monarch."

"I can think of torture devices that might be more fun." The words slip out of my mouth, and I half-expect Penelope to pull away.

Instead, her eyes darken and her gaze drops to my mouth. "Asher Gerhard," she chides, sending lava pumping through my veins. "You are not the boy I remember from boarding school."

Does she have any idea what the sound of my name on her lips does to me? What it makes me want to do? When her tongue slides out to lick her bottom lip, I follow the movement with sick fascination. My pulse thickens, and I can't think of anything except how perfectly shaped Penelope's mouth is. Always has been.

Holding her shoes in one hand, Pen flashes a smile at me and threads her fingers through mine. A sizzle of heat flows through my skin where it touches hers, and I want more. More, more, more. All of her. Whatever she'll give me, then more again.

I glance around and, seeing no one, hurry toward a side door. Grinning when I find it open, we sneak inside. It's a dark, narrow hallway with bare stone walls.

"Servants' entrance," I say in a hushed whisper. Delicious

thrills thread through my body and it feels like we're doing something very, very wrong. No one would question us, of course, but being here with Penelope...it makes my ribs crush inward.

Penelope nods, her eyes shining with a light that wasn't there before. Her lips tug at the corners, and a bolt of lightning passes through my chest. I'm twelve years old again, sneaking away from the drudgery of boarding school with my best friend and partner in crime.

This is better than hunting companies. It's better than talking to men like Reggie Donovan. It's better than seeing the satisfaction in my father's eyes when I lay another wounded business at his feet, ready for official acquisition.

Being with Penelope beats all of that, because she makes my blood pump hot in my veins. I feel alive for the first time in years. Decades. For the first time since we were at boarding school together, hiding on the roof and spending hours together away from everyone else.

We tiptoe down the hallway, ducking into a deserted room when we hear voices around the corner. I close the door and lean my ear against it, listening as the voices pass. I turn the lock in the door as softly as I can, listening for the soft *snick* as I keep my ear pressed against the rough wooden panel. Staff members hurry down the hallway as Penelope giggles, staring at me with fire in her eyes.

More voices approach, and Penelope lets out another laugh. She clamps her hand over her mouth, eyes flashing.

"Shh," I say, lifting a finger but not wanting her to stop laughing at all. "They'll hear us."

The voices get louder, stopping right outside the door. We hear doors opening and the clinking of plates and cutlery. My eyes widen. "They're getting ready for the meal service. We must be near the kitchens."

"Should we go back?"

"Do you want to?"

Penelope bites her bottom lip and I have to stifle a groan. In the dim light of the room, she looks like a fallen angel. Beautiful and dangerous, like she could tear me apart with nothing more than a look. I...I kind of want her to. Her dress glitters as sunlight filters through the sheer curtains, and her face glows with wicked light.

"I feel like a kid again," she says, shaking her head. "We used to do this kind of thing all the time."

"If we go out now, all those staff members will see us. Do you want to have those rumors swirling about us?"

Pen rolls her eyes. "I'm sure at least one person saw us walk away. If we miss dinner, the rumors will be flying anyway." She glances at the door, but makes no move to leave.

She turns to look at the room, and I finally drag my eyes away from Penelope long enough to notice we're in a disused kind of common space. The staff must use this as a break room. Saggy, worn sofas line the walls, and a bookcase leans against the corner, piled high with dusty old paperbacks. A television sits on a rickety table in the corner, and a thick layer of dust covers its top panel. Penelope looks completely out of place in her elegant gown and perfectly styled hair.

In her bare feet, she steps onto the rug in the middle of the room, making a slow turn. I drink her in, committing every angle of her face and body to memory. She stares at the furniture, the walls, the small window covered in dusty blinds and sheer curtains. Then, she lifts her eyes to me.

On the other side of the door, someone turns on a stereo. Music starts blaring and the kitchen staff let out a holler.

Penelope grins. "At least the staff is having fun."

"You're not?"

"I'm having a lot more fun than I thought I would." She

extends her hand toward me, and I find myself walking to meet her in the center of the room. She places her hand on my shoulder, taking my arm and hooking it around her waist. "Dance with me."

"This isn't exactly slow dance music."

"Shh, Asher. Just be quiet and let me feel like a woman instead of a monarch, for once. No one's watching me here."

My heart thumps. Can she feel it hammering against my ribs? I hook my arm around her waist, letting my other hand slide down her arm. I curl my fingers around Penelope's waist and pull her close.

She fits perfectly. Her body melts into mine as if she was made to be there. She leans her head against my chest, right above where the worst of my scarred skin covers my body. Thank goodness I'm wearing a shirt. I stiffen for a moment, then close my eyes and rest my cheek against her head.

No one has seen my body in years. The last time I let a woman see my bare skin, the disgust was written all over her face, her desire for me evaporating in an instant.

I don't want Penelope to look at me like that. Not now. Not ever. I don't want her to see the monster under these fine clothes. I hold her close, feeling her breath wash over my neck, trying to push the thoughts away. As much as I love having her in my arms like this, I know it would never last. She'd take one look at my ugly skin and the light would leave her eyes. I'm not sure I can handle seeing that.

Even after all these years. After all my bravado and all my toughness, the thought of Penelope looking at me with disgust in her sky-blue eyes makes my stomach turn.

Penelope removes her hand from mine, hooking both arms around my neck. Staring into my eyes, the Queen of Nord looks like the Penelope I knew in school, grown into the most beautiful woman I could ever imagine. If I took all the best bits from every person I'd ever come across and put them in one body, she'd be standing right here with danger dancing in her eyes, swaying softly in the disused common room of a foreign castle.

There's a connection between us. An unsaid understanding. An intimacy I've never felt before. She *knows* me. Knew me when I was a kid, and somehow knows me even better now. The skin on my jaw still tingles where she touched the edge of my scar—where most people are afraid to even *look*.

My hands hook around her waist, and I trace the lacy patterns of her dress plastered over her lower back. Penelope's eyelashes flutter closed at the touch, her lips falling open as her face softens.

Has anyone seen her like this, I wonder? Has she let herself relax with another man?

I tighten my hold on her waist, already knowing the answer. She hasn't. In this dimly lit break room, with nothing but dusty, stained sofas and worn-out books, I know she's showing me something special.

And, hell, I'm showing her the same. I'm not the ruthless businessman. I'm not the grotesque burned man who makes people avert their eyes.

Here, I'm just a man, and she's just a woman.

"Penelope," I groan.

She presses herself against me, letting out a soft sigh. "I love the way you say my name," she whispers.

"How do I say it?"

Pen opens her ice-blue eyes, glancing up at me. "Like you know me."

We sway in the middle of the room as my body heats up. Blood flows between my legs, and I know she can feel my arousal. She presses herself harder against me, her breasts crushing against my chest. I let my hands drift lower, resting on top of her ass as Penelope grinds her hips toward me.

We're crossing a line. Stepping over it with eyes wide-open, knowing we shouldn't go anywhere near it.

But do I care?

Staring into Penelope's eyes, I let out a sigh. "Maybe we should go back."

Pen shakes her head, her brows drawing together. "I don't want to."

"What do you want?"

A sharp intake of breath. A bite of her lower lip. A slow blink. Then, "You."

5

———

PENELOPE

I HAVEN'T HAD sex in seven years, and I can honestly say it's never bothered me…

…until now.

Desire was something I buried in the cold, dark earth beside my husband. My femaleness was something I locked away and forgot existed. I gave myself—mind, body, soul—to my kingdom.

But Asher, oh, Asher. Hitting me like a sledgehammer, my desire is overwhelming. Everything I touch is hard, muscular man. My hands sweep over Asher's shoulders, feeling where his muscles round and taper into solid biceps. His arms hold me close, the hard planes of his chest crushing against my softness.

I want him. Desperately. Ferally. Like I've never wanted anyone before.

I want to *feel*. For the first time in years, I want to feel the sweep of a palm over my thigh. I want something thick and hard buried between my legs. I want him to tangle his fingers in my hair and tug, whispering dirty nothings in my ear.

I'm not Penelope, Queen of Nord—I'm nothing but a woman in a man's arms.

Asher's eyes darken, his eyelids hanging low. "Are you sure this is a good idea, Pen?"

"No, but does it matter?"

He exhales, leaning his forehead against mine. His hands cup my ass, pulling me close. His hardness presses against my stomach, and desire whips through me like a hot blaze. My cheeks are burning. My hands claw hungrily at his arms, his shoulders, wrapping around his neck.

I don't want to beg him to make love to me, but I will if I need to. That's how deep my desperation goes. How violent my thirst is. I need his touch. His kiss. I need him to give me just a taste of pleasure, when my life has been a barren, loveless void for so long I don't remember anything else.

Would it be so wrong to give in, just this once? Would I regret it if I let him take my body, if nothing else? It doesn't have to mean anything.

Asher doesn't make me beg. With one hand on my ass, his other hand sweeps up my spine and curls around the nape of my neck. He pulls me back, devouring me with his eyes. Yearning stares back at me, as fierce as my own.

I'm bare before him. My soul is cracked open, and I want to show him everything I've been holding inside. I want to offer it to him on a plate and let him heal me, hold me, love me. Heat curls low in my stomach as my desire mounts. Every stitch of fabric is sensitive. My breasts feel heavy against his chest, aching for his touch. His mouth.

Then, Asher lets out a sigh, leans in, and kisses me. There's no preamble. No question. No need for me to beg at all. He sees what I want—what I *need*—and gives it to me without another word. His lips are soft yet demanding, and I yield—to him, to his kiss, to my own fervent need. His kiss tastes like danger, taking my own lips between his and sweeping his tongue into my mouth. I moan against him, loving the way his hands hold me tight.

Unlike any kiss I've ever had, Asher's lips transport me to another place. Another world. One where I can let desire rip through my veins like molten metal, and let him lay claim to my body, my lips, my heart. *Claim*. That's what his kiss does. It claims me, demanding, uncompromising. It teases my lips open and shows me what I've missed. It makes me *feel*.

The fire in my stomach spreads lower as I roll my hips against him. My heart pounds against my ribs as I kiss him harder. *More*. I need more. I let my hands drift over his shoulders, his chest, curling into the fabric of his shirt. I wish he weren't wearing it. I sweep my hand up his neck and grip the back of his head, pulling him for a deeper kiss.

It's hungry. So utterly inappropriate it makes my whole body ignite. My underwear clings to my body, already damp with my arousal. Every time I feel Asher's cock pressed hard against me, another wave of heat crashes against my thighs.

Asher, feeling my need, lets out a low growl. Oh, what that noise does to me, it's indecent. So completely at odds with my life as a cold, heartless queen. Asher's growl is pure fire. Pure heat and desire and lust, rumbling through his chest and into mine. He drops his hands to my thighs and claws at the fabric of my dress, bringing it up above my hips. When his palms touch my bare skin, I let out a whimper.

When was the last time someone touched me—really touched me? When was the last time I felt a palm sweeping over my ass, gripping it tight, pulling me close?

His touch feels like magic. My skin sparks against his palm, core clenching, and I forget who I am. I forget where I am, and what I'm supposed to be doing. Queen who? All that matters is me, and Asher, and the locked door that ensures we're alone.

"You're perfect, Pen," Asher growls, using both hands to grip my ass and spread it apart. I gasp. The cool air on my skin only heightens the heat coursing through my veins.

I'm dizzy. Breathless. My lips find his, kissing him hungrily.

I need this so badly and I didn't even know it was missing. I need him to fuck me. To treat me like a woman. To take me and show me what it means to be alive.

Need.

I don't say that lightly. I feel like I'll die if I don't taste his kiss. If I don't feel his cock.

Asher drops his lips to my neck, leaving a trail of kisses down to my shoulder. His hand rests on top of my breast, teasing the neckline of my dress. I want to give him everything. Bare myself for him and show him I'm real. I'm a woman. I need this. Him.

Asher growls again, wordlessly this time. I feel his teeth gently biting against my neck, and I let my head fall back. I feel like I'm floating in space, my only anchor being Asher's body. His arms around my waist. His strong legs propped up against mine.

"I want you." My voice is a rasp I barely recognize. I pull away from Asher, staring at his eyes. "I want you, Asher."

Dark eyes stare back at me, desire etched into every feature. He nods, sliding his hands down to my thighs and picking me up. I wrap my legs around his hips and let him carry me to one of the sofas, where he lays me down across the cushions more gently than I expected from a man who looks as fierce as he does. His hand sweeps up my dress and finds my ruined underwear, tugging it off in one motion.

Asher leans over me, kissing me hard. This kiss is bruising, and my back arches. Yes, I want this. I want it hard and fast and dirty and *now*. Desperately. I want him to devour me. Show me what it feels like to be his. His hand sweeps up my thigh and slides between my legs, and he lets out a low groan when he feels the wetness there. His fingers feel warm and thick as they drag through my arousal. When he brushes against my clit, desire pierces the pit of my stomach.

Seven years of buried needs. Seven years of buried emotion. Seven years of loneliness, all coming to a head in this moment.

Ice that had grown thick and permanent within me starts to melt and crack. Heat flows through my veins for the first time in years.

Asher groans, dropping his lips to my jaw, my earlobe, my neck. His fingers slide inside me as we both moan, my hips rolling to get more, more, more. I close my eyes, unable to think of anything except the fire burning in my veins. He's doing something with his thumb on my clit and the pressure is just right, so good, oh—

I come apart, arching my back as I cling onto his shoulders. My orgasm rips through me, making my legs tremble and my back arch. I cry out, but Asher clamps a hand over my lips.

"Quiet," he says, lids hanging low. "They're just outside. They'll hear."

Do I care? Not really, but the heat in Asher's eyes makes me want more. His hand over my mouth winds my desire even tighter.

I shouldn't like this. I shouldn't enjoy being fingered on an old sofa in the servants' quarters of a foreign castle. I shouldn't be sleeping with a man I knew two decades ago, with only a thin door separating me from scandal, but the naughtiness of it all only makes me hotter.

"I don't have a condom," Asher says, regret in his eyes. His breath comes in short gasps and when I reach down between his legs, I feel the throbbing hardness of his erection.

"It's okay." I shake my head.

"You're on the pill?"

"Yeah," I answer, even though it's not true. I just don't have the time or energy to explain that I'm infertile. The only thing on my mind is Asher. His body on top of mine. His cock buried between my legs.

"I'm clean," he says. "I swear."

I nod. "Me too."

We're both gasping for air, choked by our desires. I try to reach for the buttons of his shirt, but Asher grunts. His eyes darken, and he grabs my wrists.

"No," he says.

He doesn't want me to take his shirt off?

Sweeping a hand under my back, he lifts me up and turns me around, planting my feet in front of the sofa and pushing me down so I catch myself on the back of it. He kicks my feet wider, clawing at my dress to push it up over my hips.

I shouldn't like this—being exposed with my ass in the air —but if I'm honest, it's turning me on like never before. Xavier was never like this. Never commanding. Demanding. Dirty. He made love to me, but after a while I was so focused on conceiving that sex with him felt more like a chore or a medical procedure than it did something we were doing for pleasure.

This—this is different. Asher wants to fuck, and so do I.

I hear his zipper, then feel his hand on top of my ass. He lets his fingers drift down between my cheeks, just brushing my asshole and sending a delicious, dirty shiver coursing through my veins.

I'm not a queen. Not right now. Not for the next few

minutes. Right now, I'm a woman, and I intend to enjoy every second of it.

His fingers find my opening, sliding inside as he groans.

"Are you always this wet, Pen?" Asher lets out another growl, and the noise makes me push back against his fingers. I want more. Deeper. All of him.

"No," I answer. "Just with you."

Squeezing my eyes shut, I try to catch my breath. It's hard to think straight. Hard to make sense of anything except my overwhelming hunger.

My fingers curl into the back of the old sofa, my knees pressed up against the seat. Asher's legs push against my own, one hand on my lower back to hold me still. Bent over with my dress pushed up to my waist, I know I look nothing like a monarch. I don't want to look like a queen right now. I want this exactly the way it is.

When I feel Asher's cock slide against my slit, I let out a sigh. When he puts his hands on my hips and pulls me back, angling me just the way he wants me, a dirty, delicious shiver slides down my spine. And finally, when I feel his crown against my opening, I know I'm about to get exactly what I asked for.

He pushes inside me, and I gasp. Long, thick, and hard. I haven't had anything like this in years. It stretches me, invading my body. I'm so tight against him, resisting the intrusion. I hear him grunt, pausing, giving me a second to get used to him.

I pant, clinging onto the sofa as heat unfurls in my core.

"Okay, Pen?" Asher's voice is a low growl.

I nod, unable to speak. His hands mark the skin on my hips, fingers digging into my flesh.

Then, he thrusts all the way in.

I see stars. Gasping, grunting, I brace myself against the

back of the sofa. His hands grip onto my waist as he thrusts deeper and harder inside me, making me moan with every movement.

"Shh," he says, hooking an arm around my chest. He pulls me up, covering my mouth with his other hand. I let him own me. Positioning me just as he wants me and giving myself over to the wicked fire claiming my body. He thrusts mercilessly, and I'm completely powerless in his arms. I let myself fall into the pleasure of it all, loving the way he possesses my body. He puts a foot on the seat of the sofa, angling to go deeper. I lean against him, eyes closed, mouth covered, like a dirty, dirty girl.

I'd fall over if he wasn't holding me up. With one hand still covering my lips, Asher's other hand slides up my stomach and cups my breast. His thumb teases my peaked nipple and I moan against his hand, feeling fire erupt inside me. Molten heat flows through my veins as he slides his hand under the bodice of my dress, kneading my breast and teasing my pebbled nipple as he thrusts hard and deep inside me.

My back arches, everything tenses, and I come.

This orgasm is deeper than the first. Where we're joined, heat and pressure release as I tremble against him, completely supported by his arms and body. I let myself go. Right now, no one is relying on me. There are no hard decisions to make, no political tightropes to walk, no appearances to keep up.

I'm just a woman, coming apart in a man's arms. I let my orgasm rip through my body, releasing everything I've held inside. I clench around Asher's cock, loving the way he fills me up so completely, so perfectly, that it feels like we were meant for each other. Wave after wave of pleasure wash over me as Asher's moans grow louder. He likes feeling my orgasm. He wants me to feel good.

Then I feel it. His body tensing. His balls tightening. The thick, hot spurts of his orgasm lashing against me, filling me up with his seed. He grunts, the sound so deliciously male that it sends another wave of heat coursing through me.

I haven't had this in years. Nearly a decade. Too long to remember what I've been missing. We fall onto the sofa, tangled in each other and still joined. His lips are near my neck, his breath coming in hard gasps.

"Fuck, Pen," he says.

"I know," I reply. I know that was special. It went deeper than just sex. It was a release of something more than just my body. It felt like I found someone who understood exactly what I needed and how I needed it, and he didn't hesitate to give it to me.

I pull away from Asher, smoothing my dress down and slouching on the sofa. His hand lands on my thigh and he glances at me, a lazy smile gracing his lips. In the low light of the room, with bliss painted on his face, he looks so handsome I'm afraid of what his smile will do to me. How quickly it'll infiltrate my heart.

"I wasn't expecting that to happen today," he says, lifting his finger up to brush my cheek. He tucks a strand of hair behind my ear, every touch delicate. Soft.

I chuckle, leaning into his hand. "Me neither. I haven't..." I trail off, not wanting to speak those words out loud. I don't want to think of the pain of my losses, or how it felt to forget them, even just for a moment. I don't want to go back to the woman I was a few minutes ago. If only I can enjoy these moments, float in this feeling for just a few heartbeats longer.

After a pause, Asher glances at me. His broad features are

relaxed, with none of the guarded desire from before. His lip tugs. "What's Nord like?"

"You've never been?"

He shakes his head.

I let out a happy sigh, shaking my head. "It's incredible. Cold, of course, but this time of year—summertime—it's magical."

"If I wasn't so busy in Farcliff, I'd come visit."

"You should," I say.

"I wish I could." He smiles sadly.

I return the smile, but there's a distance between us. He's already giving me an excuse as to why he can't come. Telling me he's busy. Letting me know where we stand. This was a one-time thing, and I hear him loud and clear. A spear pierces my heart, and I feel so stupid and so oddly ashamed of what just happened—of how completely I let myself go.

But Asher leans over, brushing his lips against my earlobe. The touch is soft. Intimate. It sends warmth flowing down my body and scatters my thoughts in an instant. His hand moves to my thigh, where it makes soft, gentle movements along my inner leg. I resist the urge to spread them for him.

"What's it like being Queen?"

I huff out a laugh. "Tireless. Nord is facing a lot of unemployment right now, and we've had to close down a lot of heavy industry. Sometimes it feels like there are no good decisions. Whatever I do, someone suffers. Even now, at this wedding, I was expecting to be talking to an old mining executive about his proposal to mine in Nord, even though the company is less than reputable. Just another day as the head of state." I laugh, but it dies down when Asher stiffens.

It only lasts a second. Just a small flash across his eyes, a tiny pause in the movement of his hand, then the hesitation is gone. He leans over and kisses me again, then stands up to readjust his clothing.

When he glances at me and winks, the strange moment has passed, but I can't let the uneasiness go. Watching as he buttons his pants, I feel as though I've said something I shouldn't have.

I know Asher works for a company that deals mainly in resources and mining. Isn't that how his father made his fortune? I shouldn't have said anything about Nord's business.

This is what happens when I let myself be a woman instead of a queen. I make mistakes. I say things I shouldn't. I expose myself and my kingdom to people I barely know—because at the end of the day, I barely know Asher. We haven't seen each other in twenty years. He made it clear that he doesn't want to see me again. I shouldn't be talking about Nord's affairs.

As I stand up, my heart thuds uncomfortably. I try to straighten my dress and walk over to the television in the corner to use it as a makeshift mirror to fix my hair. There's a layer of ice covering my skin, and my face has returned to the still, unmoving mask I usually wear. Neither of us says anything, and I know the moment is over.

And it should be.

I'm not Pen. I'm not Asher's friend from boarding school.

I'm the Queen of Nord, and if I ever forget it, I know I'll have to pay for my mistakes. Glancing at the man behind me, I feel like I've just made the biggest mistake of all.

I DIDN'T SLEEP with Penelope to get information out of her. I slept with her because...I don't know why. Because she called out to something primal in me. Because I just couldn't resist the draw I felt to her. Because for once in my life, I felt *whole* with her in my arms.

In no universe did I think she would tell me about mining moguls sniffing around Nord. Inadvertently, she told me exactly the information I came to this wedding to get, and I didn't have to get near Donovan's sniveling face to get it. She's just made my job much, much easier.

But if I act on that information, will she think I was sleeping with her to get her to spill state secrets? Will she feel used?

Normally, I wouldn't care. I'd store that little piece of gold in the *things I'll definitely use later* box. You don't successfully hunt companies by being a nice, stand-up guy.

But this isn't some random victim of my schemes. This is Penelope. The Queen of Nord. The girl across the roof, who made my days at boarding school happy, who hauled mini rose bushes up to her windowsill because she couldn't get them back home. The girl who treated me like a real person, and not like a peasant who was beneath her. Can I really use information she let slip after we...well, after we did what we just did?

Penelope runs her hand over her dress, removing an invisible piece of lint off her skirt. Her hair already back in place. Golden strands twist into a knot at the nape of her neck as she smooths her palms over her head to catch the last little flyaways that halo around her head. Her face is stoic, serious, and completely different from the picture of bliss it was a few minutes ago.

When was the last time I saw a woman come apart like that in my arms? A woman who wanted to tear my shirt off, who wasn't afraid to let her hands drift over my scars? A woman who looked at me with hunger in her eyes, without wanting anything from me but pleasure?

I...I can't remember. Sex is usually transactional for me. Not with money, but...needs, just trading orgasms with someone who will disappear from my life as soon as the act is over. It's no deeper than the physical act.

This felt different. Still, when Penelope straights up and faces me, looking every bit a queen, I can't help but feel that something has changed between us, and not in a good way. There's distance between us. A coldness that wasn't there before. Was this casual to her? Did she not feel the connection I thought was there?

She nods. "It's been a pleasure, Asher. We should probably get back."

"Of course." Unable to resist, I let my hand drift to her lower back as I lead her to the exit. She squares her shoulders, dipping her chin as I open the door up for her. Dishes clatter on the other side as a servant yelps, seeing the Queen of Nord emerge from a staff common room.

Penelope ignores them, moving down the hallway like she owns it. Nothing about her says we've just had sex. Nothing about the way she walks, the way she holds her head, the way her clothing still somehow looks perfectly put together.

It's like it never happened.

Grinding my teeth as I ignore the uncomfortable tension in the center of my chest, I follow her down the hallway. Am I upset that she doesn't look as frazzled as I feel? Embarrassment winds its way through my core, squeezing my heart. I shouldn't care about Penelope. I shouldn't care about anyone! Why would I be upset that she's acting like nothing happened? Like what we just shared meant nothing? Of course it meant nothing—it was a quick, dirty fuck at someone's wedding. Two lonely people scratching an itch.

I should be thanking her and going on my merry way. I'm here to get information, and I got it. I know she was talking about Donovan, and now I know he's planning to expand in Nord. He has no chance of slithering out of this merger. I should be happy. The day was a success.

But my mouth tastes like ash.

When we get back to the reception, speeches are happening. I see Gabriel, lost in his own world, with his arms around his bride.

Good for him. Bitterness tugs my lips down as I stare at the joy in my old friend's eyes. I cast an eye over the assembled people in all their finery, feeling every bit the outsider that I am. I don't belong here. I don't belong in the arms of someone like Penelope.

Imagine if she saw me without a shirt! If she saw me the way I am, there's no chance would she let me touch her the way she did today. She'd recoil, just like everyone else does. Just like she's doing right now. Penelope throws me an indecipherable glance, then slips away through the crowd. Walks away like nothing happened.

I take a deep breath, jumping when I hear my assistant's voice beside me. "Any progress? Donovan's been drinking. If there was a time to start extracting some information from him, it would be now." Nico scans the crowd as I stare at Penelope. The last thing I want to do is talk to Reggie Donovan. My assistant runs his palm over his dark blond hair, squinting against the sun. He pushes his wire-rimmed glasses up and swings his gaze to me, questioning.

Nico's been my second-in-command for years. He's as ruthless as I am. Ambitious, hard-working, and deserving of success. He marched into my office five years ago, slapped a résumé on my desk, and told me I'd be a fool not to hire him. The hunger in his gaze convinced me to give him a chance, and it was one of the few decisions I've made that I'm proud of. The man is a workhorse and better at coddling difficult egos than I am. He's cleaned up more than a few messes I've made, but I'm not sure even he'd be able to clean up this one.

"Nord," I answer.

Nico frowns, arching a brow.

"He's trying to expand into Nord. Not sure what kind of resources he's planning on mining, but it shouldn't be too hard to find out."

Nico's lips pinch as he nods, a glimmer of admiration in his eyes. "Well done, sir."

"Don't sound so surprised."

"You always get the information you need," he replies, throwing a glance toward Donovan. His eyes narrow, and I know I'll have a report on my desk by the morning confirming Donovan's plans to expand into Nord.

The mining tycoon is drunk, half falling over as he throws his arm around a poor, scared-looking waitress. I have no desire to talk to him right now. Even if I did, he probably wouldn't even remember it. Plus, I got what I needed. I can get back to work now.

Ice chips freeze in my veins as I glance at the Queen, feeling oddly queasy about using that information. She has no idea I came to this wedding to squeeze Reginald Donovan. She has no idea that she handed me a secret on a platter and saved me hours of negotiation and investigation work.

But she did it after...after we...

Pinching the bridge of my nose, I suck in a breath to try to regain control over my rioting emotions. Why do I even care what Penelope thinks? We're not together. I haven't seen the woman in twenty years. We're not children anymore, and she knows who I am. Who I work for. If she didn't want me to act on that information, she shouldn't have said anything.

I hunt companies, and right now, I'm hunting Donovan Enterprises. Whatever happened in that break room, it's over now, and it doesn't change the fact that I have a job to do. "Let's go," I grunt, jerking my head toward the exit.

Nico frowns but doesn't complain. A prickling on the back of my neck draws my gaze across the tent. Penelope's bright blue gaze makes my whole body turn rigid. I freeze, caught up in her eyes. There are a hundred people between us, with cheering and clapping and speeches, but the whole world exists in her stare. She looks almost yearning. Like she'd want to be here, beside me.

And I—well, I'd like that.

Then the Queen blinks, and her face is shuttered again. She turns her head toward the speaker, and I follow Nico out of the tent. Pushing down the discomfort raging within my chest, I ignore the smell of roses and the laughter at my back.

I don't belong at this wedding. I don't belong with these people. Penelope took me to a dirty back room and we did what we wanted in a few quick, filthy minutes. It doesn't mean I'm worthy of standing beside her.

I found out about Donovan's plans in Nord from Penelope, but that's her problem. Not mine. Donovan is on his last legs, limping away from a hostile merger that my family's company is initiating. If we find out what he's doing in Nord and stop it—or take it for ourselves—he'll have no choice but to sign on the dotted line.

If Pen didn't want me to find that out, she shouldn't have said anything.

But, but, but...

I walk away from the tent. Away from Penelope. Away from her eyes of crushed ice and the fire she ignited in my core.

MY FATHER IS a man in his early sixties. His hair used to be dark, almost black, with only two patches of white hair around his temples. Now, though, he's starting to show his age. New lines have appeared on his skin and his hair is almost completely gray. His face is clean-shaven, and his eyes are dark like mine.

We would have looked similar, if not for the fire. I curl my hand into a fist to stop myself from running my fingers over the border of the scar on my cheek.

Father sits behind his desk like a king on a throne, hands resting on the arms of his chair. "So," he starts. "What have you discovered about Donovan?"

I hesitate. The wedding was two days ago, but I still can't shake the feeling that saying something about Nord would be a betrayal. In the past two days, Nico confirmed that Reggie is hoping to expand into Nord, and even planning a trip up there in the coming weeks. I still don't know what mines he wants to develop, or how good his information is about the resources up there. It could all be bullshit, but something tells me it's not.

But I haven't acted on the information. I haven't delivered the killing blow. I can still see Penelope's eyes, staring at me across the tent. I can feel the way her gaze made my body heat up. The way she made me feel when her arms were wrapped around my neck. How her lips drifted over the scarred skin on my cheek almost reverently.

She didn't recoil from me. She came apart in my arms like I was sent to that wedding for the sole purpose of making her feel alive.

But my father doesn't know that. No one knows what happened in that room. I gulp, staring at the man who's made me feel small since I was a child.

His eyes drift down to my cheek, to the pink skin that's shinier and paler than my normal complexion. If I weren't looking for it, I'd miss the twitch of disgust in his lip. I wouldn't notice the flash in his eyes, or the way he drops his gaze all too quickly to the papers on his desk.

Before I can answer, the door behind me opens. My little brother enters, shirt half untucked and hair disheveled. His bright, green eyes shine, and a disarming smile graces his lips. His unmarked skin has a thin sprinkling of stubble on it, as if he hasn't shaved in two or three days.

"Father," he says, dipping his head. Logan's eyes shift to me, to my scar, then back to my eyes. "Asher."

"Thank you for joining us, Son." My father gestures to the armchair next to mine, and I bristle. *Son*. He never calls me that. Asher, yes. *Boy* sometimes, when he's angry. Mostly, he doesn't call me anything at all.

But Logan is *son*—even though Logan spends his days chasing supermodels and socialites. Even though Logan is

Farcliff's most popular bad boy, gracing every front page of the tabloids every week. He has brought more controversy to this family than the rest of us combined.

Yet my father's eyes still soften when Logan walks in. He plans to pass the company onto my brother, even though I'm the one who's made it grow beyond what anyone could have ever imagined. I'm the one who's brokered every major deal in our company's history. I'm the one who's laid other businesses at my father's feet, presenting them like an offering to a god. I'm the one who's made my father richer than he could have ever imagined.

But Logan is *son*, and I'm just *boy*.

My brother lowers himself onto the chair next to mine, slumping down and letting his legs stretch out toward the desk. My father folds his arms on the desk, leaning toward the two of us.

"Logan, I wanted to thank you for your work with the Farcliff Times. The newspaper sent me a preliminary version of the article you worked on, and the company comes off really well. You've done good work."

Pride glows in my father's eyes, and I clench my jaw so hard pain spears into my head.

Good work? Logan? Is he insane?

I guarantee you my lazy, party-animal brother hasn't done good work. He probably pawned it off to his assistant and just showed up for the photoshoot looking like the perfect male model he is. Logan hasn't done *good work*, because Logan wouldn't know work if it hit him across the face, which, incidentally, I have an urge to do right now.

But my father looks pleased, and Logan nods, accepting the praise as if he deserves it.

Anger peppers my chest like a thousand tiny daggers. They cut my flesh as I sit here and bleed.

Father swings his eyes over to me. "And you? I gave you the task of completing this merger with Donovan Enterprises. I've heard talk he's making a move, and he might not agree to this merger. If the shareholders side with him, we'll lose the deal. It's worth multiple hundred millions of dollars, Asher." His lips pinch, deep lines bracketing his mouth.

At least he used my name.

I sit up, Logan's stare prickling on my neck. I resist the urge to adjust my collar to hide my scar, choosing instead to grit my teeth before I speak. I shouldn't say anything. I know I shouldn't. I'm mad that Logan gets a gold star for showing up to work two hours late while I get a slap on the wrist for making my father a billionaire. I'm resentful and bitter, and I hate the way my father's lips twitch whenever he's forced to look at me.

I feel his disgust like an oily film on my skin. I see the look in his eyes that says he'd prefer it if I'd died in the fire, rather than have to look at my imperfect body for the rest of his life. The weight of his expectations makes me small.

But I could hand him the biggest deal of the company's history if I bring Reginald Donovan in. I could use the information Penelope let slip and become my father's favorite son. If I find out what he's planning in Nord, I could deliver the killing blow to Donovan Enterprises, ensuring he's swallowed up in our family's company without so much as a word of protest.

If I open my mouth and speak, I can show my father I'm worthy of being his son. I'm better than Logan at this. I deserve to take over when Father retires.

I don't owe Penelope anything. What happened at Prince Gabriel's wedding was a blip. A mistake. A moment in time. That feeling I thought I felt? The connection? It was lust, that's all.

This, right here, is my life, and I'm not going to let Logan take over the business I helped build. My shoulders straighten as I nod. "Donovan is looking to expand into Nord." Every word feels like a stone sinking into a still pool, causing ripples to spread out, out, out. My fingernails dig into my palm to scatter the image.

Father frowns, two deep lines appearing between his brows. He leans forward, and I love the way he waits for me to speak. He knows this is important.

"I'm not sure what he's planning yet, but it's big. It's giving him enough confidence that he'll be able to keep the shareholders on his side and refuse our merger. Whatever he's planning in Nord has got to be in the hundreds of millions."

My father's eyebrows twitch, a faint trace of approval in his eyes. Ignoring the hot spear piercing my chest that feels a bit too much like shame, I hold his gaze. I know this information is new to him, and I know no one else could have discovered it.

"And you're sure about this?" my father asks, his praise for Logan forgotten. Father's eyes are on me, with no trace of disgust. No flick to my scar. No sign that I'm anything less than the son who made his company what it is.

I dip my chin. "Positive."

"How do you know?" Logan asks, his voice sounding a lot like a whine. I know my father pits us against each other every chance he gets, but I can't quite resist the urge to play along.

Triumphant, I swing my eyes to my brother. "I have contacts."

"And you trust this information." Father drums his fingers on his desk, tilting his head in a slightly predatory way as he stares at me. He can smell Donovan's blood now. He knows we're close.

"I'd bet my life on it." After all, it was the Queen's own mouth that spoke the words. If anyone in Nord would know the value of the land, it's her.

My father leans back in his chair, brows tugging together. "What is he planning?"

"That, I'm not sure. I'd like to go to Nord to find out. I could leave this week."

My father's frown deepens. "You want to go yourself? What about your responsibilities here in Farcliff?"

"This could be big, Father. Bigger than any other deal we've done." It's the truth, too. The merger with Donovan Enterprises is significant—but if it came with new prospects to expand in Nord? Massive.

There's another reason I'd like to go to Nord, but I can't tell my father or Logan. A blond, blue-eyed beauty with a crown nestled in her hair. A woman I'd kill to see again—but who says that's going to happen even if I do go to Nord? It's not like I can walk into the castle to say hello. Does a queen even have a cell phone?

Wanting to see Penelope again—it's a silly fantasy. I know that. It doesn't mean it isn't pulling me toward Nord. My more reasonable motivation is needing to find out what Donovan is doing. That could pay off in a big way. *That's* why I want to go to Nord. Not the Queen. At least that's what I tell myself as I sit in my father's office.

My father tents his fingers. He's not thinking of a stupid newspaper article, or the way Logan's pretty green eyes sparkle when they're on the cover of a magazine. Father's thinking about *me*, and how much money I can make him if I go to Nord.

"You might spook Donovan if you show up in Nord," Logan says, scowling.

I know I shouldn't hate my brother. I *don't* hate him,

exactly. It's just...he's been given everything. He's treated with respect. He has this entire company—a company *I* helped build—headed his way, and for what? Because he takes a good picture? In the logical corners of my mind, I know it should be my father I resent. He's the one who makes me feel small, who pits me against my brother, who sends me off to do his dirty work. When I look at Logan, though, I can't help the anger that threads through my heart. The unfairness of it all—all the love and attention and worship he gets for being whole. Healthy. For being fucking beautiful.

I shrug. "Spooking him might be exactly what we need to do. If I show up in Nord while he's there, he'll know he has no choice but to accept our deal. He's got nowhere else to turn."

Father grunts in approval. "Asher's right." His eyes swing to me. "Go."

Pushing myself off the chair, I throw my brother a dark glance before walking toward the door.

Father's deep voice makes me pause. "Asher," he calls out, and I turn. "Good work." Satisfaction fills his eyes, and he can taste the thrill of the victory on the tip of his tongue. He knows we have Donovan on the run, and whatever I find out in Nord will make us even richer.

I nod, accepting his praise as if it were water and I've been walking through the desert for days. I gulp it down desperately, trying to hide how much it affects me. I turn my back on my father and brother and slip out through the door, only letting my shoulders drop when I'm well out of sight.

The Queen told me that information in a moment of weakness. She didn't even tell me, really. She let slip that there was a mining executive trying to come to Nord. Is it wrong for me to investigate further? Is it wrong for me to use that information for my benefit?

I want to say no. We don't owe each other anything, and

it's not like she cares what mergers I complete. All we did was fuck at a wedding when we both felt a bit too lonely and a bit too horny.

...So why does this taste in my mouth remind me of regret?

PENELOPE

USUALLY, when I get back to Nord after a trip abroad, I feel the relief of being home. I taste the crisp, cool air and let it fill my lungs, confident in the fact that this is where I belong. Stirling, the capital city, is the jewel of Nord. Rich with life and culture, it's the place where I feel most at home.

But when I step off the private jet and feel the soft, summer breeze ruffle the hem of my dress, it sends a chill walking down my spine.

This homecoming isn't so sweet. It feels...lonely.

Summer in Nord is incredible. Green and lush, it bursts into life without warning after a long, dark winter. It's not muggy like Farcliff. Summer here is the perfect temperature, with just the right amount of breeze. The sun will be out until late tonight, past ten o'clock. People in Nord will celebrate in the streets, and the whole kingdom will be alive and outdoors until the cold weather sets in again come autumn.

Usually I love it, but right now it reminds me a bit too much of what happened in Farcliff. I'd prefer the cold.

Silas follows me off the plane. Sunglasses firmly in place all morning, my brother hasn't said a word to me. Hungover.

We've been traveling through Farcliff for two weeks now, and my brother has spent most of his time drinking and getting—ahem—*acquainted* with the local female population.

My brother's antics never bothered me before. Sure, the Crown has had to put out a fire or two whenever a woman feels like she has the right to cause a controversy—but Silas is Silas. My little brother, the boy who was always able to make me smile. He's been a hurricane since he was in school, so much so that he had to be homeschooled just to get him through. His antics turned to partying when he got older, and now he's mostly mellowed out in comparison to how he was in his teens and early twenties.

Sure, he often has a few too many drinks and a different woman every night—but sometimes I think he's just trying to fill some kind of void. I filled mine with ice, but maybe alcohol and sex would have been more effective.

My two other brothers, Wolfe and Jonah, are decidedly more serious. Wolfe has lightened up a bit since he got married last year, taking on the role of husband and father like he was born to do it. He's moved to the Summer Palace full-time, which used to be our summer home as a family. It rests on the Arctic Circle and is an unforgiving place in winter. He and his wife seem to love it, though. The isolation suits them both.

And Jonah? Well, Jonah is level-headed. He has a good mind for politics, and I've relied on him heavily for years. He's been in charge while I've been away with Silas.

Things would have been easier if Jonah had been born first. Or Wolfe. Maybe even Silas, if he decided to grow up sometime this century.

But the crown came to me. Little old Penelope, who just wanted to run off and catch rainbows. That little girl feels like a different person now. Like I'm staring at some distorted mirror, seeing my past through the eyes of a stranger.

I try not to let bitterness overwhelm me, especially when I think of Wolfe. We used to understand each other—he lost his fiancée, too. Neither of us thought we'd move on, but he has, and I've seen him become happier and healthier over the past year. I've always known my brothers would find wives and marry. Their happiness is important to me, but I can't shake the feeling that I've lost something I'll never get back.

Two weeks ago, I slept with a man for the first time in seven years. I let him run his calloused palms up my thighs, feeling lava pour into my veins. I tasted his kiss and drank in his scent. I was a woman, not the Queen, and it was glorious.

But it's over.

I have responsibilities, and I can't afford to cause any controversies like the ones Silas seems to attract. Plus, it's never been something I've sought out. Never been something I needed. There hasn't been a man who's made me feel any bit of arousal.

Well, not until Asher.

As I'm led to the waiting royal car, I try to let the cool breeze blow my thoughts across the land. I try to push the memory of Asher aside, but I can still feel the roughness of his stubble against my cheek. The feel of his hard length pressed up against my stomach, and the absolute hunger in his kiss.

Our time together was...it was incredible. It felt like nothing I've ever had before. Explosive.

I've been drifting through a gray life since my husband died, and that hour with Asher was in full color. Bright, vibrant, and oh-so-wrong. I'd die happy if I got to do it again...

...but I can't. All I can do is take that memory and lock it somewhere safe. Somewhere no one can find it but me.

WHEN WE GET to the castle, it feels like I'm sliding on a familiar coat of armor. This is my home. My workplace. My kingdom. This is where I rule, and where all my responsibilities are fulfilled.

Leaving Silas to go nurse his hangover, I head for the office. No doubt there will be a huge stack of paperwork waiting for my signature. Jonah could hold down the fort while I was gone, but his signature doesn't belong next to the royal seal. I walk through the empty hallways, listening to the echo of my shoes on the stone floors and ignoring the haughty gazes from the oil paintings of ancestors long gone.

Who will be my successor? Who will take the crown after I'm gone? Wolfe is the next oldest, and he already has a child. The newspapers are calling him and his son the heirs—as if I'm already dead. The Queen who failed to produce an heir. The end of her royal line. Up until Gabriel's wedding, I would have agreed with them, but now...

...I feel the furthest thing from death. Asher made me feel so deliciously alive—but it doesn't change the fact that I'll never have an heir of my own. That particular scar is mine to bear, and mine to bear alone.

My office is a large room with big, floor-to-ceiling windows. The curtains have been opened and the bright summer sunshine pours into the room. My desk gleams, and on the left side of it, a large stack of folders awaits.

I call for the staff and ask to have them serve my lunch in the office, then take a seat behind my desk. Skimming through paperwork, I sign where I need to. Most of it is inconsequential. Daily logs of castle security, a new law passing through parliament that's been hotly debated for months, photos to autograph for Nord's lucky citizens who have reached their hundredth birthday.

The usual.

As I flick through the paperwork, signing where I need to, making notes where I have questions, I let out a long sigh. My thoughts crawl back to Asher and the way I felt in that room. I wonder if I could call him. I could get a secure line and ask him if he'd like to come up to Nord.

Shaking my head, I squeeze my eyes shut and try to get a grip on myself. I'm not that desperate. It's been two weeks, and I haven't heard a word from Asher. He told me himself he didn't want to see me again. Not in those words, exactly, but I've been around politicians long enough to know what he really meant. Being *too busy to come up to Nord* isn't exactly subtle. At Gabriel's wedding, he left just a few minutes after we returned to the reception. He got what he needed, and I can't help feeling a bit unclean for giving it to him. Asher doesn't want to see me again. That's one thing I know for sure.

A soft knock pulls me out of my head. I call for the visitor to come in, and my brother Jonah pokes his head through the door. "You're back less than a couple of hours and you're already neck-deep in paperwork." He flashes a smile at me as I motion for him to enter.

Behind him, two palace staff members enter with a silver tray carrying my lunch. The smell of the chef's special chicken noodle soup wafts toward me, and I let my lips curl into a smile. The man carrying the tray stares at me, wide-eyed, and I wonder if he's ever seen me smile before. Have I really been that cold?

Jonah takes a seat as I clear a space on my desk, and two staff members arrange my lunch, cutlery, and cloth napkins for me to eat. The daily newspaper is folded neatly on the edge of the tray. They bow and back out of the room without a word. My brother motions for me to eat. "I already had lunch earlier."

I tuck into the soup, finally feeling like I'm home. "No problems while I was away?"

Jonah shrugs. "Protests are still happening almost daily. I'm told they're under control, but... I don't know. We received an application for mining rights near Roston." Jonah's brow darkens. "Donovan Enterprises wants to open three large diamond mines."

"Let me guess, the parliament wants to grant it."

"They say we need more industry. We could be entering another recession, and new mining projects opening up might just save the economy. And our reputation."

"Every year I've been wearing the crown, they've told me we're entering a recession." I shake my head and take another spoonful of soup. I tilt my head, staring at my brother. "Why don't you like Donovan?"

"I've seen the way Reginald Donovan does business, and I don't like it. My contacts in Farcliff, Canada, and the States tell me he's shady. If we grant him the mining rights, we're almost certainly opening ourselves up to serious financial and environmental messes."

"But he'll provide jobs and money, so the government wants to proceed." I shake my head, sighing. Nothing is ever simple.

Jonah grunts in agreement. Not for the first time, I'm glad to have my brother near me. With Wolfe in full-on nesting mode, and Silas still in his never-ending party years, sometimes it feels like Jonah's the only one I can trust. Like me, he's a responsible family member. The one who knows his duty.

After filling me in on the rest of the news from Nord, Jonah leaves me to finish my lunch in peace. He closes the door behind him, and my heart feels slightly easier. I'm not *that* lonely here. I have my brothers, and Wolfe's new wife Rowan is quite nice. Life is far from bad.

I just had a wobble at Prince Gabriel's wedding. A moment of loneliness. It's over now, and Asher's made it clear by his silence he feels the same way. We can both move on with our lives and go back to the way things were before—even if I feel like something inside me has shifted, and I'll never get it to shift back.

As I push my bowl away and grab the newspaper on the edge of the silver tray, my eyes widen. I unfold the paper and it opens. A gasp escapes my lips.

There, on the front page of the Stirling Times, is none other than Asher Gerhard. The headline screams at me in big, black letters.

Farcliff Executive Bashes Nord's Unemployment, Lack of Industry

My own words staring back at me. The things I said to him in a post-coital haze, splashed on the front page of a newspaper. Anger is too kind a word for what I feel right now. Bitter heat sweeps through my veins, turning everything inside me to dust. Thick, black smoke fills my veins as I struggle to keep my rage at bay.

I can't read the article because my hands are trembling too much. I lay the paper flat on the desk and stand up, leaning over it. Blinking a few times, I try to clear my eyes. That fucking *dog*. I can't believe I slept with him! I can't believe I let him lead me away from the wedding and do... do...do *that* to me. I need a shower. I need to wash this grime out of my pores and clean my tongue from the taste of him.

The article hypothesizes about his presence in Nord and what it means about the future of Nordish industry. Gerhard, Inc. is expanding into Nord, they say. Heat rushes through my chest, spearing me straight through the heart.

Was he planning this trip when he saw me at the wedding? Why wouldn't he mention it? Was he already intending to work in Nord?

Not *once* did he say anything about visiting my arctic kingdom. Not once did he say he'd want to see me again. Not once did he say *anything* about the possibility of a trip here—he said the opposite! He said he didn't have time to come here. Then, two weeks later, he's on the front page of a newspaper? He's *here*?

I read through the article three times, fuming. Written by Jacinthe Crawley, a woman who has a serious abolitionist streak and would love nothing more than to see my head roll right off my shoulders, the article praises Asher's business savvy, proclaiming him the most successful closer in his father's company's history. He's the king of mergers, apparently.

I...I didn't know that. I didn't know anything about him when I saw him. Why wouldn't he tell me?

Hurt and anger feel very similar, but mostly I feel embarrassed. I don't even know *why* I'm angry. He had no obligation to tell me he was coming to Nord, but...I guess I wish he had. This just makes it seem like he didn't want me to know. He didn't want to see me again.

My fingers drift over the image on the newspaper, tracing the outline of his lips. Perfectly formed, I remember exactly how they felt to kiss.

Blinking back tears, I crumple the newspaper and toss it aside. My throat burns as I turn toward the windows. Icicles form over my heart as my eyes widen. I look over my shoulder at the crumpled paper, every cell in my body slowly stilling. Was he just using me? That special connection I felt —did it even exist?

Evidently not, if he didn't even have the decency to mention he was planning a trip to my own damn country. He *lied*. Denied it. Told me he wouldn't come here. Said he didn't have *time*.

I...*argh*. I want to smash this window to pieces with my silver lunch tray. Smack *him* across the head with it. I'm too full of emotion right now, like I'm about to boil over.

After seven years of cold distance from my emotions, anger feels *good*. It burns through my veins like poison, and I want nothing more than to see Asher and tell him exactly what I think of him. He thinks he can use me for sex, then turn around and never speak to me again? He thinks he can expand his father's business into Nord after tossing me aside like a used tissue?

Think again, Gerhard.

Rage is hot and bright. In a life where I've been cold and distant, the fiery bite of anger is almost addictive. I dive into the feeling, swimming in my own fury.

He used me. He took me into that room, turned me around, and fucked me from behind with his hand over my mouth, then sent me on my way.

How fucking *dare* he?

In a small, quiet corner of my mind, I think my anger might not be justified. He doesn't need to tell me his travel plans just because he sleeps with me. He's welcome to visit Nord, and having more companies expand into Nord would probably help the whole political situation. It would give me options other than Donovan Enterprises, for one.

But anger feels too good to ignore, and I push those rational thoughts aside.

He *told me* he had no time to come to Nord, and then came straight here. How am I supposed to ignore the sting of that slap?

I jump when the door opens. A staff member curtsies and asks to remove the silver lunch tray. She's young—barely a teen. I haven't seen her before. Her eyes climb up to mine then dart away. "Do you need anything else, Your Majesty?" Her voice is thin. She's afraid. She can sense the anger washing over me in waves.

I'm used to that reaction. Many people have heard stories about me. I never smile. I'm cold. Heartless.

"Get me Frederick," I tell the trembling woman. She curtsies again and scurries out of the room. I sit down and lean against the back of my chair, feeling the sun warming my neck through the window, and I feel hot for the first time in years.

So hot I might combust. Like my whole body is on fire, and I need to fix this. Throw something. Kill someone.

Preferably Asher fucking Gerhard.

Frederick, my private secretary, enters the room. He has a thick, black mustache and equally black hair. His father served my father, and his family has been in service to the Crown for generations. He gives me a low bow. "You called, Your Majesty?"

I lift my chin. "Find Asher Gerhard and take me to him. He arrived in Nord this week."

"Ma'am," Frederick starts, stuttering. "You want…"

"I want you to call a car, find an address, and take me there. Is that a problem?" My voice is frosty. So cold the sunlight seems to dim.

Frederick bows. "Right away, Your Majesty."

Standing, I pick up the crumpled newspaper article and smooth it out again. I fold it as neatly as I can and tuck it under my arm. My steps are purposeful as I walk toward the entrance of the castle. The haughty gazes of ancestors on oil paintings no longer make me bow my head, they only fuel whatever rage is simmering in my chest.

I am *the Queen*, and I will not be disrespected in my own land.

When I get to the front door, a footman is already waiting with my hat and jacket. I slip them on, then tug gloves on over my hands. It's warm enough not to wear them in summertime, but I feel like I'm donning armor before a battle. The footman holds up a mirror and I check my hair, then walk to the palace's front doors.

Frederick is there. He nods. "He rented an office in the city," my personal secretary explains. "Not hard to find. We can send a car for him if you'd rather stay here—"

"No." I don't want Asher in my castle. I want him in his shitty little office, and I want to make him feel *small*. I want to fill up that space with my staff and my presence and show him exactly who I am. But I don't tell Frederick that, because I don't have to explain my reasons for wanting to go to Asher. I don't need to explain anything to anyone.

My anger winds tighter when I think of Asher's office—an office! He's here a few days and he's already rented an office! The fucking *nerve*.

Two staff members open the double doors for me, and another staff member stands at the back door of the waiting vehicle. I slide inside, tucking my feet in as the man closes the car door. My face is unmoving, my jaw clenched. My heart feels hot. Too hot. Like it might burn a hole right through my chest.

But it thumps, and I haven't felt my heart beat this hard in —well, since I was last with Asher. This is different, though. This is righteous, burning anger.

I lean into the feeling, letting my thoughts circle back to his excuses. Too busy to come to Nord, he reckoned. How *dare* he. How dare Asher use me like that, then turn around and think he can establish his company here. How dare he touch me and kiss me and put his—*ugh*—put his cock in me, then leave the wedding and say *nothing* to me? Then he thinks he can come here and start a business? Ha! He thinks he's some brilliant businessman? The best closer in his family's history? Give me a fucking break.

My hands don't tremble as we drive through the streets of Stirling. My pulse hammers, but my body behaves. Anger settles into my pores, making me feel bigger and taller and stronger than I've felt before.

When we stop in front of a tall office building, a security car in front and another behind, I see heads turn. Royal security agents stream out of the two cars, standing next to my vehicle and the front door of the building as my driver rushes to open my door.

I hear a gasp when I exit the car, as passersby point their phones at me to record my entrance to the building. I turn to look, lifting an arm to wave. I don't smile, but that's nothing new. No one expects me to smile. Ice Queens don't smile for photos.

Agents surround me as we walk into the building. The lobby is vast, with marble tiles on the floor climbing up the walls. Very fancy, Gerhard. Prick.

We ignore the reception desk, where a woman stands with her head bowed. My security team leads me to the elevators, where one agent is already waiting with the elevator door open.

My head is held high. My steps ring out in the vast space. I keep my face steady and hide my rage under layers of ice.

For the second time in two weeks, after twenty years of

absence, I'm going to see Asher Gerhard. This time, though, I can guarantee it won't end the way it did the first time. No one will be kissed. No one will touch my body. No one will make me feel like anything other than the reigning monarch of the Kingdom of Nord.

I'm not the little girl Asher used to know anymore. I won't be used and tossed aside. I won't be disrespected like this.

If he wants to do business in Nord, Asher Gerhard better get on his knees and beg.

8

ASHER

PENELOPE WALKS into my office with fire in her eyes. Her anger is palpable. It rushes toward me as soon as I look up from my desk, hitting me in the chest like a poison-tipped spear. The air feels thick around her, as if every molecule in the room vibrates according to her will. Her security agents stream into the room as she strides forward, then filter out when she waves her hand.

She moves to the tall windows lining the interior wall of my office, flicking a switch that closes the automatic blinds. We're alone, which sends excitement tripping down my spine. I bury it down, knowing Penelope isn't here for a repeat of what happened at Prince Gabriel's wedding. I can hardly believe she's here at all.

Clearing my throat, I stand. "Penelope."

"Sit. Down." Blazing eyes stare at me, and a dagger of heat pierces my stomach. I like the way she looks at me. Like she wants to tear me limb from limb and send me back to Farcliff in pieces.

Why does that make my blood rush between my legs? There's something seriously wrong with me.

The Queen takes a step forward, letting her eyes drop down my body and back up again. Her full, pink lips are pressed together, but I can't forget how it felt to kiss them.

Shame is sour at the back of my throat. I know why she's mad. I know why she's here. Does she know about Donovan? Does she know I figured it out from what she said about him?

I knew it was a betrayal. She has a right to be mad—but damn, she looks good. Wearing a navy pantsuit and a gauzy, pearl-colored blouse, the Queen stands with her feet together and her hands clasped in front of her, a crumpled newspaper dangling between her fingers. Her chin is high, and I see two glittering stones winking from either earlobe.

She's powerful in her femininity. Completely in charge. Completely, utterly furious.

Lowering myself onto my chair, I bow my head. "I wasn't expecting you," I say, lifting my eyes as my head stays bowed. I watch her throat clench as she swallows, her eyes flicking from me, to my desk, to my father's company logo on the wall. A decal sticker has already been applied after moving into these offices a few days ago.

The newspaper skips across my desk when she tosses it. I catch it with my hand, flattening the crumpled page, and glance down at my own face.

"If you think you're going to set up shop in Nord, you can think again, Mr. Gerhard." The Queen's voice is so cold, my heart slows down. Frost clings to every surface as I crawl my gaze up to meet hers. The only thing not completely still is my raging heart.

"Pen—"

"Call me anything but *Your Majesty* again, and I'll have you deported within the hour."

My lip twitches, but I will myself not to smirk. Why am I

enjoying this? Am I so sick in the head that I like feeling the emotion pulse through her? Do I enjoy her anger?

...or do I deserve this kind of rage, and I'm enjoying the punishment I think is owed to me?

Sighing, I pull open a drawer and take out a bottle of amber alcohol. Whiskey—my weakness. Well, that and powerful, angry women. I need a drink to take off the edge and give myself time to let my body cool down. How can I explain this deal with Donovan? How can I tell her that I wasn't using her when we had sex, I just figured it out based on the hint she dropped? It was...an accident.

Heat curls in lazy circles down my stomach, resting somewhere between my legs. My cock throbs at her nearness, remembering how it felt to have the Queen of Nord bent over in front of me with her skirt bunched around her waist.

"Drink?" I ask, taking out two crystal tumblers.

"Tell me something, Asher," the Queen says, turning to look at the company logo on the wall. "Do you always go after foolish women when you want a quick lay? Do you always tell them you're too busy to see them afterward?"

"I wouldn't call you foolish." I pour two drinks, sliding one across the table toward her.

"So that's a yes?" She arches a brow, swinging her icy gaze to meet mine.

I throw my drink back, swallowing it in one gulp. Putting the empty glass down, I shake my head. "I never planned for that to happen."

"What, you and me?"

I nod, throat tightening. "And coming here. I meant it when I said I was busy in Farcliff."

She stares at me for a moment, as if she's trying to gauge whether I'm lying or not. "I didn't think it would happen either, but I was stupid enough to follow you to that dirty room. Stupid enough to bend over like you wanted me to."

Images flash in my mind, and I will myself to keep my face steady. There's so much bitterness in her voice that it makes my heart ache. "Do you regret it that much?"

"Hmm, let's see," Penelope says, taking a step toward me to lean over the desk that separates us. She smells like sweet candy with a hint of rose. "You made me feel like a cheap, used whore, then walked away without saying goodbye. So, yes, I regret it."

"There's nothing cheap about you, Pen, and you used me as much as I did you."

"Is that right?" Her delicate fingers touch the edge of her glass of whiskey, and I half-expect her to grip it tight and toss it at my face. Instead, she drinks it down as fast as I did, grimacing. "You have terrible taste in whiskey."

"That's the nicest thing you've said to me all day."

"Fuck you."

"Aren't you supposed to be the Queen? That's no way for a monarch to talk."

Fire sparks in the pit of my gut when Penelope's hands grip the edge of the desk. I can taste her anger on my tongue, and I want more. I want to taste every part of her. Angry, hot, and alive.

"I will never let you work here. You can take your father's business and walk away right now, because the Gerhard Corporation will not do business in Nord, Asher."

A groan escapes my lips before I can stop it. It's just...the way she says my name makes my gut clench. I haven't felt this alive in years. I keep my face steady, my gaze clashing with hers. "Why not? I haven't even applied for a business license. As far as you're concerned, I'm a tourist...a tourist with an office in downtown Stirling."

"And it's going to stay that way." Her eyes don't leave mine, and—I want to kiss her. Right here. Like this. I want to stalk to the other side of this desk, roll that designer dress over her waist, and bury myself inside her. I want to swallow her anger whole and have her come apart on my cock.

I want everything she'll give me. Every part of her. Anything. All of it.

Catching her fingers across the desk before she can move away, I press my lips against them.

Penelope gasps, her eyes widening. Yanking her hand away, she slaps me across the face. Hard. I suck in a breath, gripping the edge of my chair. Pain explodes across my cheek as I grunt, turning back to face her.

"I could have you arrested, Asher." There's an edge to her voice now. A slight tremble. The ice is cracking.

I shouldn't taunt her, but I like seeing her like this. I like watching her come apart. The mask is slipping, and I feel like I'm seeing the real her—even if she wants to slap me around and throw me in jail. A wicked, smoky smile spreads across my face. "Does that involve handcuffs? Because I could get on board with that."

The Queen slaps me again, harder this time. I probably deserve it. I gasp, skin burning. My teeth grind together and I speak through a clenched jaw. "That wasn't very nice."

"Neither was you using me then tossing me aside without even telling me you'd be coming here. You said you were too busy for Nord. Too busy for me." Her bottom lip trembles ever so slightly as her eyes grow watery.

Is that why she's mad? Because I came here without telling her? Because I left Gabriel's wedding without talking to her? My heart twists painfully. I...I don't want her to look at me like that, like I'm the cause of her pain. Dropping my head, I shake it from side to side. "I'm sorry, Pen." Glancing up, I meet her gaze. "I mean, Your Majesty. Please don't arrest me."

Penelope sinks into a chair across from me, deflating as she leans back. She looks...exhausted. Worn out.

Hurt.

Because of me?

When I was in my father's office, I didn't think she'd pay me a visit. I thought I'd never see her again. I thought, maybe, she wouldn't even notice, even though I hoped... I don't know what I hoped. Maybe I hoped for exactly this. I wanted to see her again, but she's a queen and what am I? I'm not someone beautiful women chase. With these scars covering my body, I'm the one who makes pretty women run away. I'd never deserve someone like her.

"I'm sorry," I say quietly. "I didn't think you'd want to see me again."

Penelope flicks her eyes up to mine, icy blue and vulnerable. My chest aches. Every thump of my heart feels like it's cracking ribs, so I look away. I grab my glass and the bottle of whiskey, moving around the desk and sinking into the chair next to hers. I fill up both our glasses, my fingers brushing Penelope's as I hand her the tumbler. My skin sizzles at the contact, heat rushing up my arm.

She takes a sip, wrinkling her nose. "My earlier comment stands."

"I didn't know you were a whiskey connoisseur."

"You don't know anything about me." Her eyes stare out through the window behind my desk, and my heart does that painful twist again.

I stare at her profile from my seat next to hers, unable to look away from her neck, her jaw, those perfect lips I haven't stopped thinking about since I kissed them. Before I can stop my hand, my fingers are drifting over her cheek. Her perfect, smooth skin. Unmarked. Unscarred.

Her scars are hidden.

Penelope doesn't flinch away from my touch. She closes her eyes, letting my fingers drift down her cheek and over her jaw. Her skin feels like warm satin. I never want to stop touching her. I'd run my hands over her body for hours at a time, just to prove to myself she's real. She exists. This beautiful creation is alive, and she's doing me the honor of letting me caress her skin. "I wanted to see you again, Pen. I was curious when you said you were talking to mining executives, so I pitched the trip to my father as a business trip." That's... mostly true, right? Penelope hasn't mentioned Donovan—does she know about the merger? I pause, trying to find the right words. "What I really wanted was to see you."

It's not a lie, exactly. But it's not the full truth. My motivations weren't altruistic. I came here to find out more about Reginald Donovan, to make sure I can cut his legs off at the knee and ensure this merger goes through. But is that the main reason? What really pushed me to come here? Without even having to ask myself the questions, I already know the answer. I stare at the beautiful woman next to me, letting out a sigh. "I was hoping I'd see you here."

Penelope turns to look at me, ice-blue meeting my gaze. She searches my face. Her brows tug together and the faintest line appears on her forehead. "Why wouldn't you just call me?"

"You're not exactly easy to get ahold of. Do I just call up information and ask to be connected to the Queen?"

"At least you'd be making an effort."

I grin. "I'd give my left arm to have you storm into my office like this every day."

"Shut up, Asher. Why would you tell me you had no time

to come to Nord if you were planning on setting up an office here?" Her voice is thin and reedy, and I know she's showing a side of her that usually stays hidden. I'm...honored, but...

Still no mention of Donovan. No talk of the merger. My heart thumps as I clear my throat, staring at the wood grain on my desk. The truth sings in my veins—she doesn't know. Doesn't know about the merger. Doesn't know why my father really sent me here.

I know I'm hiding something from her. Maybe you would call it lying. Hell, who am I kidding? It's a lie. I should tell her about the merger, about Donovan, about everything.

Penelope hasn't so much as mentioned Donovan's name —her main complaint is the fact that I didn't tell her I was planning on coming here. But if I tell her about the merger with Donovan Enterprises, will she still believe that I came here in the hopes of seeing her, too? Or will she feel angry and used?

Swinging my eyes to stare at Penelope, there's a tightening in my chest. A deep kind of pain at the thought of losing her again, letting her walk away from me. So, I tell her what I *really* want—the thing that might be truer than any merger or business deal. "I wanted to see you, Pen. That's why I'm here."

"I don't believe you."

"I'm not asking you to."

"I've heard stories about you," she says, arching a brow.

"All good, I hope."

Penelope lets out a dry, humorless laugh.

I bring my glass to my lips. "Do you regret what happened at the wedding?"

She pauses for...a long time. Too long. Then she whispers, "Yes."

I wasn't expecting that to hurt so much. My chest feels

like it's caving in, my heart squeezing into a tight ball. I nod. "Oh."

"I don't like feeling like this. Out of control." She takes a sip of her whiskey. I'm so incredibly fascinated by the movement of her lips, her jaw, her throat.

"You're completely in control, Pen."

"What did I say about calling me that?"

My lips curl. I shrug. "Can't help myself." I laugh, and her eyes brighten. She stares at me, at my mouth, then back at my eyes. I let out a long sigh. "Can I see you again?"

Penelope sets her glass down on the edge of my desk. It's mostly full, the alcohol rocking gently from side to side. She stands up, brushing her thighs as she purses her lips. "I'll think about it."

Her eyes are cold now. The heat is gone. But behind the chill of her voice, there's something. An edge. A roughness. Penelope *wants* to see me again. She's fighting this feeling, this connection between us.

I stand up, turning toward her. She's so close. Her chest just an inch from mine. Her eyes staring at my chest. If she just tilted her head up, I could lean over. I could brush my lips against hers. I could taste her sweetness once more.

But the Queen clears her throat and takes a step back. She glances at me through thick lashes, then blinks away. "Sorry for slapping you. Your cheek...it's red."

My fingers brush the still-stinging skin, the pain long since dulled into something else. Another kind of heat that rests lower in my body. "I liked it." I shrug.

Penelope's head whips toward me, and I can't help but laugh at the shock on her face. "You're sick in the head."

"You say it like it's a bad thing." I don't even try to hide my grin.

"You need help."

"Maybe I just need to be slapped around a bit." I arch a brow, loving the way her eyes drift down to my lips.

But before I can move, Penelope shakes her head and walks to the door. She pauses, turning to glance at me. "How long are you in Nord?"

"As long as it takes."

She holds my gaze, as if she's trying to decipher my words. I don't even know what I mean. Do I mean as long as it takes for me to close this merger with Donovan?

Or do I mean as long as it takes to see Penelope again? To make her understand what she means to me?

The Queen doesn't answer. She opens the door and walks away. I listen to her footsteps fading, trying to control the violent thudding in my chest.

9

PENELOPE

I SHOULD HAVE HIM DEPORTED. Or arrested. Or arrested, then deported. And fined. Definitely fined. He can pay for it, with the gazillions he's made in all the business deals that article was boasting about.

A thought smacks me in the face. Did he plan the news article? Was it some ploy to get me to notice he's here?

He said he came here because he wanted to see me...but then why wouldn't he just try to contact me? It doesn't make sense. I want to trust him, but...

Squeezing my eyes shut, I lean back against the seat of the car and let out a long sigh. The privacy screen is up and the windows are tinted dark, so I'm as alone as I can be.

Heat whips through my core even now, many minutes after I left Asher's office. The way he looked at me...it was sinful. It made me want to kiss him in a desperate kind of way. My cheek burns with the whisper of his touch. Heart stuttering uncomfortably, I shift in my seat and try to regain control over my rioting body.

Letting out a sigh, I stare out the window. There's something wrong with me. I can't get involved with him. I should never have done anything in the first place. What happened at the wedding felt good. It was special—or at least, it felt special to me.

But Asher was able to turn my life upside down and take my focus off the kingdom. I slept with him *once*, and he had me stomping into his office in a completely inappropriate way. What will the newspapers say about me tomorrow, I wonder? Will the headlines scream about the two of us? Will they say I'm too busy worrying about my love life to focus on the looming recession and rising unemployment?

I shouldn't want to see him, but, but, but...

Seeing him in his office made me feel alive in a way I've missed. In a way that makes me forget about my responsibilities.

I've been the Queen for so long, it feels like a betrayal to my people to feel like a woman, for once. My cheeks burn at the thought of the things we did in Prince Gabriel's castle. If anyone were to find out...

The car jerks to a stop, jarring me from my thoughts. I look up ahead as a mass of people push onto the road. Angry, snarling faces scream, the noise dampened by the thick bulletproof glass protecting my car. Police officers push the crush of people back as protesters lift signs.

Craning my neck, I read one of them.

Give us work. Give us dignity.

My shoulders drop. Unemployment has been on the rise in Nord, and with winter only a few months away, many people will be struggling. It's only the beginning of June, but the summer is short here—and the winter is harsh. I've tried to expand social services, but it doesn't change the fact that the talking heads on the television are right. Nord is entering a recession. Maybe the parliament is right to push for new businesses to invest in Nord. Maybe Donovan Enterprises wouldn't be so bad. If we were able to keep a short leash on them, they could provide jobs for thousands of people.

The police force clears a path through the crowd, allowing us to snake through the angry faces and make our way inside the palace gates. I spin around to watch the gates close, protesters rattling it from the outside.

The car intercom buzzes. "*Are you okay, ma'am?*"

I press a button on the center console. "Who were they?"

"*Mostly workers from the oil refineries in the east. They lost their jobs when the refineries closed.*"

Grimacing, I turn to look behind the car again. I knew things were getting bad in Nord, but I hadn't realized just how much discontent was brewing. The push to open new industry makes sense. We closed six oil refineries for policy breaches. Thousands of people lost their jobs.

I, as their Queen, should have an answer. I should be able to provide work for the people who live in my country. I should be a head of state with a vision for the nation.

I thought I was doing something good by closing those refineries. The working conditions were atrocious, with small, dirty camps for the men and women who relocated to work there. Aquifers were polluted around every oil reserve. Closing them down had been a hard decision, but a good one.

Or so I thought.

Now, thousands of people stand at my gates, unemployed, demanding their dignity back.

Isn't that my sole responsibility? To serve the people? To provide them with fruitful, stable lives?

The car stops in front of the entrance to my castle, and when a footman opens the door for me, I can still hear the shouts of the protesters in the distance. Gritting my teeth, I make my way inside and back to my office. I close the door, glancing at the stack of papers on my desk, then move to the window.

There are many hundreds of people out there. Truck drivers. Machinery operators. Scaffolders, carpenters, electricians.

They need work.

Sighing, I close my eyes. How could I possibly worry about Asher coming here without telling me when I should be caring about my own people? I'm not some jilted woman who needs to be coddled by a man. I'm a queen. I'm *the* Queen.

Doing what I do best, I shove my own feelings aside. Now is not the time to think about the way Asher's stubble felt when he kissed my neck, or how good it felt to have him pressed up against me. I gave up companionship when Xavier died. Being with a man like Asher doesn't change that. I don't deserve a companion. I *can't* have a companion. Even if I could be with Asher, I'd be denying him the opportunity to have children. My infertility would take that choice away from him, and what kind of woman does that make me? How could I ask a man—*any* man—to give that up for me?

I need to take those minutes in the break room in Westhill and shove them somewhere deep and cold and inaccessible.

Now is the time to act like the monarch I am—even if it means giving up the only man who's made me feel alive. I know what I need to do.

An idea sparks. A plan.

My chair groans when I drop into it, reaching for the phone. I pick up the receiver and hear my secretary greet me on the other side of the line. "Get me Mick Burgundy." The

CEO of the Nord Resources Group has been under a lot of pressure lately, but I need to know exactly where he stands—and if he'd agree to this plan I'm concocting.

As soon as the line connects, I hear the older gentleman's deep voice. "Your Majesty."

"Thank you for taking my call," I say, even though I know no one would refuse a call from me. "I want to know exactly where you stand with regard to taking on new projects, and if you'd be open to a joint venture."

There's a slight pause, then Mick clears his throat. "I'm listening."

After a long conversation with NRG, where Mick tells me about their restructuring efforts, and just how much—or how little—work they'd be able to take on, I hang up the phone and take a deep breath. That was the easy part. I'm used to dealing with Mick—as the head of the national resources company in Nord, he's an important government employee. He's been a solid partner for many years, and I trust him. The other half of this plan, on the other hand...it's not quite so easy. Or so clean.

With a trembling hand, I pick up the phone again and hear my private secretary's greeting on the other side of the line. I squeeze my eyes shut. "Frederick, can you connect me with Asher Gerhard?" Even saying his name sends a thrill rushing down my spine.

"Right away, Your Majesty." Frederick hangs up the phone and I do the same, folding my hands on the desk as my heart thumps. My mind spins circles around me as I sit there, staring at my desk.

Am I doing this because I'm thinking of the kingdom, or

am I doing it because I want to talk to Asher again? Does it matter, if the outcome helps the people of Nord?

I jump when the phone rings.

"Well, well, well," Asher's deep, resonant voice says on the other end of the line. A thrill skips down my spine, diving somewhere in the pit of my stomach. "I wasn't expecting to hear from you so soon."

Ignoring the thumping of my heart, I grit my teeth and keep my voice as cold and emotionless as I can. "We may be able to make a deal after all, Mr. Gerhard."

Asher lets out a soft groan.

I frown. "What?"

"I like when you call me that."

"Mr. Gerhard?"

There's that growly moan again, sparking fire in my veins. "Yeah. That."

"Focus, Asher," I snap. "I'm not calling you about...you know." *Ugh*, am I the least smooth person in the universe? I think I must be. I suck in a breath, squeezing my eyes shut. "I'm calling because I might be able to help your business interests in Nord, after all. I have a proposition for you."

A pause. Asher clears his throat, and his voice is cooler when he answers. "Of course, Your Majesty. I'm willing to hear your proposal."

How does he somehow have control over this situation? I know he didn't stage the protests. I know I have the authority between us—but still, I feel like I'm asking *him* for permission. It irks me and...excites me. Heat buds in my stomach, and I resist the urge to squirm in my seat. "Come to the palace tomorrow. I'll have Frederick arrange an appointment with you." I hang up the phone before Asher can say something else that will surely knock me off balance. My heart stutters as I close my eyes. I massage my temples, letting out a long sigh.

This idea, this plan…it's the right thing to do. My people need me to think about something other than the heat moving lower in my abdomen. Asher Gerhard came to Nord for a reason, and whether or not part of it was to see me, it's irrelevant now. I need his help—and his business.

My fingers drift to my lips, and I can almost taste Asher's kiss. If I go through with my plan tomorrow, and he accepts, it'll be the end of anything more between us. We'll be professionals, and our relationship will be nothing like it was at Prince Gabriel's wedding.

But for my people, for Nord, I'll give anything up. Even Asher.

ASHER

I'M NOT A NERVOUS PERSON. Business deals are where I feel most comfortable, but when the car slides through the tall gates leading to Stirling Castle, I have to admit I feel a tremor in my gut.

I wasn't expecting a call from the castle so soon after Penelope left my office. I wasn't expecting a call from her at all, if I'm honest. There's something between us, but when a woman slaps you twice within the space of five minutes, that sends a certain message.

Not that I minded.

Penelope said something about a business meeting. She told me she would let me expand my business in Nord, but what does that mean, exactly? When she left my office, she seemed completely focused on *not* letting me do business here.

There's something underneath my nerves, too. The buzz of excitement, warm and spicy. It tastes sweet on the tip of my tongue.

It's her—the Queen. Penelope. The thought of seeing her

again, of being in the same room as her, watching her lips move every time she talks, hearing her call me Asher or Mr. Gerhard or asshole or whatever other name she wants to throw at me...I'll take it all and beg for more.

As a staff member opens the door for me and gives me a low bow, I'm not thinking about a business deal or being the successor in my father's company. I'm not thinking about serving on the board or making millions for the man who told me I looked like a monster. I'm not thinking about Logan, or how he doesn't deserve to inherit Father's company instead of me.

I'm thinking about Penelope and the way she holds her head high. How regal she looks in everything she does. How badly I want to wrap my arms around her again, or drop to my knees in front of her and pledge my life to her.

As my steps resonate on the polished floor, I try to regain control over my racing heart. I'm supposed to be the man who brings in business. The man who sees opportunities where there were none before, then exploits them. Right now, I feel more like a hormonal teen going to see his first crush.

"This way, sir," a man in his thirties says. He's wearing a crisp, black uniform, his hair gelled back. His mustache is so thick it would make Burt Reynolds jealous.

"Can I ask you a question?" I say as we walk down the castle hallway, nothing but old paintings and statuesque guards to keep us company.

"Of course, sir." The man inclines his head but doesn't look back at me.

"Do you carry a comb around for your mustache? Or does it just naturally lie so perfectly?"

He bristles, every proper bone in his body recoiling at my question. I fight to hide my grin. He sweeps a hand toward a door to the right of us, and I nod.

When I step through the door, I'm led down a slightly narrower hallway. Smaller, but still opulent. White marble floors with gray and black veins, expensive paintings, chandeliers dripping with crystals. Every inch of this place has crown molding and intricate finishes. The paint is a delicate white color, with accents of red and purple. We pass a living room with walls painted blue—the exact blue of Penelope's eyes.

Tension builds in the pit of my stomach. I can almost sense her. The Queen. She's close. I can see it in the way the staff members stand up straighter. The buzz of excitement in the air. The unnerving silence, where all I can hear are my footsteps and the thumping of my own heart.

Stopping in front of a timber-paneled door, I wait for my guide to knock. He raps on the door twice and waits for a voice to come through from the other side.

My breath catches. The door opens, and she's there.

The woman I haven't been able to stop thinking about. The goddess that made me feel like a man, and not a monster. The woman who touched my scar and didn't recoil. Who clawed at my shirt and would have taken it off if I hadn't stopped her. Who slapped me across the face then let me caress her cheek as if nothing had happened.

The woman who filled my mind when I had my fist wrapped around my throbbing cock this morning.

Today, the sun streaming through the windows silhouettes her sheer dress, leaving very little to the imagination. I want to tear every scrap of fabric off her body, lay her down on that polished oak desk, and feast on her. I want to worship every inch of her body, kiss every part of her, make her feel the heat of my desire.

I need her. My cock is so hard it hurts.

She stands tall as she greets me with a slight nod of her head. "Asher."

"Your Majesty."

A twitch of her eyebrow tells me she's surprised I'm using her title. She glances at the man who led me here, and that's enough for him to bow to her and back out of the door. We're alone.

The Queen takes a deep breath, watching me. "Thank you for coming."

"I wouldn't refuse you."

Fire flashes in her eyes, sending sparks flying through my chest. "How long are you planning on being in Nord?"

"As long as it takes," I answer without thinking.

"You said that yesterday. For what?"

As long as it takes to make you mine. "To explore options... for the business," I answer, my voice stilted. I clamp my mouth shut, and the Queen motions to a sofa to my right. I wait for her to sit down across from me in a high, wingback chair, then take a seat where she indicated. Penelope folds her hands on her lap, looking regal and calm, but her eyes drill holes through me.

"I'm sure you're wondering why I called you here."

"I'd come here no matter what you wanted."

"Asher..." Her voice is a breathy whisper. She ducks her head, angling it to the side so I can see the graceful column of her neck. I want to lick it. Every part of her. Head to toe. Glancing back up at me, Penelope takes a deep breath. "I have a proposition for you, Mr. Gerhard."

I stifle a groan. Whenever she calls me that, it makes me imagine her on her knees in front of me, mouth open...

I nod. "I'm listening."

"I'm sure you've noticed the unrest in the capital."

"The protests?"

She inclines her head. "There have been a few major oil refineries that have closed recently, and a number of people have been left without jobs. Truck drivers, machinery operators, engineers. Unemployment is on the rise."

"You need new industries to open."

"I need people I can trust," she replies, her eyes searching mine. "Can I trust you?"

"With your life."

Penelope pauses, staring at me for a few moments. I try to hold her gaze, but all I want to do is rush over to her and take her in my arms. How is it possible for a woman to have this hold on me? I'm supposed to be listening to her business proposition, and all I can think about is how good she looks in that dress. My eyes drift down to her chest, tracing the soft curve of the neckline.

"At Prince Gabriel's wedding, I mentioned I was supposed to talk to a mining executive. I was referring to Reginald Donovan, of Donovan Enterprises."

I freeze, my eyes climbing back up to meet hers. Is this when she mentions the merger? Tells me she knows I've been hiding it from her?

Penelope continues. "Mr. Donovan has been trying to buy Crown land in the eastern part of the kingdom, near Roston. It's the second largest city in Nord, and a major industrial center." The Queen's voice is steady, but her hands tighten around each other. She's hesitating. With a breath, she continues. "Donovan Enterprises is planning on opening at least three large diamond mines in the area."

Air whooshes out of my lungs. *Diamonds*. That's why Donovan is here. All my investigative work over the past weeks has returned nothing, but the Queen just dropped that information in my lap without even knowing I needed it.

Again.

Discomfort churns in my gut. I should tell her. I should be honest about the merger. I should tell her why I came here...

...but then she'd think I was lying when I said I wanted to see her. I wouldn't be in this room if I'd told her I'm in Nord to find out what Reginald Donovan is up to. It's only been a couple of weeks since Gabriel's wedding, but I can't let this connection go. I can't bear the disappointment in her eyes. I can't imagine going on with life without the promise of seeing her again.

So I say nothing.

When I nod, Penelope continues. "The government would prefer to keep those mines under the control of the public resources conglomerate in Nord—the Nord Resources Group. But for reasons I won't go into, NRG isn't in a position —financially or managerially—to take on a project such as the diamond mines near Roston. There have been questions posed about the suitability of Donovan Enterprises. They have a less than stellar reputation, and I don't want to open my country up to companies that aren't reputable."

"I understand."

"I'm not sure you do, Asher," Penelope says. She leans forward. "I want you to provide a proposal for the land and mines. I can give you the contact details for Mick Burgundy, the director for the Nord Resources Group. I'd like you to put forward a proposal for a joint venture for the development of diamond mines in Roston. From what I understand, the Gerhard Corporation has a great track record and would have the capital to at least match Donovan's proposal. With NRG on board, your proposal would be even more attractive since you'd have Nordish local industry on your side. I can't guarantee you'll get the contract, but I *can* tell you parliament isn't completely satisfied with Donovan Enterprises. If there were another company in the mix, and especially one that's willing to work with a public company..."

The Queen is handing me a victory on a silver platter. She's giving me Donovan on his knees, and she doesn't even know it. A lump forms in my throat, and I struggle to swallow past it. "What about Donovan?"

She shakes her head. "I don't trust him. I'd rather work with someone who has a reputable company with a good history. You've already had good press in Nord, and you've only been here two weeks. We could help you grow your business here."

"We?"

Her lip tugs. "The royal we."

My mouth goes dry. Penelope is delivering the killing blow to Donovan Enterprises and making my job incredibly easy. By offering me the opportunity to bid on this land, this mine near Roston, the Queen is ensuring I go back to my father with not only Donovan Enterprises ready to merge with our corporation, but a new mine under construction with all the approvals in place. A sprint to the finish line with a royal head start.

It would be an unimaginable victory for me. Father would have no choice but to recognize my success. It would be enough to show him that I deserve the company, not Logan. No one—*no one*—would be able to close this deal as decisively as me.

I'd be a fool to refuse. I *can't* refuse. All the work I've done for my father has led me to this room. This deal. This conversation.

But...I should tell Pen about the merger. I should be honest about why I'm here. I should tell her I came here with the intention of finding out what Donovan was planning, and I should tell her she just made my job easier. I should tell her that once I submit a proposal for these mines, my father will no doubt proceed with the merger, and Donovan Enterprises will be part of our company, too.

No words come out, though. If I tell her, will she retract the deal? Or worse...will she cut off whatever connection is forming between us?

Gulping down my worries, I nod. "I'm interested. Get me in touch with NRG. I can have a proposal put together within two weeks, and I'm sure my company will be able to release the funds for the purchase of the land near Roston."

"Two weeks. That's sooner than even I expected," Penelope says softly. She takes a deep breath, stands, and extends her hand for me to shake. My palm slides over hers, and heat flows through my arm. I resist the urge to tug her closer and crush my lips to hers, but in Penelope's eyes I see something faint. Something hidden.

Yearning.

Penelope nods, making a soft, closed-mouth noise. "Good. I'll let my staff know to expect your proposal." She pauses, her cheeks slightly red. "Come with me." Penelope walks toward the door, her gauzy dress flowing around her legs like smoke. Her blond hair is twisted into a low bun, and those twinkling diamonds still garnish her ears. I want to kiss them—they're the only diamonds I care about right now.

When she stops at the door to wait for me, I scamper closer. I inhale her sweet scent, immediately forgetting why I'm here. Reginald who? I follow her out of the office, trailing in her wake like a dog on a leash.

Usually, I'd hate this. I've never been one to follow behind a woman—behind *anyone*. My father gives me free rein in the company because he knows I don't do well with authority. My results speak for themselves. I'm his best performer, and the person who's made him a very rich man.

But trailing behind Penelope...I have to admit I like it. I like the cool way she delivered her business proposal. I like the rational side of her, and the angry, slapping side of her, the undone, passionate side of her and every other emotion she's shown me—because none of those emotions are pity. None of them are disgust. She doesn't stare at my neck and jaw, trying to keep her face steady. Her eyes don't drift down, wondering just how much of my body is scarred.

No, Penelope doesn't even seem to notice. She gave me her pleasure and laughter at Prince Gabriel's wedding, she gave me her fury and annoyance, and now she's showing me that she, too, knows how to do business. I'll take it all. Anything. All of it—because to her, I know I'm not a monster. She sees *me*.

We walk in silence for a few moments, until we spill out into a large foyer at the back of the castle. Penelope glances over her shoulder at me. "I was angry yesterday," she says.

"You were."

"It was inappropriate of me."

"Are you trying to apologize right now?" My lips tug at the corners. "If so, you're not doing a great job."

"I'm trying to establish the boundaries of this relationship."

"And what are those?"

She pushes open a door, walking out onto an outdoor patio area. Potted plants line either side of the door, with a wide, paved path leading to the vast castle grounds. "I've decided I need you."

A jolt of heat pierces my gut.

Penelope cuts me with a glare. "Professionally, I mean."

"Right."

We walk for a few minutes, across a lawn and into a more wooded area. A fountain sprays into a pond at the end of the path. She pauses, glancing behind her, then turns to me. "We need to talk."

I nod. "I'm listening."

"I'm serious, Asher."

I bite back a groan. I love the way she says my name. It's sweeter on her tongue, somehow. Like it would sound good if she cried it out in ecstasy.

Penelope takes a deep breath. "What happened at Gabriel's wedding—"

"I understand."

"Let me speak," she snaps. Her eyes flick to mine, icy-blue and clear. "It...It was fun. But it can't happen again. This relationship must remain professional."

"Of course."

"No comments, Asher. No innuendo. No kisses. No touching. No slapping."

"To be fair, *you're* the one who slapped *me*."

She lets out a frustrated huff, and I can't quite hide my grin. "Asher, I mean it. The only reason I'm even considering this deal is because of the economic situation in Nord. We need heavy industry. Our workers need jobs."

"And I can provide them."

She holds up a hand. "But if anyone thinks I gave you that project because of some kind of...personal favor...it would look very, very bad. For both of us."

A soft breeze teases a strand of hair out of her bun, making it whip across her face. Before I can stop myself, I'm tucking it behind her ear. Her skin is so soft. She closes her eyes for just a moment, and everything goes still.

I forget that she's a queen, and I'm only a lowly business executive. I forget that she's telling me there can be nothing between us. I forget that my body is scarred and ugly, and no one will ever be able to love me when they see what the fire did to me.

Because in this moment, Penelope closes her eyes and lets out a soft sigh, and it's easy to forget everything around. "Asher," she whispers.

"The more you say my name, the more I want to kiss you." My voice is full of gravel. I take a step toward Penelope, letting my hand slide behind her ear to caress the nape of her neck.

"Did you not hear anything I just said?"

"I heard every word, Pen."

Her eyes meet mine, emotion warring within them. "So why are you doing this?"

"Because it feels too good not to."

"I'm not..." She shakes her head. "I'm not a regular woman, Asher. I need to be a queen to this country before everything else."

"I'm not asking you to give up the throne."

"But you are." Her voice is nothing but a whisper. "Touching me like that..." she trails off, closing her eyes.

With one hand drawing small circles over the nape of her neck, I slide my other hand over her hip. Her dress feels silky, and I let my fingers crawl down to rest on top of her ass. One step forward, and her chest is against mine.

"You can tell me to stop, Pen, and I will."

She lets out a sigh, conflict written all over her face.

"I wasn't pretending at Gabriel's wedding," I say. "I swear. What happened between us...it felt..."

Real.

The words don't come. We stand there, in silence, with her body melting into mine as I pull her near. Her lips part, and everything in my heart screams at me to kiss her.

"Pen, I really want to kiss you right now." My voice is a growl. A rasp. It's pure need.

"We can't," she whispers.

"Why not?"

"Because I'm the Queen, Asher." Her eyes are closed, her voice so soft.

"You're Penelope Stone."

"But I'm the Queen first." She pulls away, and it feels like she's ripping the air between us in two. Like the atmosphere is being shredded, throwing up an invisible shield between us.

I inhale deeply, dropping my head. "You're right. I'm sorry."

"We can't."

"I know." I know but oh, I hate it. I hate the fact that she's the Queen, and I need to work with her. I hate the fact that I care about the future of my company, and I know I need this diamond mine to inherit my father's business. I hate that not telling her about the Donovan merger feels a lot like a lie. I hate all the barriers between us.

I lift my hand to my neck, feeling the too-smooth skin of my scar. Penelope doesn't know it covers a third of my body. She doesn't realize I'm not like other men. I'm not beautiful and flawless like her husband was—perfect for photo opportunities and official paintings. I'm not worthy of her.

"For this to work, we have to keep things professional," Penelope says. The breeze flutters through stray strands of hair again, but I resist the urge to touch it.

I nod. "You're right. I apologize."

She sighs, shaking her head. "It's my fault. I never should have done anything with you."

Her words pierce my heart, spreading an ache through

my chest. I clear my throat and turn away from her, but I know the truth.

She doesn't feel what I feel. This connection I thought existed? It's one-sided.

Penelope needs me to employ her citizens, and I need her to earn my inheritance.

It's business.

11

———

PENELOPE

MIND REELING, I walk back to the castle with Asher and excuse myself. I hurry to my chambers and lock the door, dropping my head in my hands.

I'm in trouble.

How can I say I want to keep things professional when my body screams at me to act? To lean in and kiss him? To take his face in my hands and run my fingers over his lips?

How can I pretend to be a worthy queen when I'm so easily prepared to turn my back on my responsibilities for the sake of...lust? Or is it something more?

When Xavier died, I turned to my duty for comfort. The part of me that was open to love got buried in the ground beside him, and I resigned myself to my fate.

But now...

Shaking my head, I strip off my dress and take a shower. I need to wash off the embers Asher sprinkled all over my skin. I need to cool down my heated core and remind myself why I'm here. Who I am. What I need to do.

The water does nothing to temper my feelings. I find myself sliding my hands down lower, bracing myself against the tile wall. My fingers slip through another kind of wetness —one not caused by the shower. I shouldn't. I can't.

My hand doesn't listen, though. Fingers slide through my own arousal and I find that bundle of nerves promising sweet release. All I see is Asher. His broad hands, and the feeling of his palms on my hips. The hard planes of his chest. The taste of his kiss.

This finger sliding in and out of me? I wish it were his. The pleasure teasing through my thighs feels like a whisper of the real thing, but I still let myself go there. I picture his dark hair curled around my fingers, and his thick, hard cock driving inside me. I imagine his strong, broad body caging mine, and the feeling of letting go. Letting him take control. Letting him give me what I need.

Under the shower stream, I stifle a cry as an orgasm washes over me. My legs tremble as my core clenches on nothing, Asher's face burned in my mind. Panting, I stand under the shower for a while longer. It doesn't cool me down or wash away the feeling that I'm making a big mistake.

Asher may be beautiful. He might make my body feel more alive than it has in years. He might have a disarming smile and mischief in his dark brown eyes, but that doesn't mean I can pursue him—or anyone, for that matter.

I'm the heirless Queen of Nord, and my duty is to my people.

I SUCCEED in keeping things professional with Asher by avoiding him entirely—well, except for my dreams. More than once, I wake up tangled in my sheets with an ache between my legs. A week passes, then another. He communicates with me through official channels but not directly with me, which is fine. We're professionals. I don't normally talk to mining executives personally, anyway.

Whenever I see his name, heat blasts through my core. I wear an almost permanent blush. As the days roll into one another, I pretend I've regained control over myself. I almost forget the way it felt to be in the same room as him.

Almost.

But two weeks after our talk in the garden, my office receives the Gerhard Corporation's official application for mining rights and purchase of land near Roston. The proposal, as I requested with Asher, is for a joint venture between Gerhard Corporation and Nord Resources Group, with the former providing the capital and management oversight, and the latter providing the labor and diamond mining expertise. When I review the application, I'm impressed. Two weeks isn't a long time to put something like this together. It's almost unheard of—but this deal is too sweet to pass up. I knew it when I asked him to submit a proposal. I handed him a big, fat paycheck and a new market to explore.

I make a few comments, asking that the contracts stipulate a minimum percentage of local workers to be employed at the mines and construction sites at all times. I can tell by my staff and legal team's comments that this application is much more desirable than the Donovan one.

By making this deal with Asher, I might have just saved my kingdom from doing business with Donovan Enterprises —but I've cut myself off from ever being with Asher as anything other than a distant professional acquaintance.

THINGS MOVE QUICKLY. The protests in the kingdom are gaining steam, and the government is keen to announce something positive to the people. Gerhard Inc.'s application is approved within two more weeks, and the sale of land proceeds. Four weeks after I tell Asher about the diamond fields, his company officially purchases the land from the Crown.

Our relationship is officially professional and must remain that way. When I see the news break about the sale of the land and see the positive reaction of almost everyone in the country, I know I made the right decision. Nord needs new industry, and Asher is perfectly positioned to provide it.

Still, I can't help the feeling that I've lost something. A chance at...something. Love, maybe. Or at least companionship.

A week later, at the beginning of July, we receive an invitation to a ceremony to officially announce the start of the project. We'll be unveiling the preliminary plans to the locals and announcing the new mine to the world.

My presence would be appreciated, as it would make it very clear where the Crown stands. Royal approval of this project will be good for the mine—and good for my image. I've sustained so much criticism over the past few weeks that any good news will need to be blasted to the public.

As soon as the invitation comes through, I know where my duty lies. For once, it's aligned with what I want—and I want to go to Roston. I want to see Asher.

Travel preparations are made, and I try to quell the excitement that trills in my chest. I haven't seen Asher in five weeks. The day I'm supposed to travel to Roston, the eastern-most city in Nord, nervous butterflies tickle my stomach. I check my hair and touch up my makeup, then curse myself for caring.

But I don't care what Asher thinks of how I look—I just know there will be lots of photos taken...right? These are professional worries. It's not his presence that makes my stomach twist in knots.

A car takes me to a royal jet, which carries me up in the air toward Roston. I try not to fidget, choosing instead to review the official press release and the agenda for the day. We have a few scheduled stops to make in the city—the hospital and an elementary school, to start, then we'll head to the new mine site for the announcement. I'm to make a speech ratifying the agreement between NRG and Gerhard Incorporated.

They'll unveil the plans to start exploratory tests this summer, then spend the winter planning the construction of the mine. The official start of the project will be at the beginning of summer next year, but jobs will be available to Nordish locals throughout the next few months.

I should be relieved, but all I feel is a nervous kind of excitement.

The flight is bumpy. Turbulence shakes the aircraft like a paper plane, and I grip the edges of my seat until we're safely on the ground. It's hard to be graceful when my stomach is twisted up in knots—but is it due to the flight, or the fact that I'm going to see Asher again?

I smile and shake hands when I'm supposed to, and I'm ferried from one stop to another. The sky grows dark, and the wind starts to howl.

Even though I meet a hundred people, I see no one. I'm sure I do all the right things, because I've been doing these duties since I was ten. I've been the Queen for a long time. I smile when I'm supposed to and congratulate school kids on their achievements. The hospital visit is just as smooth, and I take all the required photos.

But when the royal car takes me toward the future mine site, I tense.

Asher will be there. I'll have to look at him, knowing I felt something when we were at Gabriel's wedding, but I'll have to ignore it. I'm the one who told him this had to stay professional. I'm the one who's stayed locked up in the castle and has avoided any business meetings where I knew Asher would be present.

If the connection between us has fizzled, it's my fault—but I did it for my duty to my people. I gave up that connection, let it die out, because it's what I *had* to do. What I still have to do to save my kingdom from recession and mass unemployment.

We arrive, and I'm led through a pack of reporters to a small stage. Asher's already there, along with Mick Burgundy. I barely see the second man. All my focus is on Asher, and the way his eyes track my every move. Despite the harsh wind, heat blazes through my body. Even the sight of him reminds me what it felt like to have his palms on my body, his lips on mine, his cock buried deep inside me.

And—I want that again. I want to feel like something more than a queen who stands in front of cameras and makes wooden speeches. I want to bare myself for him and know he sees me not as the Queen of Nord, but as Penelope Stone, the girl he knew in boarding school.

Gritting my teeth, I push the thought aside. That's not the life that was laid out before me. I was given a chance at love, and it ended in tragedy. I'm destined to walk through life alone—and after living through the agonizing heartbreak of my husband's death, I have no desire to re-live that experience.

I'm the Queen. Nothing more.

Asher keeps his head down in a show of deference, only flicking his eyes to mine when he rises from a bow. There's a hint of laughter in his gaze, and a whole heap of insolence.

I resist the urge to roll my eyes. At least he hasn't changed —and he's acting appropriately in front of the cameras.

My gaze flicks across his broad shoulders and down to his tapered waist. In a well-tailored wool pea coat, Asher looks like he belongs in the streets of New York, not a mine site in Nord. A scarf covers his neck, with only the barest hint of his scar showing above it on his jaw. Briefly, I wonder if he did it on purpose—hiding his scar for the pack of cameras that flash before us.

It's hard to keep my eyes to myself when he looks so wonderfully delicious. My fingers itch to unbutton his jacket, slowly revealing more of his muscular body. He never let me undress him when we had sex. I've been left wondering what he's hiding under those clothes, and my curiosity burns hot somewhere low, between my thighs.

Stop, Penelope. Be professional. He was off-limits before, and even more so now.

The ceremony starts. I make my speech, cameras flash, and I do my best to keep my voice steady. I don't look at Asher. Why would I? He's a businessman, and I'm the Queen. We shouldn't even know each other at all.

My heart tugs when I leave, and a deep sense of longing opens up in my chest. I didn't get a moment alone with him, but the fact that he was near made me feel warmer than I have in years. I barely even felt the wind—am I really ready to give that feeling up for my kingdom?

I've given so much to this place. Duty has worn me down to a shell of my former self, and I know the Crown will suck the life out of me until there's nothing left—but isn't that the duty of the Queen? To serve?

These feelings—longing, regret, red-hot lust—they don't matter. Not in the face of providing for my people.

On the way back to the airport, the intercom buzzes. Frederick, who's sitting in the front seat, speaks. *"Ma'am, we've just heard from the pilot. The wind is too strong to fly. We'll have to stay in Roston for the night."*

"That's fine, Frederick," I reply, settling back in my seat.

The intercom buzzes, then flicks off. There's a pause, as if my private secretary is hesitating. Finally, his voice comes through again. *"The hotel is undergoing renovations, and the rooms they do have are occupied by NRG's people, so they don't have an adequate suite for us. But...Mr. Gerhard has generously offered his home for the night."*

My eyes snap open, heat unfurling in my core. A whole night in the same building as Asher? What if I have a...*dream*? Will I be able to look in him in the eye in the morning? What if he sees the desire in my gaze and knows what I've been trying to resist?

I shouldn't stay at his house. But if I refuse, and the media catch wind, would it cause a controversy? If there truly was nothing behind Asher and me, then I would accept his offer graciously and thank him for his generosity. I need to act normal. The unruffled, cold Queen—but being in the same house as him is dangerous, and I'm not sure I have a choice.

Heart thumping, I press the intercom button. "Thank you, Frederick. We'll stay at Mr. Gerhard's residence." Mercifully, my voice doesn't tremble. I lean back in my chair as a gust of wind shakes the car, rattling my whole body. My thoughts scatter, and the only thing I can focus on is Asher. His face, his lips, the way it felt to have his hands on me in the royal gardens.

He makes me feel *warm*. Everywhere, all at once. It's intoxicating, even after all this time apart. As we pull in through a gate and I see a mid-sized house loom up ahead, I can't deny the excitement curling in my core.

My driver pulls up outside and Frederick rushes to open

the door for me. I'm hurried inside, where a maid is waiting to take my jacket. She's not alone. Asher stands a few steps behind her, a teasing grin playing over his lips. I flick my eyes to his, immediately regretting it.

Fire rips through my core at the sight of his gaze, which promises trouble. Delicious, mischievous trouble. Yearning rises up inside me like a hungry wolf, howling to be heard above the wind.

Clearing my throat, I nod. "Thank you for your generosity, Mr. Gerhard."

"Of course, Your Majesty," he says, saying my title with a hint of irony. He gives me a low bow, which on the surface, looks appropriate, but I can tell by the tug in his lips that he means it to be a joke. His hand moves to touch his cheek, and when his eyes flash, I know he's thinking of the slap.

I'd slap him right now if no one were watching.

He sweeps an arm toward the interior of the house. "I've had my team prepare rooms for you and your staff. I only moved in here a week ago, so you'll have to excuse the, uh, minimal furnishings."

I follow his gaze, noting the empty living room to my left. I follow him to a kitchen, which does have a table and chairs, but looks equally as bare as the living room. There's nothing on the walls. No decorative pillows or throws. It looks...soulless. Like Asher doesn't plan on staying. Why does that thought make my heart sting?

We head up the stairs, and Asher points out a row of doors to the left. "Those are for you and your staff. Once again, I apologize for how bare the rooms are."

"I appreciate you housing us, Mr. Gerhard."

His eyes glimmer, and I feel like I'm roleplaying. We're acting appropriately, when all I can think of is how badly I want to taste his kiss again.

No. Stop. That's not why I'm here. That's not why I approved this project or came here to celebrate the announcement. I'm doing this so people have jobs and I try to avoid mass unemployment during the next few years. I'm doing this for the people, because it's my responsibility to make sure my citizens are safe and fed and employed.

I'm definitely not here because Asher makes me feel like my body is on fire. It's not because he melts the ice that has clung to my veins for seven years. It's not because he makes me want to double over and laugh—and slap him silly at the same time.

"I'll be just down the hall," Asher says, pointing to a door, "if you need anything." I can hear the teasing in his tone. The slight emphasis on the word *anything*. The laughter dancing in his eyes.

The urge to slap him is strong.

"Much appreciated." My voice is frosty, but my core burns hotter. "I'm surprised you have a house here at all. I thought you'd be back in Farcliff as soon as you broke ground."

Asher shrugs. "Maybe I'm planning on staying longer than that."

He holds my gaze for a few moments as fire erupts low in my belly. My heart thumps hard at the thought of him staying—so close to me. Accessible. After a pause, Asher bows and heads back downstairs and out of view. I follow Frederick to my room, where my staff is unpacking an overnight bag that had been stowed in the plane. They bow to me and back out of the room, and I'm left alone to gather my racing thoughts.

With a sigh, I sit down on the edge of the bed, staring at the bare surroundings. There's a nightstand and a double bed, and a closet with no coat hangers in it. If he bought this place, does it mean he intends to spend time in Nord? Maybe the reason he's here isn't just money for his father's company.

Maybe he was telling the truth when he said he was drawn here for another reason...for me.

My heart thumps and I squeeze my eyes shut. Those are dangerous thoughts, and ones I can't afford to have if I'm going to be the Queen Nord needs me to be.

FREDERICK HAS my chef prepare a meal for my dinner, which I eat alone at the kitchen table. I pick at my food, barely finishing half the plate. I wonder where Asher is. After dinner, I ask to be left alone. Frederick is staying in the room next to mine, my security staff have rolled out sleeping mats on the ground floor, but I feel lonelier than I do in my big, empty castle in Stirling.

I lie back in bed, knowing sleep won't come. Asher's presence is everywhere. I hear a floorboard creaking down the hall, and my heart takes off.

Eyes squeezed shut, I try to regain control over my body. Asher and I talked about this. We have to keep things professional. What happened at Prince Gabriel's wedding was a mistake. A slip of judgement. I should never have done it.

Now, we need each other professionally. He needs my approval for his diamond mining operation, and I need him to provide jobs and housing for the workers along with a boost to NRG's operations. He'll help prevent widespread protests and strikes, and I'll make him a very rich man.

It's business.

So why does it feel like so much more? Why does it feel like fate?

After twisting and turning for an hour or three, I finally swing my legs off the bed. Taking my silky, white travel robe off a hook on the door, I wrap it around myself and head downstairs. Not even knowing where I'm going, I find myself padding toward the kitchen. My stomach grumbles, reminding me that I barely ate my dinner.

Silently, I tiptoe through the empty house. Guards are stationed outside, with their untouched sleeping mats laid out for later in the night. Most of them will probably stay outside until the small hours. I peer into living rooms devoid of furniture, wondering if Asher will actually establish himself here. Did he buy this house to stay, or is it just an empty symbol as a show of his commitment?

When I turn the corner to the kitchen, I let out a yelp.

Asher turns around, plate in hand, eating my leftovers from the fridge.

Oh—and he's shirtless.

My eyes drift down his strong shoulders and over his perfectly formed chest. His skin is taut over his broad frame, cords of muscle moving in fascinating ways as he turns toward me. His stomach shows every ridge and valley of abdominal muscle, ending in deep grooves that lead all the way down between his legs. Loose, gray pants hang low on his hips. I stare at him, taking it all in. This is what I wanted to see at Gabriel's wedding. This is what he hid from me, not letting me undress him.

My eyes snag on the left side of his body, where his scar extends down from his neck, covering part of his chest and wrapping around his side. The burn marks are still clearly visible, even decades after the accident. The skin is discolored and slightly raised, with wide bumps and ridges where healthy skin was grafted overtop. It looks like a patchwork of suffering and scars—the history of his pain, right there for the world to see.

"Asher," I whisper, unsure what I want to say.

"Majesty." His growly voice rattles through me, his eyes trained on mine. He lowers the plate of food to the counter, letting his arms hang loosely at his sides. One hand rises to touch the edge of his scar, near his heart, and my eyes flick up to his.

Slowly, Asher turns. I see the burn marks on his body extending all the way around his back, with rugged edges that look like the map of an unknown land. Somehow, I find myself walking toward him. Drawn to him. I step around the kitchen island as he glances at me, eyes dark.

"I guess it'll be easier to keep things professional now that you've seen what lies beneath," he says, dark smoke shrouding his words.

My fingers reach for his skin. It's warm as my hand skates over his chest, teasing the edge of his scar. The skin, uneven and strangely smooth, feels like magic under my fingers. Heat teases through my chest, sinking low down into my stomach. "You're beautiful," I whisper. It's a stupid thing to say to a man with a body like Asher's. He's all muscle and brawn, with a scar that makes him look like some kind of warrior god. He's arrogant, cocky—he knows how good he looks.

But when my eyes flick up to Asher's, I see surprise in his eyes—and something else. It's the same thing that's plagued me for weeks. The same thing that's twisted my stomach in knots since I crossed the threshold of his new home.

Hot, needy desire.

12

───────

ASHER

WHEN PEOPLE SEE MY BODY, they usually recoil. Sometimes it only lasts an instant, but I see it. There's a flash of surprise, then disgust, and occasionally pity, which is somehow worse.

Penelope, though...she doesn't look like she pities me. Her voice is reverent when she tells me I'm beautiful, and my heart inflates in my chest. It hurts to breathe. There's a lump in my throat that makes it hard to speak, and all I can do is stare at her fingers as they sweep over my damaged skin.

No pity. No disgust. She's...She's being honest. She likes the way I look. Is that...a joke? Why isn't she looking away? Why isn't she saying anything? Why is she still touching my skin like she loves the way it feels?

In the cool air of the kitchen, my body feels almost too sensitive. Goose bumps pimple over my skin and when Penelope sweeps her hands over my chest, she sends sparks flying through my body. She doesn't pause at the edge of my scar, choosing instead to lay her palm flat against my skin and slide her hand up to my shoulder. Her thumb teases the edge of my jaw as her eyes take me in. All of me. Scars and all.

117

"You didn't want me to take your shirt off at Gabriel's wedding," she says in a low rasp.

"No," I answer.

Her eyes meet mine, hot fire dancing in their icy blue depths. "I wish you'd let me."

"I was afraid," I whisper, surprising myself with my honesty.

"Of what?"

"Of the face you'd make when you saw me."

"How does my face look now?" Her brows draw together, and my hand cups her cheek.

Heat curls low in my stomach, but there's something else. A tugging in my chest. A twinge, deep inside me, telling me I'm not here just for a diamond mine. I'm not here to show my father I deserve to inherit the company. I shake my head, letting my eyes close for a moment. "You look like an angel."

Air is sucked in through her full, pink lips. Her thumb makes slow movements over my jaw, over and back. It's making me dizzy. With one hand cupping her cheek, I let my other hand find her hip. She notches one leg between my thighs, pressing her body against mine. She fuses herself against my mottled skin, holding me close as if there's nothing wrong with me at all.

"Pen," I say, pushing the word out past the obstruction in my throat. "I'm not sure I can stay professional. Not when you're here, like this..." Her robe feels silky beneath my fingertips and it would be so easy—so fucking easy—to slide it off her body and show her just how much I've missed having her in my arms.

Pen's eyes close, face tilting toward mine. I let my gaze sweep over her face, her lips, her jaw. Her neck is graceful, and her body perfectly molded to mine. She melts in my hands, clinging onto me as her thumb keeps moving on my jaw, so soft and consistent that she might be putting a spell on me. That movement—back and forth, back and forth—makes my head spin so fast I can't think about anything other than her, her, *her*.

"Maybe we can make an exception," she whispers, eyes still closed.

My heart thumps hard enough for her to feel it. It's bursting out of my chest. I tighten my grip on her hip, loving the way my fingers press into her flesh. When she rolls her core toward me, the heat between her legs rushes toward me and makes fire dance in my veins. Glancing down, I see her dressing gown slipping open. Her bare leg is against mine, gently grinding against my thigh. I groan. "I want to kiss you, Pen."

Opening her eyes, she lets a soft smile drift over her lips. "So what are you waiting for?"

Nothing, is what I'm waiting for. Sliding my hand to the nape of her neck, I tilt Penelope's face toward mine and crush my lips to hers. Somehow, her kiss tastes sweeter than the first time. A moan slips through her lips as she parts her mouth, deepening our kiss. She tastes like candy. Like roses in bloom. Like everything that's been missing from my life.

The newspapers are wrong about her. Nothing about Penelope is icy or cold. She's hot fire and sin.

My Queen.

Dropping my lips to her jaw, I leave a trail of kisses down her neck. I brush my lips over the shell of her ear, worshipping every inch of skin my lips come across. Penelope rewards me with whimpers and moans, sinking her fingers into my shoulders and pulling me close. Both shoulders—scarred and unscarred alike. Her hips roll against mine, gown falling open.

I let my hand sweep up the bare skin of her waist, feeling

sparks ignite against my palm. Her body—my God, I missed this. One of the shoulders of her dressing gown falls down, and my lips are drawn to her shoulder. Clawing at the silky fabric, I pull it down lower to expose her upper arm, her chest, the top of her breast.

Under the dressing gown, Penelope's wearing a thin, blue tank top and a tiny pair of matching shorts. I feel like an animal. Hunger for her sweeps through my core, and I see nothing except her soft, pliable body molding against mine, her swollen lips, her eyes full of need.

And I need her too. I need to feel her palms running over my skin—every inch of me. I need to feel the heat between her legs pressed up against my thigh. I need to feel her nails sinking into my shoulders as she pulls me closer. I need her to *touch* me. Touch the skin I've grown to hate and tell me she likes the way it feels. I need her to tell me I'm beautiful and *mean* it.

When I sweep my hands up her sides, my thumbs tease the undersides of her breasts. She trembles, lips parting. Her eyes meet mine, and I see none of the distant, cold Queen that was there before. She's all heat and fire, and she's all mine.

"Tell me what you like, Pen," I whisper, dropping my lips to her chest. I lay a kiss on the swell of her breast, then on the neckline of her shirt. Dipping down lower, I drag my teeth across her nipple, with only the thin fabric of her top keeping me from tasting her skin.

Penelope bucks against me. She gasps, clutching me tight as her head falls back. I grin, loving the way her face loses all its harshness. I'm seeing the real Penelope—just as she's seeing the real me.

Dragging my tongue over her breast, I suck her pebbled nipple into my mouth. Pen's fingers tangle into my hair, pushing me closer and tugging me away all at once. She arches her back, gasping again. I groan. I want her to make that noise again. Heat spears my core as I grind myself against her. I know she can feel me—my hardness. The steel pressing up against her stomach that tells her exactly what she does to me.

Moving to the other breast, I leave a wet patch on her blue top. With hazy eyes, Penelope glances down at me. She leans back against the kitchen counter, spreading her legs wider.

My heart is beating so fast I have to grip the edge of the counter to steady myself. When Penelope sweeps her hands over my shoulders and down my sides, she doesn't hesitate to run her palm over my scars. She holds me close, exploring every inch of my body with her hands.

No hesitation. No recoiling. No disgust hidden behind a thin veil of pity.

"This doesn't mean anything." Penelope gasps when I cup her breast and suck its peak between my teeth. Her fingers tug at my hair. "Whatever happens tonight, it doesn't mean anything, Asher. We go back to professionalism afterward."

"Okay," I answer, moving to kiss her clavicle, her neck, her ear. "It doesn't have to mean anything."

"I'll be the Queen again in the morning."

"What does that make you right now?"

She sucks her bottom lip between her teeth, staring up at me through thick lashes. "Yours."

13

PENELOPE

HALF OF ASHER'S face is cast in shadows with moonlight cutting the harsh angles on his face. Sharp cheekbones frame his features as his eyelids hang low and dark. His hair curls at the temples, inky black against his skin. I let my fingers drift over his lips, swollen from our kiss.

Every stitch of fabric on my body feels too sensitive. His hands are broad and strong and warm, and they send thrills of pleasure rushing wherever they touch—but it's his eyes that do the most to me. Dark, brooding, and dangerous, he looks at me like no man has looked at me before.

I'm not a conquest or a queen. To Asher, I'm just a woman and oh, it's intoxicating to feel that way. To strip off all the expectations of my station and just let myself...be.

I want to ask him if he meant it when he said he came back to Nord because he was drawn to me, or if the reason he bought this house was because he intends to stay. I want to ask him if he sees me as anything more than a means to an end, a way to make himself richer.

I want to ask him if he feels what I feel when we're together.

But...I'm scared of asking those questions because I don't want to hear the wrong answer. And what is the wrong answer? If he says yes, he feels this connection between us—it doesn't change the fact that we can't be together. I can't shirk my duty to be with him. I can't be anything other than the Queen, always the Queen.

And if he says no, he doesn't feel what I feel...well, I don't think I could handle that. I may be cold and shuttered and cut off from most people, but underneath it all, I'm too fragile. Too weak to hear those words aloud.

There's no good answer, so I don't ask the question. Tonight, we give in to temptation. We let our fingers roam and our lips taste, and we let ourselves need. Nearly alone in this big house with him, I feel like a new woman. Heat winds its way through my core and all I want to do is squeeze my thighs together against the emptiness between them.

Instead, I walk my fingers up Asher's chest, exploring every bit of exposed skin. I let my eyes wander over his body, taking it all in. I want to remember this.

Tonight, I'm not the Queen. He's not a mining executive. We're two old friends, drawn to each other in our loneliness. We're scratching an itch, that's all.

"You're not going to slap me tonight, are you?" His eyebrow arches.

I purse my lips. "I wasn't planning on it."

"That's disappointing." He pouts, his bottom lip looking too good not to kiss.

I roll my eyes. "There's something wrong with you."

Asher pushes his leg between mine and I stifle a whimper. His hands slide over my breasts, tweaking my nipples and sending another jet of heat straight between my legs. How would it feel to have his lips on my breasts without any fabric between them? Suddenly, I need to know. I need to feel his lips on me everywhere.

Closing my eyes, I arch my back and shamelessly roll my core toward him. The loose, gray pants that cover his strong thighs is soft between my legs, but I wish he were wearing nothing at all. I let my fingers drift down past the waistband, stopping just above his ass.

"You can touch me." He grins. "I know you want to."

"You're too arrogant for your own good, Asher." I try to purse my lips, but I can't quite hide my desire. My hands slip lower, feeling the curve of his powerful muscles. He thrusts against me, gently, and I feel his ass clench and move beneath my palms. At my front, against my stomach, I feel the thing I've been missing for weeks. The hardness that will quench this relentless ache inside me.

Sucking in a breath, I meet his eyes. Asher's gaze lowers to my lips, and he shakes his head. "Do you know how I know you've been through hell and lived to tell the day?" His hand slides up underneath my shirt, and the heat of his palm against my stomach makes my head spin.

"How?" My eyes are closed, and I tilt my head back, enjoying the movement of his palm. His fingers sweep just below my navel in intoxicating circles.

"You didn't flinch when you saw my body."

I open my eyes, frowning. "I'm not sure you've looked in the mirror lately, Asher, but your body isn't exactly hard to look at."

His eyes soften, his hand sweeping higher. When his thumb brushes over my pebbled nipple, I let out a shiver. Yes, that feels incredible without any fabric between us. Fire burns a wide path straight between my legs.

"Not many people would agree with that statement, Pen." His voice is dark. Rough.

I meet Asher's eye, searching his face. "Why? Because of this?" My hand slides over the ridges and soft bumps of his scar. I shake my head, sighing. "Every part of you is beautiful." Flicking my eyes up to his, I grin. "I hope I don't regret saying that. You're arrogant enough as it is."

A corner of his lips tugs. "It's an act."

"Are you telling me your attitude is a defense mechanism?" I give him a teasing smile, but Asher doesn't return it.

Instead, he dips his head and angles his mouth against mine, gently brushing his lips over my own. It's barely a touch. Not quite a kiss. Embers burn through my veins as my whole body reacts to his touch, arching toward him, as if on a primal level, I know I need more.

"No one's seen me shirtless in years," he whispers. Before I can answer, Asher crushes his lips to mine. His kiss is ravenous. Hungry. Almost desperate. He lets his hands slide down, one wrapping around behind my ass and the other slipping down the front of my shorts.

We're in a kitchen, with security staff all around outside the house and my private secretary upstairs. Anyone could see us. It's highly inappropriate and completely out of character for me...but I can't stop. It feels like I *need* this. I need Asher's touch, his kiss, his cock. I need to feel his skin against mine and let him show me what I've been missing.

And, in a way, I think he needs me too. We're two lonely souls, scarred and broken, and we've found each other in the long, endless night. What's one more moment of bliss? Why wouldn't we give in, just this once?

Asher's hand slides over my mound to the wetness between my thighs. He groans when he feels my arousal, kissing me hard. "You're wet for me, Pen."

I moan, angling my hips toward him. If only he knew how aroused I've been all day, or how many times I've touched myself to the thought of him. His fingers brush against my sensitive bud, sending a violent shiver through my body. Asher grins against my lips, a low chuckle escaping his throat. The sound winds the tension inside me tighter, as if every sound he makes, every touch, every kiss—it all just serves to make me want him more.

When he slides his hand through my slit and teases the edge of my opening, I let out another whimper. There are no words. My brain isn't functioning. Heat curls in the pit of my stomach, causing every muscle to bunch and tighten. The wet fabric on my breasts clings to me, rubbing in the most deliciously sensitive way.

But it's Asher's body against mine that sends my body spiraling. His broad shoulders caging me against the kitchen counter. His strong leg nestled between mine. His long, hard cock pressed up against my hip.

When he slides a finger inside me, I gasp. His thumb finds my bud and the pressure inside me builds. He kisses my earlobe, my neck, the corner of my lip. He grunts when he feels me buck, and my hands fly to his shoulders, his body. I claw at him, pulling him closer.

He slides another finger inside me, stretching me as I gasp. My hips grind against him, and I don't even have the energy to be embarrassed that I'm losing control. I rub myself against his hand as he urges me on with low moans and soft grunts.

Asher's teeth scrape across my throat, and a shiver of pleasure tumbles through my veins. I clench around his fingers and before I know what's happening, Asher's on his knees in front of me and tearing my shorts off my legs. He hooks one leg over his shoulder and covers my wet slit with his mouth.

Stifling a scream, I bite my lip. His tongue laps me up

from back to front, sucking and kissing and *devouring* me. My hands are tangled in his hair, black strands curled around every finger. My leg is hooked on his shoulder. I grind myself against him and—I come apart. Sucking in a breath, my whole body tenses. In this moment, with ecstasy coursing through my veins, I don't have time to think about what this means or why he's here. I can't think about who I am. What I'm supposed to be doing.

I'm just a woman coming apart, loving the way Asher moans as he tastes my orgasm. He's enjoying this too.

When my body relaxes, Asher stands. His breath comes in short, sharp gasps as his eyes hang low. "Penelope," he rasps, staring at my lips, my shoulder, my breasts.

Cool air brushes against my most sensitive parts, but it does nothing to dim the fire burning inside me. I reach for his sweatpants, sliding my hand inside. A growl rumbles at the back of his throat when I feel his length. As I wrap my fingers around him, he stares at me and shakes his head.

"You are unlike anyone I've ever met, Penelope." His lips tease mine as I grip him. His cock is like velvet-covered steel, and the feel of him in my hand makes me ache with painful emptiness. Fascinated, I watch as he hooks his thumbs into his waistband and lets his pants drop to the ground right next to my shorts.

My breath catches. He's...beautiful. Gloriously male. Power incarnate. I stare at him, taking it all in, as my heart thumps and my body temperature cranks up a few more degrees.

"I want to see your face when you come this time," he says, his eyes promising sinful ecstasy. When he slides his hands over my hips, I lift my arms and let him take my top and robe off. Before they even hit the ground, his lips are on my breasts. I gasp, wrapping my arms around his neck and holding him close. He slides his hands to my lower back and tugs me closer so I can feel him pressed up against my stomach.

Hard as a rock. For me.

Hot lava pours into my veins as he sweeps his tongue over my breast, tugging it gently with his teeth. I let out a sigh, knowing I need more. I need *him*. My arousal is making my head spin, and if I don't feel him inside me, I think the ache in my body might kill me.

Lifting myself onto the edge of the stone countertop, I wrap my legs around his waist.

His eyes cut to mine, then drift down my naked body and come to rest between my legs. His lids hang low and the look of pure pleasure on his face makes fire lash through my body. With one hand gripping my waist, Asher grabs his shaft with the other and angles it against me.

We don't speak. There's nothing to say. We both want this—desperately. We both want to feel like we've found someone who understands.

And just for tonight, we're not alone. I can pretend I'm just Penelope, and he's just Asher. I can close my eyes and enjoy the feel of his skin beneath my palms, without worrying about what it means to feel him close.

Asher pushes into me, and the pressure is almost too much. I'm not used to feeling something so long and thick between my legs. I whimper, and he pauses.

"Are you okay?" His hand moves gently over my waist.

I nod. "Yeah."

Gently, he thrusts another inch. And another. My body slowly stretches to accommodate him, and I flick my eyes up to his. He's staring down to where we're joined. His cheeks are red, lips still glistening with my arousal. He looks totally, completely enraptured, and I let myself relax.

He groans, pushing deep inside me with one long movement. I shift the angle of my hips and wrap my legs around him, taking him deeper. He falls forward, catching himself on the counter with hands on either side of me. I let my fingers slide over his temple, curling into the strands of hair that fall over his forehead.

When we had sex the first time, it was hot and dirty and rough. I loved every second of it. It made me feel alive.

But this...this is different. Asher drags himself out of me and pushes in deep and slow. It's torturous, as if he's dragging the pleasure out of me and teasing me for endless seconds before pushing back in. He knows how badly I want his cock filling me up. He knows how desperate I am to feel him bury himself inside me—but he pauses, slows, and stretches every second of pleasure out longer than I can bear. His mouth hovers over mine. I can feel every sigh. Every grunt. Every moan. I rock my hips against him as we move slowly, my hands exploring his beautifully scarred body.

This isn't a hot fuck in a dingy old break room. This is intimate. It...it feels almost...*real.*

Asher's hands wrap around my waist and he holds me close, spearing me over and over in steady, slow movements. We fall into a rhythm that has me quickly spiraling out of control. Still, Asher refuses to speed up. Even when I buck my hips against him and try to take charge of the pace, he stills until I sigh, whimpering. His slow thrusts continue, urging me higher and higher as I struggle to maintain control over my own rioting body.

Every time he pushes inside me, heat pulses through my veins. The build is sweet, slow torture. A bundle of heat tightens deep inside me, coaxed to life by his thrusts. He moves as if we have all the time in the world. As if there's no risk of someone walking into the kitchen. As if there's nothing between us that says this is a bad idea.

His eyes watch me, hanging low, taking in every bit of me as if he's mesmerized.

When Asher reaches between us and presses his thumb over my bud, I gasp. When he rocks against me at just the right angle, I cry out, the noise muffled by his body. He cages me against the countertop and drives his cock inside me again, slow and deep and—

My orgasm rips through my body like wildfire. Everywhere he's touched in the past hour lights up, as if my cells have memory encoded specifically with him. My breasts tighten, my core clenches. I cling onto him, wrapping my arms and legs around him as my teeth sink into his shoulder. He urges me on with low grunts, kissing wherever his lips land.

"That's it," he growls. "Come on my cock just like you came on my tongue a minute ago. Give it to me."

No one has said those things to me. Not even my late husband. No one has said dirty, delicious things in my ear as I come, urging me to let go and let my pleasure take me higher and higher.

Asher's fingers don't stop moving over my clit and before I know it, another wave of pleasure is crashing into me. I'm trembling. Panting. Saying his name over and over like a mantra. A prayer.

With a grunt, Asher finds release. Our orgasms twist and wind around each other as I hold on for dear life, my nails sinking into his skin as he fills me up with his seed.

I...I love it. I love feeling him inside me like this, throbbing and panting as pleasure relaxes every line in his face. I love feeling connected to him on a primal level. I love knowing his orgasm is inside me, as if it belongs to me now. *Mine*.

When we pull apart, Asher's eyes are clear. I kiss his cheek, his jaw, his chest. It's only when I pull away and see his face that I notice the way his eyes shine. His hand drifts over the spot where I kissed his chest, where the burn scar covers his heart.

Asher leans over and kisses my lips. He's trembling. It's a soft kiss, but it contains a thousand unsaid words, hidden emotions, and layers of pain.

I know what his kiss means, because I feel exactly the same thing.

I've found someone who knows me—the real me. The only problem is we can never have each other.

14

ASHER

MY FINGERS DRIFT over Penelope's skin as I nuzzle my lips into her neck. She tastes sweet, and I know we've just shared something special.

Her eyes drift over my neck, following the jagged edge of my scar all the way down to my hip. She runs her fingers over the skin as I try my best not to wince.

No one's touched me like this before—almost reverently. Flicking her eyes up to meet my gaze, Penelope smiles. "You look like some kind of gladiator," she whispers. Her hands sweep around my back, and there's no disgust in her face. No hesitation at touching the scarred skin.

It covers a third of my body, and Penelope...likes it?

I try not to frown as she lets her hands drift over me, struggling to understand how she could see me as anything more than damaged. Because isn't that what I am? Broken? Marred?

"Do you remember the fire?" Pen asks, smoothing her palm over my shoulder and sliding it up to my neck. Her thumb teases my jaw, and I lean down to nip the tip of her finger, grinning when she yelps.

I nod. "I do."

Biting her lip, Penelope glances at me through long lashes. "What was it like?"

"Terrifying."

"I'm sorry," she whispers, but there's no pity in her voice.

I lean over to hand her the discarded shorts and top, then help her slip on her robe. Pulling my own pants up over my hips, I shrug. "You've got nothing to be sorry about. It wasn't your fault."

"I know, but I had just left the day before. If I'd stayed..."

"I wouldn't have been moping in my room missing you when the fire started?" I grin, teasing. Penelope's face falls, as if I've just spoken her deepest fears. "Hey," I say, sliding my hands over her hips. "It wasn't your fault."

"Did it hurt?" Her brows draw together, and for the first time, I feel like someone really wants to hear about that day.

People have asked me about it, of course, but there's always been some sort of sick curiosity underlying their words. Behind their well-meaning stares full of pity and sadness, there's always a hint of pleasure at my misfortune, like they're watching a gruesome true crime documentary play out on my face. Those conversations always leave a bitter coating in my mouth.

With Penelope, there's none of that. She asks me about the fire as if she wants to know—not because she wants to feel better about herself or because she wants to pity me, but because she truly wants to understand what it was like that day at boarding school.

Roughing my hand through my hair, I take a deep breath. "Yeah, it hurt," I finally answer, my thoughts faraway. It's like remembering an old movie, as if my brain has shielded me from the true horror of that day. "I was stuck on the top floor, and I ended up crawling down the stairs to the entrance. The fire was blocking my path."

Penelope's hands reach for my chest, drawing soft circles over my skin. I slide my hands around her waist, loving the closeness of her body. I haven't talked about this in a long time. I don't like remembering the years of doctors' appointments and skin grafts and operations.

It's a visible scar no one wants to acknowledge—least of all me.

I gulp. "I had to run through it. My shirt caught fire, but they said I was lucky I didn't inhale more smoke. They said by crawling to the exit and running out, I saved my own life."

Penelope's shoulders drop as her hands slide up to the nape of my neck. She wraps herself around me, leaning her cheek against my chest. Her skin rests right above my heart, where the edge of my scar begins. "I'm so sorry, Asher."

"It wasn't your fault."

"I feel like I have no right to be upset about anything. My life has been easy."

"Just because you don't show your scars doesn't mean they aren't there." My voice is soft, and I let my hand drift through Penelope's hair. I tuck a strand of gold behind her ear, kissing the top of her head. Here, like this, alone in a house on the edge of the world, it almost feels like nothing else exists.

I'm not my father's son. I'm not here to start a new mining project. She's not the Queen. We're just two people who understand each other. Need each other.

"I've never really talked about the fire," I admit. "Whenever people ask me about it, it always feels like they're doing it to satisfy their own perverted urges."

"That's how I feel about Xavier's death," Penelope says, her voice soft. "Sometimes I get the impression they used my grief as a symbol of virtue for me. Like if I ever wanted to move forward, I wasn't allowed to."

"The people of Nord?"

"The media. My family. My advisors." She lets out a dry laugh, shaking her head. "It's not that bad. Cost of wearing the crown, I guess."

"You're allowed to struggle."

Penelope glances up at me, smiling sadly. "No, I'm not."

"That's how I feel sometimes, too. Unless I'm achieving more than everyone else at the company, I'm just the boy who was in the fire. I have to perform better than my brother, bring in more business, be more ruthless—all in the hope that people see me as something other than the sum of my scars."

"You're a lot more than that, Asher."

"Am I, though?" I think of the way my father's eyes drop to my neck whenever I walk in the room. How he averts his eyes whenever a sliver of skin is showing. How even after everything I've done for him, he still plans on giving the company to my incompetent, pretty-boy brother.

"You'll be providing jobs for a lot of people who need them."

"And they'll be providing my father with healthy profits." Bitterness soaks through my voice, and I wonder why I'm doing any of this. For my father? For the money?

It all seems so...meaningless.

Penelope sighs, pulling away from me. She puts her hands on either side of my face, pulling me down for a soft kiss. "You walked through fire and lived, Asher. That's nothing to be ashamed of."

I open my mouth to protest, but nothing comes out. In the few times I've seen Penelope, it's like she understands my deepest fears. My greatest shame. And, amazingly, she doesn't judge me for it.

Penelope smiles sadly, shaking her head. "I feel a lot of shame for never having given Xavier an heir. He died knowing I couldn't give him the one thing he really wanted."

"A child? Were you trying?"

Penelope lets out a snort. "Trying? We were desperate for it. *I* was desperate for it. We tried for many years. I...I'm infertile." When her eyes meet mine, I see nothing but sadness in them. There are no tears, but it's something deeper. An old wound that refuses to heal. Scar tissue so thick, it's impossible to ignore. Penelope pinches her lips. "I have polycystic ovary syndrome," she explains. "The doctors kept telling me there was nothing wrong with me because I was a healthy weight and things seemed normal. They couldn't find anything wrong with me. But there were little things, you know. My cycle was messed up, and we found out later I wasn't ovulating. I *knew* something was off. I let doctors push me around and tell me I was fine. I guess, I just...I never advocated for myself. Maybe if I'd known sooner, I could have done something. I don't know what, because we tried every single fertility treatment we could find, but..."

My heart squeezes. I hold Penelope, my fingers sliding over the silky fabric of her robe. She doesn't meet my eye. Tightness in my throat makes it hard to swallow, but I manage to take a full breath. "That's not your fault, Pen."

"And the fire wasn't yours, but we still have to deal with the consequences, don't we?" Her voice has sharp, jagged edges. She shakes her head, dropping her eyes. "Sorry."

"Never apologize for speaking your mind."

"It's not something I'm supposed to do." She grins. "I'm the Queen. I don't have a mind of my own."

"You have a mind, and it's beautiful." My voice is gruff as I sweep my finger over her cheek. Penelope closes her eyes, tilting her head toward me. She melts into me as if my touch is made of magic, as if there's some connection between us that can't be ignored.

I feel it, too.

"I wish you were here under different circumstances," she whispers.

"What do you mean?"

"Not business related," Penelope says, her eyes still closed. "So we could...spend time together."

So there was no conflict of interest. So you didn't feel like I'm using you to make a profit.

I hear her unsaid thoughts, and I want to respond. I want to tell her that I wish the same. I wish I'd had the courage to walk away from my father's company so I could stand next to her. I wish I'd come to Nord without pretense, without needing a shroud of business to give me an excuse. I wish I hadn't lied about Donovan. Lied by omission—but a lie is a lie, and this one hangs heavy on my mind.

I wish I'd had the courage to come to Nord simply because I wanted to see Penelope again—because after all, isn't that the truth?

15

PENELOPE

ASHER and I share a late night meal in the kitchen. It's intimate and quiet and...nice. He makes me laugh when he teases me about my time at boarding school and makes my heart warm when I catch him glancing at me across the kitchen island.

I feel nothing like a monarch and I forget the responsibilities I'll have tomorrow. For a few hours, I just...exist.

Then, with one last soft kiss, I head upstairs and disappear into my room. Lying in bed by myself isn't where I want to be, but I know it's what has to happen. After all, what happened in the kitchen felt special, but I have to remember who I am and why I'm here.

If word got out that I was sleeping with, well, *anyone*, it would cause a splash. But if word got out that I was sleeping with the man who had just been awarded the right to mine Nordish land? That would be more than controversy. It would taint not only my reputation as Queen, but put a stain on Asher's reputation, too.

The best thing for me to do is stay away from Asher until the discontent in Nord subsides and the mining operation is well underway…but it doesn't make it any easier to stay on my own. Asher's the first person to make me feel almost whole.

I turn onto my side, hugging a pillow to my chest, enjoying the soft warmth that permeates my stomach. Closing my eyes, I do my best to push the thoughts of Asher out of my mind.

My team ushers me away from Asher's house in the early hours. We say a rushed, polite goodbye, with nothing but a flash in Asher's eyes to remind me of what we did last night. Then I'm whisked off to the plane and back to Stirling.

Once I'm home I feel somehow colder. I walk to my office and bury myself in work, asking not to be disturbed.

I don't hear from Asher that day. Or the next.

Protesters still picket outside the castle gates, but their numbers seem to lessen. Then, on the third day after the official announcement of the mine, I turn on the television in my office to see Asher doing an exclusive interview with one of my greatest critics.

Jacinthe Crawley, the woman who wrote the front-page article on Asher, is on the screen. She's a staunch abolitionist, wanting to strip me of my titles and make Nord a republic. With deep, black hair and angular features, she makes a striking image on the television.

Across from her, Asher sits. My eyebrows arch when I see the top button of his shirt undone, revealing more of his burn scar than he usually does. He gives Jacinthe a smile, and bitter jealousy twists somewhere deep in my stomach.

Irrational, sure. But it's there.

Gulping, I turn up the volume.

"…The new mines will provide jobs for over two thousand people during construction, and seven hundred and fifty permanent jobs during the operating phase." Asher's hands are folded on his lap as he reclines against the back of the chair, looking powerful and completely at ease. "If phases two and three of the project are approved, those numbers could triple."

Jacinthe shifts in her seat, crossing one leg over the other. She leans forward, a dangerous look dancing in her eyes. "Mr. Gerhard, is it true the Queen initially rejected your proposal to open the diamond mine? She stood in the way of Nordish progress until you were able to convince her otherwise, happy to let thousands of people remain without employment while Nord threatens to enter a recession?"

I grind my teeth together. That's a total lie. I'm the one who told Asher about the diamond fields and encouraged him to submit a proposal. *Me*. Crawley has always been able to twist the truth for her own agenda—but then, I suppose, she *is* a reporter. She has headlines to sell and an agenda to push—one that includes the end of the monarchy in Nord.

Asher chuckles, the sound low and warm, with just a hint of menace. I clench my thighs together, leaning toward the screen. "The Crown has been nothing but supportive of our efforts near Roston. The Queen herself even made the trip and managed to get us to commit to thirty percent more jobs guaranteed to Nordish citizens. She was in full support of the joint venture with NRG, ensuring that Nordish interests were front and center in the project. She very clearly stated she didn't want us to bring in workers from elsewhere when there were hundreds of qualified tradespeople and professionals in Nord. Her Majesty wasn't standing in the way of Nordish progress. Quite the opposite—she advocated for her people every step of the way."

Warmth curls in my heart as my cheeks grow pink. Asher didn't have to say that. Yes, it's true I asked him to guarantee jobs for my people. But to admit it on television? That makes me look good at his own expense. He could have played it off as a quality of his own company. Instead, he chose to shine a favorable light on me.

My breath catches as the camera stills on Asher, his upper body in the frame. The pinkish, pale skin on his neck is on full display, and he makes no move to cover it up. Pride swells inside me, and I wonder if our evening together had an effect on him. Did he feel the shift between us, as I did? Did it hurt him to see me leave? Has he been thinking of me as much as I have him?

Shaking my head, I lean back in the chair and listen to the rest of the interview. I wouldn't have that kind of effect on him. What we shared in the kitchen—and at Prince Gabriel's wedding, if I'm honest—was special, but that doesn't mean it changed the fabric of who Asher is.

If he's showing off the scar, it's either because he's always felt comfortable doing so, or he thinks it'll be beneficial to the reception he gets in Nord. Nothing more. He's a businessman and an incredibly clever one at that. His interview today has nothing to do with me.

Still, when I flick the television off, I clutch the remote to my breast and let out a long sigh. Something is changing inside me. I no longer feel like the world is muffled under a layer of frost. My emotions aren't cold and distant.

Heat is melting the ice inside me. Fire is making me feel alive. Asher's presence is bringing me back to life, and I don't know what to do about it.

If I pursue these feelings, I open myself up to criticism, ridicule, and rejection. I could be accused of signing off on the mining rights at Roston because he's my lover, and not because it's good for Nord.

But if I turn my back on Asher, can I really face a lifetime of cold distance? Can I keep my feelings at arm's length and pretend that nothing has been awoken inside me? Can I say goodbye to Asher and resign myself to a life of loneliness?

As I sit in my office, with the same four walls that have surrounded me since I became the Queen at ten years old, conflict rages within me.

On one side, duty. On the other, life.

Both have been one and the same until Asher walked into my life and showed me what I've been missing. My life *was* my duty until now.

Until Asher.

16

ASHER

REGINALD DONOVAN'S whole head is bright red. Fire sparks in his eyes as steam curls out of his ears. "You bastard," he sneers, leaning his knuckles on my desk.

I lean back, tenting my fingers in front of my chest. Popping a brow, I look the man up and down. The buttons of his poor shirt are straining against the effort of remaining closed. His hair is sticking up at odd angles, and it looks like he ran the whole way here. Not that he'd be able to run very far. Cruel, tangy satisfaction tickles my tongue as I allow myself to smile. "Hello, Reggie."

"Don't fucking *Reggie* me, you piece of shit." Spittle flies from his mouth, spraying my forehead with saliva.

The diamond mines have been all over the news. I've been doing interviews and press releases day in, day out. The people of Nord are happy about the new industry, and Gerhard, Inc. has gotten more good press since the announcement than we do in a full year. The partnership with NRG is the best deal I've made in years.

Suck on that, Logan.

I have Penelope to thank for it—and I've been making

143

sure to make that clear in every interview I have. She might be the Ice Queen of Nord, but she deserves the credit for this.

Shaking out a handkerchief, I dab Reginald's spit off my face. "I assume you heard about the diamond fields near Roston."

"You snake. You little fucking dog. I bet your father's happy with you. Did he give you a tasty little dog treat, you…you…you…"

"If you're going to keep calling me names, Reggie, I'm going to have you escorted out of here."

"How did you get an application in so fast? My contacts at the government told me I was the only applicant interested in the land in Roston."

"I guess your contacts were wrong." I don't even attempt to hide my grin, enjoying the nice shade of purple that sweeps over Reginald's cheeks.

"Something's fishy here."

"Are you just going down the list of animals, or…?" My grin widens. Nico, sitting in the corner of the room, chokes on a laugh.

Reginald spins around, huffing out a grunt. He walks back and forth across the room, throwing me hateful glares. "I'll find out who told you about this and wring their neck."

"Doubtful."

"You did something illegal. I've heard how you operate, Gerhard. You did *something* wrong, and I'll find out what it is."

"You'll sign on the dotted line and let the Gerhard Corporation absorb your company."

"Over my dead body."

"Cute." I push my chair back, standing up. Turning my back to Reginald, I stare out the Stirling office window at the city sprawled at my feet. I feel like an explorer discovering new lands. Donovan's protests only make me hungrier for more. More success. More money. More business.

In the distance, the castle gleams in the bright, summer sun. I stare at the building, wondering what Penelope is doing now.

"I'll never hand my company over to you, Gerhard."

"Of course not." I glance over my shoulder, grinning. "You'll still maintain some control over your operations, Reggie. On paper, at least. The only thing that will change is you'll have to report to us."

"I'd rather die."

"That can be arranged."

Donovan huffs, kicks the leg of a sofa, and winces. "I found that land months ago. It took weeks to get the geotechnical reports approved to prove the existence of diamonds. Putting the proposal through to purchase the land took even longer. How the hell did you manage it so quickly? A few weeks ago, I was assured no one else knew about it."

"Someone did," I answer.

"Who?"

"That, I can't say." My eyes flash. I would never throw Penelope under the bus. I'd never tell Donovan or anyone else that she approached me. All Penelope did was tell me about an opportunity and arrange a conversation between me and Mick Burgundy. She had no say in who was sold the land near Roston, or whose application for mining rights was approved. The parliament handled the actual application.

Still, I feel the need to protect her from any criticism. There's no corruption here, just an opportunity—but would the public see it that way?

Donovan swears, then turns on his heels and leaves without another word. I wait for the door to close behind him, then let out a sigh. Sinking down into my chair, unease gurgles in my stomach.

"He's mad," Nico says from his chair on the edge of the room.

I glance at my second-in-command, shrugging more nonchalantly than I feel. "It's understandable. I scooped his get-out-of-merger-free card out from under his nose." And I did it with the blessing of the Queen. "He knows he has nowhere to go, and he knows his shareholders will accept the deal we propose. He's done."

"How the hell did you manage that? You still haven't told me your source."

Scrubbing a hand over my jaw, I glance out the window at the castle again. "Confidential, Nico."

"Even from me?"

I grin. "Don't get your panties in a twist. Where's the progress report on the design of the site offices? We need to break ground within weeks."

Nico throws me a glance as if to say, *I'll find out your source eventually*, which I ignore. He stalks out of the room and I finally release a long breath. My shoulders slump.

What will happen when Penelope finds out about the merger? Will she know I failed to tell her about my interest in Donovan's company? Will she think I used her for information?

Did I use her? Have I done something wrong here?

Guilt tastes bitter on my tongue. I can't shake the feeling that I've done something I'll regret—but why would I feel that way? Penelope was clear that she couldn't influence the approval of the project. We won it fair and square—all she did was tell me about the opportunity. She was also clear that she wanted to keep things professional between us...although our night in Roston wasn't exactly following those rules.

She'll find out about this merger, which means she'll think I lied and used her.

I shouldn't care. Normally, I wouldn't. It's business. Lies are part of the game. Using people is how you get ahead. This is how I've become successful, and it's how I'll prove to my father that I deserve to inherit the company.

Somehow, though, this feels different. I don't want to treat Penelope the way I've treated others. She deserves better than that...better than me.

WORK SENDS me to Roston as the preparations are made to start construction of the site offices, but my mind is in the capital with Penelope. I learn of an industry gala happening in two weeks' time and hear a rumor that the Queen might attend. I immediately buy a ticket.

Those two weeks are spent thinking about the merger with Donovan Enterprises, and resigning myself to the fact that I'll have to be honest with Penelope. I need to tell her about my father's intentions to take over Reggie Donovan's company. I need to tell her it was in the works long before she told me about his interests in Nord. I need to tell her the truth—the whole truth—and accept whatever consequences come with that.

She might hate me. She might never want to see me again—but I know I need to open myself up to her. She's the only person who's seen me as I am and accepted me. She deserves for me to be truthful to her. She deserves to know about the merger.

If she pushes me away, so be it. I never deserved a woman like her to begin with, so I know I'm on borrowed time. I'm not worthy of a woman like her, let alone a queen. The least I can do is be honest.

By the time the gala rolls around, it's been three weeks since she stayed at my house in Roston. Three weeks of thinking about her night and day. Three weeks of staring at myself in the mirror and wondering what she saw in me that made her say I was beautiful. A gladiator. The man who walked through fire and lived. Three weeks of worrying I'll never see that look in her eyes again if I tell her the truth about Gerhard, Inc. and Donovan Enterprises.

Torture.

The gala is held in a big, glamorous convention center near the castle. It's a fundraiser for some charitable organization or another. Wine to be poured, dinner to be served, and awards to be handed out. Boring as hell.

There are hundreds of guests, and more than a few eyebrows rise when I walk in the room. Gazes flick down to my neck, where I've made no effort to hide my scar. Why should I? I'm not ashamed of what happened to me. It's like Penelope said—I'm a warrior. Whether that causes disgust, or awe, or strikes fear in the people in this room makes no difference to me.

She was right. I should be proud of where I came from. Proud of my scars because they made me who I am. If I hadn't suffered those burns, would I have ended up like Logan? A coddled rich boy who expects the world to be handed to him on a silver platter?

The experience I've had can't be traded for anything. I've built a reputation for myself *despite* the scars marring my body—not because of them. So I keep my head held high and resist the urge to touch my jaw and neck. I wear my scars like a badge, daring the other guests to stare. I feel oddly empowered, as if I've left the shame of my appearance behind, and I can finally show myself fully.

It's...incredible. There's a shift in the other guests, too.

They no longer shrink away from me—many of them actually approach me and start speaking to me. A man introduces himself as the union leader for truck drivers. He shakes my hand and congratulates me on the approval of the mining project, then leans in and asks me for a meeting later in the week.

There's no glance at my neck. No wrinkling of his nose. The only thing in his eyes is...respect.

Is this all because of the way I'm carrying myself? Or is it because of my association with the Queen?

After doing my first round of the room, shaking hands with a few union leaders and industry bigwigs, my heart starts to sink.

No Penelope.

I make it through the main course, craning my neck every time there's movement near the entrance, and finally give up. Dejected, I head back to my hotel. My shoulders curve inward and it's hard to keep the scowl off my face.

Am I really so desperate that I just want to catch a glimpse of her? That being in the same room as Penelope gives me a thrill?

It's not like I can just march up to the castle and ask to see her. She's kept behind a high fence with hundreds of guards around. I probably wouldn't even be admitted onto the property, let alone be allowed into her presence.

She made it very clear what she wants from me—professionalism. Even after our night in the kitchen in Roston, she told me it was only for the night. We'd go back to being business associates by the morning. Why do I think I owe her the truth? She should understand if I don't tell her about the merger. It's not a lie or a betrayal—it's just business.

Pressing the elevator button, I lean against the side of the lift and rest my head on its mirrored surface. A sigh slips through my lips as I'm taken up to my room on the top floor, and I manage to shake my head at myself.

Pathetic.

Of course she wasn't there. Of course she didn't want to see me. Who am I to her? A lover? Am I even that?

It's sad, really. The first person who shows me a bit of dignity becomes almost an obsession in my mind. Am I really so deprived that all it takes is for a woman to notice me? All it takes is someone to touch me without recoiling? She tells me I'm special and I want to open my company's deepest secrets to her?

This is why I turned to business many years ago. This is why I became my father's best attack dog. This is why I don't look for love in anyone else—because it does nothing for me except make me weak.

Tonight, at the gala, I saw the effect I have on people. I saw how little my scars really matter. I don't need the Queen to kiss me and tell me I'm pretty.

No matter what my heart tries to tell me, I came to Nord to prove to my father that I'm able to fill his shoes. I should inherit the company. I can do more than bring our victims to their knees before we swallow them up in our own enterprise —I can lead the company. *Me*.

I came here because I wanted to prove, once and for all, that I'm worthy of inheriting the empire I helped to build. Logan has never managed a project this big. He's never brought as much money as I have, and managing this diamond mining project will be enough to show my father that I'm the one who should follow in his footsteps.

And the Queen? She's nothing. She's a pawn I used to get information. She's a woman with a warm touch who made me feel less alone for a night or two. It doesn't mean I have to chase her around the kingdom. I should be focusing on what's important—business. Proving myself. Making sure this project goes off without a hitch.

I should stick to what I'm good at.

Penelope's role in all this is only to sign the papers that will allow me to do my job. I should remember that whenever the urge strikes to travel across the country and attend stupid galas I have no time for. I should *definitely* remember it when I feel like I need to tell her my secret plans to merge with other companies. She could ruin the whole thing; then where would I be? I'd fail my father, fail my company, and I'd lose everything I've worked to achieve.

Pulling a key card out of my pocket, I barely notice the two men in dark suits stationed at either end of the hallway. I enter my suite with nothing but a glance toward them, letting the heavy door close behind me. Movement catches my eyes to my left, and a gasp stays stuck halfway up my throat.

Penelope stands, her tight burgundy gown hugging every curve. Heat sparks deep in my stomach as my eyes drink her in. The delicate lace edge of her dress dips down her back, and her thick mass of blond hair is gathered in a neat twist. The sight of her skin makes embers burn in my veins, and all I want to do is run to her.

And I thought she meant nothing? Am I delusional? The mere sight of her makes me want to fall to my knees.

She dips her head, smiling. "I hope you don't mind the intrusion."

"You're here," I breathe. I'm still rooted in place by the front door. The Stirling skyline twinkles behind her, and in the warm, low light of the suite, Penelope looks like a goddess. She's too good for this place, even though it's the height of luxury. She's too good for anyplace that isn't as beautiful as her. Too good for me.

She tilts her head. "Yes, I'm here. Is that a problem?"

"I bought a ticket to that stupid gala because I heard you'd be there." My words come out in a rush, and I blush. Me, Asher Gerhard—I actually *blush*. She tilts my whole world off-balance. I'm no longer the cold, ruthless businessman. I'm acquiring nothing here. The word 'merger' is meaningless when she's standing in front of me.

Penelope laughs, the sound sending heat rushing straight to my heart. It thumps in response, and I find myself walking toward her. My body has a will of its own, and no matter what I told myself all evening, I know I'm powerless to her pull.

Sweeping my arm around her waist, I crush my lips to hers. Soft and sweet, she melts into my embrace and wraps her arms around me. My fingers find the edge of her lace bodice, feeling the skin of her back against my fingertips. It's intoxicating, having her this close. It makes me forget who I am.

Pulling away, Penelope puts a hand to her cheek. She's flushed. "I wanted to thank you."

"For what?"

"For the interview you gave with Jacinthe Crawley, and the other press appearances you've made over the past few weeks. You've done a lot to silence the criticism I've been getting."

"I only told the truth."

"But you didn't have to tell it, so I'm thanking you." She smiles softly, staring at my eyes. I wonder what she sees when she looks at me. Does she see what the rest of the world sees? A man who's shut himself off from everything except the thrill of the hunt? A man who hasn't felt the touch of a woman—not like this—since...well, ever?

Or does she see something else? Maybe she sees the Asher Gerhard who lived in the room across the rooftop from her. She sees...*me*.

"Do you still enjoy fishing?" Pen's lips tug at the corner.

I frown. "Fishing?"

"I recall many afternoons when we'd sneak out of the dorms and go fishing in the river by the school. I thought maybe you still enjoyed it now, as an adult."

A chuckle slips through my lips. "That was just an excuse to skip class and spend time with you."

"Well, maybe you can skip work and spend time with me again." Her eyes twinkle, and her hands play with the collar of my shirt. She slides her fingers down, circling the top button. Her gaze climbs to mine, snagging for a moment on my lips before reaching my eyes. "I arranged for a week at the Summer Palace. It's just a short drive from the Arctic Ocean, where the fishing is world-class. We could make a trip of it."

A lump grows in my throat, and my grip on Penelope's waist tightens. "You want to spend the week with me?"

"Is that so surprising?" She laughs.

My heart hammers as I struggle to swallow. I nod. "When do we leave?"

"Whenever you can get away from your work."

"That's the good thing about being in charge." I grin. "We can go tomorrow. Tonight. Right now."

Her smile is blinding. It sends a jolt straight through my chest, and I wonder how I could have possibly thought she meant nothing to me.

Going anywhere with Penelope is the exact opposite of what I should be doing, which is going back to Roston and being fully involved in the mobilization of staff and materials for the start of construction.

I should be staying far away from her, because she tempts me to tell her the truth about our merger with Donovan Enterprises. She makes me want to leave behind the ruthless businessman I am and become something else...some*one* else.

But her lips are so beautifully soft, and her body is pressed up against mine and...I'm weak. I want this warmth. Her smiles. Her laughter. I want to feel this heat coursing through my veins.

The thought of heading back to Roston on my own seems like the entirely wrong thing to do.

One week can't hurt, can it? It doesn't mean I have to tell her anything about the business. After all, she's the Queen, and who am I to refuse her?

17

PENELOPE

I'VE BEEN TRYING my best to be a good queen, to keep my thoughts away from Asher and focus on the people. There's been a knot in my stomach since we were in the kitchen together in Roston. I haven't been able to eat right, and my staff is starting to notice. Everything feels...off. Physically, mentally, emotionally. Asher came into my life and shook everything up like a snow globe.

It doesn't help that every time I look at a newspaper or turn on the television, he's there.

Usually, he's saying complimentary things about me and my government. I can't help but feel like there's a hidden meaning. When he says I serve Nord with duty and honor, I can't help but remember the way it felt to be in his arms. Like he's reminding me in every interview that we shared something secret—something special.

Over the past three weeks, tensions in Nord have dissolved, and the threat of unemployment is lessening. Approval ratings are on the rise, and people crying for the abolition of the monarchy are quieting down. Even Jacinthe Crawley.

I have Asher to thank for that. Without his support in every interview and article, I doubt I would've gotten the credit for this project.

His fingers make soft circles over the skin on my back. We stand in his hotel suite, arms locked around each other. My head spins. That slow, tender movement of his hand—it...it does something to me. To my heart. Makes it stutter and skip inside my chest, as if my body has forgotten how to pump blood properly.

"You've been very kind to me in the media," I say softly, lifting my gaze up to his.

"I've told the truth. Without you, this wouldn't have happened."

"I appreciate it." I clear my throat, taking a deep breath. "I often feel like I'm on my own, always being criticized. It's nice to have someone in my corner."

Asher's eyes soften, his hand stilling for a moment. I think I see a hint of conflict in his eyes, but it passes so quickly I almost doubt whether it was there at all.

I've seen so little of him over the past weeks—months, even. It's been over two months since Prince Gabriel's wedding, but I feel like my whole world has shifted. I think about him all the time. I know I said I wanted to keep things professional, and being here is in direct conflict with that. I *know* these things...but I just can't quite bring myself to care.

Call me weak. Call me a hypocrite. Call me whatever you want—but I'm sick of resisting. I want to spend time with him. As the days have passed without him, I feel almost nauseous. Ever since Roston, it's happened in waves, like I can't quite shake the feeling that something has changed within me. Something is *different*.

It's emotional or mental—manifesting itself physically—

but there's been a seismic shift inside me. All because of Asher.

"I have a confession, Pen." Asher's eyes are dark. He looks in my eyes, then drops his gaze to my lips.

A slow tendril of heat curls through my stomach, making me want to clench my thighs together. Every night, I've thought of how it felt to have him inside me. Three weeks I've pleasured myself to the memory of his touch. I've replayed our night in Roston over and over in my mind. Being here...it makes my head spin. Pushing past the lump in my throat, I speak. "What's that?"

I don't want him to say we can't do this. I don't want him to repeat the words I said to him and tell me we can't be close. I've *done* that. I've tried to be professional. I've kept my distance.

I can't do it anymore.

Asher leans down, touching his forehead to mine. "I have to admit..." His throat clenches as he gulps, and a thin thread of fear travels through my heart. There's something wrong. His eyes...they're serious. He's going to confess something to me, and I'm not going to like it. My heart starts to hammer, and hot embarrassment creeps up my neck. I shouldn't have come here. He's going to reject me. He's going to tell me something awful.

Asher takes a deep breath, squeezing his eyes shut. Deep lines bracket his mouth, then his shoulders drop. He opens his eyes, and the conflict is gone. A thin, watery smile appears on his lips. "I have to admit, I *really* hate fishing."

Sweet, sweet relief. There's nothing wrong between us. He's not rejecting me. Am I really so weak that my mind went straight there?

Laughter bubbles through me, silenced when Asher kisses me. His lips are soft, yet demanding, and I melt into his kiss. When his tongue swipes across my lower lip and dives into my mouth, I feel every muscle in my body relax into his touch.

How could I think to resist this? How could I stay away from him when I know how it feels to be in his arms?

Heat clenches deep inside me, fire sparking between my legs. I...want this. More. I want more of him, and I don't want to keep things professional. I don't want to be the Queen. Not now. Not with him.

Pulling away, Asher grins down at me. Low, warm light from a nearby lamp hugs his face, making me want to touch his broad cheekbones and commit every feature to memory. A tremor passes through my chest, and it feels a lot like...like an emotion I'm too scared to name.

He brushes his lips to mine again, softly, then lets out a low groan. "I missed you, Pen. I don't want to keep things professional between us."

As my heart speeds up, I close my eyes and melt into his touch. "I missed you too," I admit in a low whisper. It feels like a naughty confession. Like a secret that should be said in a hushed voice.

Who am I to miss a man? Why would I deserve to have someone like Asher—all muscle and manliness and sex? Didn't I already lose my chance at love? Hasn't my body betrayed me time and time again, and I've been resigned to a life of loneliness? Why would that change now?

"Let's forget about the Roston mines," he growls. "Just for this week. Show me the Arctic Ocean and the Summer Palace. Let me see the real you, Pen."

A shiver courses through my body. This is almost forbidden. Not because of the mining contract or the sale of the land near Roston. Not because of the press, or what people would say if they found out about this...relationship. Is this a relationship?

It feels forbidden because I haven't allowed myself to soften for anyone. Even with my brothers, I've maintained my frosty exterior. I've hidden myself away beneath a layer of ice, never letting any vulnerabilities show.

Now, Asher wants me. All of me. He wants to see what lies beneath...and I want to show him.

His hand skates up my spine, curling around the back of my neck. His other arm sweeps around my lower back, so I'm completely encased in his embrace. I inhale Asher's scent, feeling more at home here than I do in my own castle. I feel more like myself than I do when I'm alone.

That can't be wrong...Can it?

Over the past three weeks, I haven't spoken to Asher at all, but he's shown me what it means to feel supported by someone. Whenever he's been challenged in the media about me or my government, he's responded with grace and tact. Singlehandedly, he's made the growing unrest in Nord quiet down and improved my reputation.

I owe him so much, but he's asking for nothing. For the first time in years, I feel like I don't have to face this life on my own.

WE LEAVE for the Summer Palace in the morning, taking the royal jet up to a private airstrip, then driving over to the newly renovated palace sitting on the edge of the Arctic Circle. Last summer, construction was completed on the castle. The design was created by none other than Wolfe's new wife.

This is the first time since the opening ceremony that I've been to the Summer Palace. The first time since the birth of

Wolfe's child that I've made a visit to my brother and his bride. I've dreaded seeing their happiness. My heart has clenched at the thought of seeing their baby. The newspapers call him the heir to the throne—something that in my heart of hearts, I know is true. I know when I die, there won't be a child of my own to pass my title to. Still, it feels like a slap in the face.

I haven't had the guts to visit them because of my own ego, my own failures, my own malfunctioning body.

Now, though, as the royal vehicle drives through the intricate wrought iron gates and onto the meadow of wildflowers leading to the Summer Palace, a smile drifts over my lips. Asher's hand is intertwined in mine, and I find myself leaning my head against his shoulder.

We haven't said much to each other this morning. There's a calm sort of energy between us. An excitement tinged with a feeling that this is *right*. This is where we're supposed to be.

When we drive up to the palace, Asher lets out a low whistle. "This is nicer than my place in Roston. I can tell you that without even stepping a foot inside." He cranes his neck to look up at the two tall turrets framing the building, the whole place gleaming with the newness of the renovation.

I smile, squeezing his hand. A thought pops into my head uninvited—this place could be his, if he wanted it. All of it. All of Nord. I'd give him the kingdom if he'd accept it—accept *me*. Gulping the thought down, I pull away from him as the footman opens my door. Whatever is happening between Asher and me, it's not that serious. It's...it's a break. A break from responsibility, not something everlasting. I need to remember that.

My brother Wolfe is waiting for us at the top of the steps. Somehow, he looks even wilder and more regal than he did before. His new bride is beside him, smiling down at me from

the top of the stairs. She drops into a curtsy, her coppery hair
ruffled by the breeze.

Anxiety pierces my belly, wondering if maybe my brother
would have made a better king. Wolfe's dark curls frame his
face as he nods. With eyes the color of warm honey, he stands
at the door as if he belongs on a throne. Head thrown back, a
huge dog at his feet and a beautiful woman by his side, he
looks like more of a monarch than I ever did. The corners of
his eyes crinkle when he sees me, his gaze shifting to the
child hanging off his neck.

My heart takes off. Anxiety ratchets up inside me at the
sight of the child, and I know it's irrational. I know it's
misplaced. I shouldn't be jealous of my brother's son, but I
can't help but feel the ache of my own losses.

Then, a hand on my lower back. A calming presence by
my side. Asher's soft voice in my ear saying, "You've got this."

Squaring my shoulders, I paint a smile on my face and
walk up to Wolfe. "Hello, Wolfe. Rowan."

Rowan nods, smiling. Wolfe shifts the babbling boy in his
arms, who unhooks an arm to point at me.

Wolfe grins. "Wren missed you."

"Wren doesn't remember me." I laugh.

The one-year-old blinks, laughing, moving his head from
side to side as he knocks into Wolfe's shoulder. The smile on
my brother's face is unlike anything I've seen from him
before. It's pure happiness. It's love like I've never experi-
enced. Love I'll never *get* to experience.

It makes me feel cold.

Asher's hand reappears on my back, and his touch melts
my anxious thoughts. I clear my throat, glancing at my
brother and his wife. "Wolfe, Rowan, this is Asher. We went
to school together."

Wolfe's amber eyes twinkle when he looks at Asher, who

bows to my brother. I resist the urge to roll my eyes. "You bow to Wolfe but not to me?" Looking at my brother, I jerk my thumb toward Asher. "This guy wouldn't know proper etiquette if it hit him across the face."

"He'll get along well with Rowan, then." Wolfe grins, glancing at his wife.

"Hey now." Rowan arches a brow. "I just didn't appreciate your sense of entitlement. It has nothing to do with etiquette." The breeze picks up, blowing her red hair over her shoulder as a smile stretches over her full lips. She looks at Wolfe like he's her whole world, one hand moving to stroke her son's back. Wren shifts in Wolfe's arms, stretching out toward his mother. She takes him in her arms, blowing a raspberry on Wren's neck as he giggles.

It's hard to be so close to all this love and happiness. It's hard to see the change in my brother, from a lonely soul to a family man...

...but it's not quite as hard as it was before. Behind my pain, something new tugs at me. Warmth soaks into my blood, and I find myself happy for my brother, for once. Truly happy for him. Seeing him with his wife and child, I still feel my own losses, but somehow they're not as loud as they were before. It's...easier.

Maybe I'm finally ready to let go.

That child could be the future King of Nord, and...that's okay.

When I glance at Asher, I find him staring at me. His hand stays on my lower back as we head toward the castle, and my heart does a funny kind of flip. When we cross the threshold, I'm like a snake shedding its skin. I'm leaving the cold, icy woman behind, and I'm opening myself up to something new.

18

____

ASHER

WHEN I'M WITH PENELOPE, everything else fades in the distance. The company, my father, the upcoming merger with Donovan Enterprises—nothing matters. All I see is her soft blond hair, her brilliant smile, her velvet blue eyes.

The tremors in my chest feel unfamiliar, but they happen every time she's around. Whenever she laughs at a stupid joke I make or slips her hand in mine, my heart squeezes in a way I've never felt before.

We watch the sun go down at the back of the Summer Palace, having eaten a big meal with Penelope's brother, Wolfe, and his new wife, Rowan, before leaving them to put their son to bed. The two of them are so in love it's sickening, but it makes me feel an odd sort of yearning.

Alone with Penelope, I catch myself glancing at her, wondering if she feels this tugging in her chest like I do.

"We used to come to the Summer Palace every year with our parents," Pen says, smiling at me. "It was my favorite place."

"It's beautiful."

Framed by two tall mountains on either side, the sunset

throws pinks and reds across the sky. An eagle cuts across my field of vision, diving down to the meadow below. Soft grasses sway in the wind, and Penelope lets out a happy sigh.

"I'm glad you're here," she says.

There it is, that clenching in my chest again. I nod, choking the words out. "Me too."

"I wonder..." She shakes her head.

"What?"

"I wonder what would happen if we stopped being...professional."

"I'm not sure we ever have been." My grin tugs at my lips, and I enjoy watching a blush sweep over Penelope's cheeks. She ducks her head away from me, watching the sun dip lower on the horizon. Clearing my throat, I reach for her hand. "It would cause a lot of controversy."

"Would you mind?" Her eyebrows arch.

"If newspapers said nasty things about me?"

She nods.

I chuckle. "No. I've heard it all before. Would you?"

"I..." Her blush deepens. She shakes her head, a tendril of gold falling loose from her braid. "I don't think so."

Tucking her hair behind her ear, I bring my lips to hers. No matter how many times I kiss her, I just can't get enough of her lips. They taste like the sweetest candy. Like the most delicious thing I've ever had, tantalizingly close anytime she's near. I slide my arm around her shoulders, pulling her closer. When she rests her head against my chest, it feels...right.

"Is that what you want, Penelope?" I ask. My voice has a rough edge to it, as if I can't quite shake the emotion off. "You want us to be...public?"

Penelope hesitates, then shrugs. "I don't know."

We're dancing around our words, waiting for the other person to speak. The more time I spend with Penelope, the surer I become that she's the most incredible woman I'm ever going to meet. There's no one else that comes close. And if she's telling me she feels the same way...

...well, that would be worth anything. It would be worth giving up my place in my father's company. Worth turning my back on business. Worth shedding the identity I've crafted as a businessman.

Being with Penelope would overtake all those things in an instant. I could wake up next to her every morning and capture her lips between mine. I could do all the things I've dreamed of doing to her with my hands and tongue and lips. I could see her smiles and try to make her laugh every day, just to watch the way it brightens her face.

"Do you want kids?" Penelope asks in the silence. Her head is still resting on my shoulder, but I can feel tension mounting in her body.

I suck in a breath, letting it out slowly. "No."

Turning to stare at me, she arches her brows. "Really?"

"I always thought I'd end up alone."

"That's sad."

"Thanks." I grin.

"So you never wanted to have kids?"

I shake my head. "Don't think I'd be any good at it."

Penelope searches my face, shifting her gaze from one eye to the other. Her brows tug together as her lips part, as if she's trying to draw the truth out of me. Seemingly satisfied with what she sees, she rests her head against my shoulder again. "So...my issues...You wouldn't mind?"

"Are you asking if I'll be your boyfriend?" I can't keep the grin from my voice.

"I'm the Queen, Asher. It doesn't work that way."

"How does it work?"

"I…" Penelope inhales, shaking her head. "I don't know. I've never done this before."

"I don't want to jeopardize your reputation."

"And I don't want to hurt yours either," she says.

"But this feels…"

"Real," she finishes, glancing up at me.

A lightning bolt passes through my chest, and suddenly it's hard to speak. Emotion chokes me, making my pulse quicken and my throat constrict. I never thought I'd meet someone who accepts me for who I am. To be honest, I never thought I'd let anyone close enough to really know me.

But Penelope knows. She's wriggled her way under my skin and made me rethink everything I used to believe mattered to me. Since we left Stirling, I haven't thought about work once. I haven't thought about my father, or the merger, or the mine.

I've been totally consumed by Penelope. I've been…happy.

As a lump lodges itself in my throat, I sweep my fingers over Pen's cheek. I can't speak because I'm afraid it'll come out as a croak. I don't have the words to tell her how I feel, because I don't even understand it myself. It feels like I'm ready to leave everything behind for her. To disappear into this northern land and leave my whole world in the past without another look.

I'm ready to give her my all.

When my lips touch hers, she lets out a delicious, soft moan. I gobble it up like a man starved, then sweep my tongue into her mouth. Within seconds, our kiss is ravenous. Demanding. Her fingers curl into my shirt, fisting it as she swings a leg over my lap. I drop my lips to her neck, her breasts, and back up to her lips. I kiss her like she's my sustenance. Like I need her to live.

In a way, that's how it feels.

Isn't she the one who said this felt real? We're two people who'd been resigned to a lonely life. We were so convinced that love and life and happiness were closed off to us, that seeing the possibility of actually having it seems like a gift from the divine.

As Penelope grinds her core against mine in the light of the fading sunset, my whole body lights up with the strength of my emotion.

I love this woman. Truly and completely love her with every fiber of my being. I'd do anything for her, including stand in front of cameras and extoll her praises, or go back in front of those cameras and proclaim to the world that she's mine.

I'd turn my back on my father's company. Let Logan have it—I doubt it ever would have been mine no matter what I accomplished. I'm done seeking approval where it'll never exist.

This, here, with Penelope—this is what matters.

She grips the back of the wicker furniture, pressing her hips into mine. "You always make me want you in the naughtiest places," she growls in my ear. "Anyone could walk out here."

Slipping my hand under her dress, I feel the soft lace of her panties. My cock throbs when I feel the dampness soaking through, and I let out a low moan. "Let them watch."

She shivers at my touch, rolling her body against my hand, demanding more. I tug her panties aside and slide my fingers through her honey, unable to hold back the groan that rumbles through my chest. I can't get enough of touching her. She's soft and warm and wet—for me. All for me. All mine.

"Penelope." I sigh, kissing her shoulder.

"Shh." She nibbles my ear, her hands curling into my

shirt as her hips keep rocking over my hand. When I press my thumb against her bud, the way she shivers makes me want to claim her right here, like this.

But I lean back against the seat, driving my fingers inside her as I twirl my thumb around her clit. I watch her eyes close, lashes fanned out over her high cheekbones, and I take in every angle of her face. Her lips drop open, head bowed, as if she can't believe how good her body feels when I touch her.

"Asher," she whispers, and my name sounds like magic on her lips.

The wicker loveseat creaks as she rides my hand, and I urge her on with dirty whispers. I want her orgasm on my hands. I want the stain of her wetness on my crotch.

With one hand inside her, I slide my palm over her outer thigh and feel the soft curve of her ass. My fingers slide down the cleft of her ass and feel the tight pucker behind, circling it with slow, steady movements. The cries that fall from her lips are my reward. My sustenance. Everything I'll ever need.

Heat winds through my core as I watch Penelope come apart in my arms, quivering over my hands as she wrinkles my shirt in her fists. She gasps, twitching, her core clenching around my fingers in a way that makes my whole body ache for her.

The words are right there, on the tip of my tongue. *I love you.* They'd be so easy to say, just three little words, but they don't come. The lump in my throat grows and all I can manage to do is kiss the corner of her lip as I slide her panties back in place.

"Asher," she whispers again, boneless on top of me. I slide my arms around her waist and hold her close, knowing she holds my whole heart in the palm of her hand.

19

PENELOPE

THERE'S nothing cold about me when I'm with Asher. Everything is warm and tingly. Heat flows through my veins like never before, and I realize just how much I've been missing.

One week turns into two. We spend our days hiking and traipsing through the countryside, taking a trip up to the Arctic Ocean to go fishing, even though Asher pretends to hate it. It's the first real break I've had in years. I sleep better than ever before, but still somehow have nagging tiredness. I don't feel quite...right. Not sick, exactly, just...odd.

The nagging nausea and lack of appetite that started in Stirling seem to get worse. I thought I was just nervous about being apart from Asher. But he's here and my stomach is still tied up in knots. I'm a schoolgirl with a crush.

During our second week at the Summer Palace, when I have to take a break in the woods for my fourth pee break, clutching my stomach as I come out from a small copse of trees, Asher tilts his head. "Are you sure everything's okay?"

"I think so," I say, putting a hand to my chest. "Maybe it was those sandwiches we had. Having a bit of heartburn."

"Let's head back. There's a doctor at the palace, right?"

I shrug. "I'll be fine."

"Pen." Asher's face is deathly serious, his brows knitted together. The fact that he cares about my well-being this much makes everything inside me flush. He walks toward me, putting his hands on my thighs and making slow circles with his thumbs. "Just get checked out and rest. I don't like you feeling like this."

His worried expression makes my heart do a funny kind of flip. He really cares, even if it's just a bit of heartburn. If only just to pacify him—and maybe to enjoy the warm flush of having him take care of me—I agree to head back toward the castle. We walk back down the side of the mountain, and all my limbs feel heavy. I lean against Asher, and he hooks his arm around my shoulders.

I haven't had someone to lean on in years. Literally or figuratively. Over the past few months, Asher's been there for me at every turn, and I'm not sure how I'll cope if he ever goes away. He's supported me in public, making sure no one says anything bad about me in his presence. And in private? Well, sometimes it feels like he's the only person who sees me as Penelope, and not as a vague shadow with a crown sitting on her head.

When we make it to the palace, deep frown lines are cut into Asher's forehead. He glances at me, then asks one of the castle staff to fetch the doctor.

"I'm fine, Ash. Really."

"You're not. You look pale and almost green. You've been peeing nonstop and I saw the way you looked at that coleslaw at lunch."

I clutch my stomach, groaning. "It's not my fault coleslaw looks like chunky, wet slop."

With one hand on my lower back, Asher guides me to my

chambers. He helps me into bed and sits beside me, holding my hand while we wait for the doctor.

After a few minutes of Asher staring at me like I'm about to drop dead right here in bed, I start laughing. "Asher, come on. I'll be fine."

"I don't like you being sick."

"I'm not sick."

"You haven't eaten right in days."

"It's heartburn." I wave a hand dismissively, even though I've never gotten heartburn in my life. Sure, my appetite has decreased—but it's not my fault food suddenly seems unappetizing. Maybe it's all the sex we've been having. It's messing with my hormones. After a seven-year dry spell, my body has no idea what's happening.

Dr. Williams knocks on the door and walks in, his eyes flicking between me and Asher. He bows, then straightens, his kind blue eyes landing on my face. "Your Majesty," he says in a slightly nasally voice. "I hear you've been unwell."

"I'm fine. Just a bit of heartburn."

Asher throws me a glance, but I ignore it. He puts his hand on my arm, running his thumb along my wrist. A small bubble of heat expands in my chest. His protectiveness—the fact that he cares—it's...nice. It makes me feel like I'm not alone in the world for the first time in a long, long time.

I'm the head of state. I'm the leader of this country, and I have been since I was a little girl. To have someone by my side who isn't *serving* me, but is standing next to me? That's indescribable. It makes my heart sing.

The slow movement of Asher's thumb continues as the doctor moves to the side of the bed. He checks my pulse, blood pressure, listens to my lungs. Asks me a few generic questions. Then, Dr. Williams glances at Asher. He clears his throat. "Your Majesty, could I have a word with you...alone?"

"I'm staying," Asher grunts.

"Ash." I shoot him a glance, popping my brows. "I'll be fine. Why don't you go see what Wolfe is doing?"

After a moment of grumbling, Asher lifts himself off the bed and pads out of the room. He looks at me one last time, scowling at the doctor. I want to shout at him that this was *his* idea. Getting the doctor to come check me out was all Asher, and he shouldn't be mad it's happening.

I can't get the words out, though, because the sight of Asher's grumpy face in the door makes my heart flip-flop all over my chest cavity.

When Asher steps out and the door latches quietly, the doctor turns his clear blue eyes to mine. "Ma'am," he starts. "You said you've been nauseous for how long?"

I tilt my head, thinking. "A few weeks. Three, four, maybe? Five?"

He clears his throat, unhooking his stethoscope from his neck and folding it into a large front pocket. "And, excuse the personal question, Majesty, but..." He drops his voice. "Is there any chance you could be pregnant?"

I laugh. I literally start laughing, because after ten years of knowing I'm infertile, the thought of a baby growing inside me must be a joke. I tortured myself with Xavier, punished myself for my failure to bear children. Does Dr. Williams not remember that? Does he not remember all the newspaper articles asking about an heir? Does he not remember how devastated I was, how many weeks I spent in bed, how many heartbreaking procedures and failures I had to endure?

So I laugh, and laugh, and laugh, but the doctor just stares at me, waiting for me to answer.

I straighten up on the bed, shaking my head. "No. There's no chance. I can't have kids."

"And your menstrual cycle has been regular?"

"It's gotten more regular in the past couple of years, yes," I answer, frowning. "It was all over the place when I was younger. Since I turned thirty it's almost been like clockwork —" I stop talking, eyes widening. Ice fills my veins as all the blood drains from my face.

Yes, my periods were irregular when I was in my early twenties. They stayed irregular for years, until my cycle leveled out when I got older. I ignored it, mostly, because it wasn't relevant to my life. Being infertile had become such a part of my identity—a painful part that took years to accept—I never considered it could change.

Clearing my throat, I swing my legs off the bed. "It's been six or seven weeks since my last one," I say all in a rush. I walk to the table on the other end of the room where a calendar sits. When was the last time I had a period? When I was in Farcliff? When I got back to Nord?

My heart hammers in my chest as my hands tremble. I flip through the calendar as if it'll give me the answer, knowing full well that what the doctor's saying rings true.

"Your Majesty," he starts quietly. "Perhaps we could double-check."

"It's not possible." I shake my head, spinning to face him. My eyes are wide, breaths short and sharp. There's a pain in my chest as my heart squeezes. This feels a lot like panic.

I can't be pregnant. I'm not *able* to get pregnant. I tried every single fertility treatment available to me, and none of them worked. I've come to terms with my infertility.

I'm. Not. Pregnant.

It's not possible.

My head shakes from side to side as my thoughts swirl around me like a hurricane. Dr. Williams takes a step toward me, holding his hands out as if he's trying to calm a nervous animal.

"Ma'am, if there's a chance—"

"I'm *infertile.*" I spit the word like a curse as my heart bangs against my chest. "I have PCOS. I don't ovulate. It's *not possible.* You *know* that, Doc. You *know.*"

"Yes, your fertility issues were caused by a lack of ovulation, Majesty," the doctor says patiently, taking another step toward me. "If your menstrual cycle has become more regular and you've started ovulating, it's perfectly possible for you to conceive."

Eyes wide, I stare at the man before me. He has gray hair and glasses perched on the tip of his nose, and is wearing a shirt two sizes too big tucked into pleated trousers. He motions for me to sit down in the chair next to me and pulls out a chair of his own. Leaning an elbow on the desk, he folds his hands and lets out a small sigh.

"We need to rule out the possibility. With your fatigue, nausea, heartburn, and the timing of your last menstrual cycle, pregnancy is a possibility."

I open my mouth, then close it to gulp, then open it again. Words...just won't come.

My head is spinning. The doctor says something else, moving to his black satchel and producing a glass vial, tubing, and a sterile needle. I stare at him, seeing nothing.

The diagnosis for my infertility has weighed heavy on my spirit for a decade. It drove a wedge between Xavier and me, and it made me feel like a failure. I've dragged it around with me for *years.* I've woven my infertility into my very identity. The cold distance at which I keep people—that's because I saw myself as empty. Barren. Broken. Failed.

I've never been a woman who can conceive, because I'm not a *woman.* I'm merely a queen. I'm a figurehead. A monarch.

But...

My heart clenches, and I shift my gaze to the floor. My eyes trace the intricate patterns in the Turkish rug at my feet, and I try to make sense of my thoughts. They fly through my fingers like fireflies, elusive. Squeezing my eyes shut, I take a deep breath. The doctor says something, but I don't hear it.

His hand appears on my arm, and he starts tapping the inside of my elbow. He's saying something else, but it sounds like it's coming at me underwater.

I nod, knowing he needs to take my blood. He needs to confirm what I already know to be true: I'm not infertile. I'm not barren. I'm not a failure of a woman.

I'm pregnant with Asher Gerhard's child.

20

ASHER

I DON'T LIKE LEAVING Penelope's room, and I hate how long it takes for her to come out. After an hour, I find myself in one of the sitting rooms in the palace, staring out at the mountain peaks in the distance.

"Beautiful, isn't it?"

I turn to see Rowan walking into the room. She's carrying the baby in her arms, and there's a soft smile on her lips. She looks...happy. Truly happy. Like her heart is at peace. She has bright eyes, and I can see in an instant why Wolfe fell in love with her. She has spirit.

She reminds me of Penelope, in a way. A strong woman with a mind of her own.

Rowan nods to the landscape. "I fell in love with it here as soon as I arrived, and that was the start of winter in one of the worst storms the palace has seen. I nearly died."

My eyebrows shoot up. "Yeah?"

She laughs, shaking her head. "It was a crazy time, but it led me here. To Wren." She puts the child down, hanging onto his hands as he takes a few tentative steps. Rowan grins. "Lord help me when he truly learns to walk. It was a lot

176

easier when I could just swaddle him and know he wouldn't be running all over the place on me."

I smile. There's a strange clench in my chest as Wren breaks from his mother's hands, making a run straight toward me. His chubby little legs run, head tipped forward, as if he's seconds away from face-planting on the floor. He catches himself against my legs, falling back onto his bottom, giggling so hard spittle drips down his chin. Wren squeezes his little fists toward me, still laughing, until I bend down and pick him up.

"I think he likes you." Rowan's eyes soften as she takes her son's hand in hers. She nibbles on his fingers, kissing every one, and Wren giggles harder.

Then, the boy leans over to me and leaves a sloppy kiss on the side of my cheek. I laugh, pulling away.

Rowan takes him from my arms and apologizes. "He hasn't quite learned how to keep his saliva to himself. I swear this year, I've seen more bodily fluids than I ever thought possible. Motherhood isn't pretty."

"You seem to be doing a good job." I chuck the boy's cheek as my chest expands.

I've never been one to like kids. They're too...soft. Slobbery. Innocent. I guess a part of me realized I'd never meet anyone who would want to have kids with me, so I just closed that part of my brain down. I thought I didn't have a parental bone in my body—it's not like I had good role models. I was shipped off to boarding school as soon as I was old enough, and my entire adult life has been a long exercise in witnessing my father's disappointment whenever he looks at my scars.

But this feels different. Rowan and Wolfe have so much love for their baby boy that it makes me think I might have missed something in this life. Maybe I've shut myself off from a type of happiness I didn't even know existed.

All three of us turn when there's a noise at the entrance. Prince Wolfe stands in the doorway, his eyes softening when he takes in Rowan and Wren. He crosses the room in three strides, takes his son in his arms, and tosses him high in the air.

"Careful, Wolfe!" Rowan's eyes widen, and Wolfe just laughs. Their son giggles and giggles and giggles, globs of spit falling from his mouth onto the rug.

I feel like I'm intruding. This feels...intimate.

Wolfe catches his son, tucking the kid into his arm as he nods to me. "How are you enjoying your time here?"

"It's amazing. I never even knew this palace existed. Feels like another world."

"You should see it in winter," Rowan says, eyes gleaming. "It looks like a foreign planet."

"Our planet," Wolfe says. He places a kiss on her temple, and I watch as she melts against his chest. The three of them make such a perfect image that it makes my chest ache. My heart seems to grow as I watch them, and my thoughts shift to Penelope.

Would she ever want that? She's been so clear about her responsibilities as queen, about her duty, that I wonder if she ever considered she could have a modest kind of happiness, too. The kind of happiness that comes from a good relationship and a child.

Heart dropping, I glance away. Of course she gave that up —her husband died and she was told she couldn't bear children. I see the pain inside Penelope's heart, and all I want to do is take it away.

A buzz comes from my pocket, and I excuse myself, leaving the happy family to look out the window together.

Moving to the far corner of the room, I pull my phone out of my front pocket and stare at the screen. Sighing, I swipe the screen to answer. "Hello, Father."

"When are you back in Farcliff, Asher? We need to finalize this acquisition. Donovan's been rumbling about sabotaging it, and I want to get this done."

"I'm great, thanks," I reply sardonically. "Thanks for asking."

"Asher, I don't have time for this. Get on the next plane and get down here. We need you here to make sure Reginald doesn't try anything funny. The shareholders know about the diamond mines in Nord, so now is the time to act. You know the Nord project better than anyone, and there are important things I want to talk to you about."

"Like what?"

"Just get down here," he snaps. The phone clicks, and I lift my eyes to the ceiling. If I had a nickel for every time my father hung up on me, I'd be nearly as rich as he is. Taking a deep breath, I count to ten. It helps the anger inside me simmer down slightly, enough for me to feel like I have control over my emotions.

Not once did my father thank me for this project in Nord. He's never congratulated me on my efforts or told me I did a good job. Even now, he just called me to chew my ear out and tell me to come, like I'm some sort of dog.

Maybe Reggie Donovan was right—I'm just my father's pet. I was a fool to think he'd ever offer me the company. He'll never put me in charge, no matter how good a job I do. My father doesn't see me as someone worthy of his legacy. He just sees me as a burned, broken boy whose body is grotesque.

And for years, I believed him. I looked in the mirror and saw something ugly...until now. Penelope has shown me another side of myself. She's opened my eyes to everything I ignored—everything good and true about me. All the things I thought were unlovable. All the things I tried to lock away.

As I put my phone back in my pocket, I know what I have to do. I'll go to Farcliff to see my father, but it'll be the last time. I'll tell him I can no longer work for him. I'll finalize this last acquisition and make sure Donovan behaves, then I'll hand in my notice.

I'm quitting my father's company and crawling out from under his shadow. I want to be the kind of man Penelope sees when she looks at me. I want to make her proud, and I can't do that if I'm the Gerhard Corporation's attack dog.

As if she can hear my thoughts, Penelope enters the sitting room. Her face is pale, jaw clenched. I fly to her side, smoothing my fingers through her hair. She closes her eyes, letting out a low groan.

"Is everything okay?" I ask quietly, leaning my forehead to hers.

"Depends who you ask." She lets out a dry, humorless laugh. There's something in her eyes I don't recognize. They shine with unshed tears as a watery smile tugs at her lips. Her brows draw together, as if she's trying to read my face.

"What did the doctor say?"

"I'm...healthy," she answers cryptically.

Sliding my hand down her cheek, I wrap my fingers around the nape of her neck. She hooks her arms around my body, resting her cheek against mine. Her body is tense, and I run my other hand up and down her spine. "Why don't you lie down for a bit, babe?"

Inhaling deeply, Penelope pulls away. She stares at the center of my chest for a moment before forcing her eyes to climb up to mine. "No, I'm okay. I need to talk to you." Turning to glance over my shoulder, she wrestles her lips into a smile. "Hi, Rowan. Wolfe. Wren."

The baby babbles, but the sound no longer fills my chest with warmth. A chill snakes down my spine when I see the tension around Penelope's eyes. Heart stuttering uncomfortably, I put my hand on her lower back and turn to face the other couple in the room.

Sensing our need for privacy, they say a few words and slip out of the room. Penelope pulls away from me, wrapping her arms around her chest. She drifts to the wall of windows, standing exactly where I was a few minutes ago, staring at the mountain peaks that surround us.

Then, with a breath, she turns her head and drags her gaze to mine. Time pauses, and my whole world hangs on what she's about to say. Somewhere deep in my heart, I know she's about to change the course of my life. Whatever she's going to say will rock me to my core. I do my best to keep my face steady.

No matter what I do to prepare myself, though, I'm not ready. Nothing in my life could have prepared me for the five words that come out of her mouth next.

"I'm pregnant, Asher. It's yours."

21

PENELOPE

I BRACE myself for Asher's reaction. I don't know what I expect. Shock, maybe? Panic? Anger?

What happens to Asher's face is not what I imagine. There's shock, of course. His eyes widen and his jaw drops, but his gaze drifts down to my stomach. Then something changes. His shock turns to awe, and a beautiful kind of softness fills his eyes.

"You're pregnant?" he whispers, taking a hesitant step toward me.

I nod. "The doctor confirmed."

"You're sure?"

"Yes."

"I thought..."

"Me too." My throat is tight. My voice is nothing more than a croak, but a balloon starts to inflate in my chest. I think Asher's happy. More than happy. I think...I think he might want this as much as I do.

Erasing the distance between us, Asher wraps his arms around me and crushes his lips to mine. His hand splays over my cheek and his lips devour me, leaving sloppy kisses over my lips, my jaw, my neck. He holds me close, clutching me tight as his whole body trembles.

"Is it healthy? Is everything okay?"

I laugh, pulling away. My vision is blurry and I try to blink away my unshed tears. "I don't know yet. You're happy about this?"

"I..." Asher's mouth closes. He opens it again, concern drawing his brows together. "You're not?"

"I didn't know what you'd say."

Asher drops to his knees, running his hands over my stomach. Warmth tugs at my lower belly, unfurling and sending tendrils of fire spreading between my legs. I thread my fingers through his silky, dark hair, closing my eyes.

He wants this. He's *happy*.

My steps trembled when I walked from my room to here, and when I saw him standing there, I thought I wouldn't have the courage to say the words out loud. But I did, and his reaction is better than anything I could have ever imagined.

Asher wants this baby with me. I could...I could have a child. I could have *love*. Everything I thought I lost—everything that's been buried under an arctic layer of ice—it could be mine again a hundred times over.

My heart feels so big, I think my ribs might crack. It expands in my chest, filling me up until I feel like I'm going to float up to the ceiling. A smile stretches my lips, and I let out a sigh I didn't know I was holding.

"Penelope," Asher whispers, rising to his feet. He slides the back of his hand over my cheek and rests his forehead against mine. "I never thought I'd be as happy as I've been with you. Tell me you want this. Me. The baby. All of it."

"I want it," I whisper in a rush. "I want it so bad."

My thoughts flick to Xavier, but the image of him is fuzzy. I still feel a tug of pain when I think about his death, but it's not so overwhelming anymore. It doesn't feel like I'm drowning in grief when I think of him. And, as cheesy as it sounds, I know he'd want me to be happy.

Asher holds me tight, and I soak his shirt with tears. He swipes his thumb over my cheek to wipe the tears away as I giggle-snort, shaking my head. "I didn't know how you'd react."

"I wasn't expecting this, but...I don't know, Pen. It feels good. Ever since I've been with you, my whole life has felt different. I was focusing on all the wrong things and you came in and smashed that illusion to pieces. My reality was just the reflection of a broken mirror, and you're finally showing me the truth. Happiness."

I tilt my head up to his and accept a soft kiss. "Meant to be." His lips taste so good that I wonder how I ever survived without them before.

"So...do we have to get married?"

I grin, hiding my face in his chest. "Probably."

"Sooner rather than later, I assume."

"Uh-huh."

"Is that going to be a problem for the mine in Roston? People will wonder why Gerhard won the project."

"I don't care," I admit. "Let people scream outrage. I don't give a shit. I just want you, and this baby, and..."

Asher's smile is blinding. He kisses my cheeks, catching a few stray tears that just don't seem to want to stop leaking from my eyes. Then he presses his lips against mine. His pulse thunders against my chest—or is that my own heart? It doesn't matter. It feels like a blanket of bliss covers us both, and I can see a future for myself that I never imagined.

Sighing, Asher lets out a groan. "I have to go to Farcliff."

"Why?" My voice sounds a lot like a whine.

"My father called, and I...I think I need to talk to him in person. I need to tell him I'm not coming back."

I nod, even though my chest squeezes. The last thing I want to do is let Asher out of my sight. Here, at the Summer Palace, it feels like the rest of the world doesn't even exist. I can understand why Wolfe and Rowan fell in love with each other sheltered within these walls. It's impossible not to feel the silence and privacy of this place.

But the real world does exist, as do my responsibilities—and Asher's. I know he has to go to Farcliff, and as much as I hate it, I give him a tight smile and nod. "Of course."

"I'll hurry back as soon as I can."

"You'd better."

Asher smiles then, and it's a full, broad, gorgeous smile. There's no guardedness. No hesitation. Just...love.

It's crazy, but I haven't even told him those three little words. I haven't even spoken them out loud. We've talked about kids and marriage, but the worst still won't come. They're there, on the tip of my tongue, ready to be released into the world.

I love you.

I love him in a desperate kind of way. I love him for being beside me, for showing me what I've been missing from my life. I love him for giving me hope. I love him for giving me a child. I love him for breaking through every barrier I've worked to erect and dragging me out of the icy wilderness and into the shelter of his arms. I love him for making me laugh and kissing me like no one's watching.

Mostly, though, I love him for being exactly who he is. Strong, protective, and so incredibly brave. He walked through fire and lived, carrying his scars on his body like a badge of honor. He's been through the kind of pain I have, and he hasn't shied away from it. He's guarded, but he opens himself up to me.

I love every inch of him, inside and out. He makes me think of the future in a way I couldn't have imagined without him—a future with *hope*. It's not a dreary, bleak future full of duty. We could have love.

We could have an heir.

Standing in that living room at the Summer Palace, I realize Asher is everything to me. I clutch his body and hold him tight, hardly believing I've found a man like him.

As if he senses the emotions roiling inside me, he leans down and presses a soft kiss to my lips. His hand sweeps over my stomach, and Asher drops to his knees. He presses his lips to my belly, resting his cheek against it. I thread my fingers through his hair and let my eyes drift closed, feeling completely happy and at peace for the first time in my life.

Just as I let peace settle into my body and hold Asher tight to my stomach, a little gremlin in my head crawls to my ear and whispers, *maybe this is too good to be true.*

I DON'T WANT to leave Nord, the Summer Palace, and definitely not Penelope's side. A violent protective streak arcs up inside me, and I find myself worrying about everything. What she's eating, carrying, doing. I can't stop thinking about the life growing inside her.

Our baby. *My child*.

The morning I'm supposed to leave, I wrap my arms around Penelope and pull her close. She lays her head on my chest and lets her fingers trail over my skin, and I know—I just *know*—that I was a fool before. To think I didn't want this? I thought I could do it on my own? I thought my father's business was what brought me joy?

I'm not the ruthless hunter of failing businesses. I'm not the man with a reputation for blood.

I'm Penelope's, through and through. Nothing else matters but how she feels in my arms. My entire universe shrinks to a pinpoint of life, with Pen at its center.

"Don't go," she whispers, nuzzling against me.

Sighing, I rest my cheek on her head. "I don't want to, but I have to quit the business. That needs to be done in person."

"I know," she says. "But I like having you beside me."

"What are we going to say to the media?"

"About us?"

I grunt in acknowledgement.

Pen sighs, shrugging one shoulder. "I'll let our media team handle it. Once you quit, there's no longer a conflict of interest. We can keep it quiet for a period of time."

"I don't know if you realize this, Pen, but we have a bit of a ticking clock." I slide my hand over her stomach, feeling her lips move into a smile against my chest.

"We can hide away at the Summer Palace. Release photos of our wedding after it happens, announce the birth when it happens, not before. People will talk, but... Who cares? My media team is used to dealing with difficult situations—except usually it's Silas who creates them. We can control the narrative."

"You'd lie to the people of Nord?"

"To protect my child from rumors? From name calling and controversy? Of course."

"And to protect me," I say in a low voice.

Penelope lifts her head to glance at me, a soft smile teasing over her lips. "That too. Not that you need protecting."

My heart feels so full it's about to burst. Pen's fingers trace the outline of my scar, from my shoulder down to the waistband of my sleep shorts and back up again. For once, I don't stiffen or jolt at the touch. She does that a lot—lets her fingers drift over the line where healthy skin meets scarred. Where the two sides of me come together.

For years, I've pushed that part of my history down. I've hidden my body. I've been...ashamed.

But Pen...God, what did I do to be worthy of her? She makes me feel *proud* of my scars. She makes me realize I was looking at my past all wrong. I was seeing the worst in people —in myself. But her touch, her love…it melted that part of me that clung onto the negative.

My alarm goes off for the fourth time and a groan rumbles through my throat. "I should get up."

"The plane will wait." Pen's lips curl into a cheeky grin as her hand slips lower, under the waistband of my shorts. "It won't leave without you."

"I could get used to these private jets," I say, tugging at her shirt.

"You're going to have to."

"You know, Pen, the day you walked up to me at Gabriel's wedding?"

"Mm-hmm…" Her lips drift over my chest, trailing kisses all the way down to my navel.

I groan in contentment. "I was thinking of you. I was staring at those roses remembering the way you dragged that little potted plant up to the roof."

"Were you?" She looks up, head near my waistband, smiling.

"Then you appeared behind me, as if I'd thought you into existence."

"Arrogant as usual," she grumbles, laughing. "I always existed, Asher. You just happened to walk back into my life at the right time."

I release a moan as she kisses a line lower still, leaning back in the pillows as my queen makes me feel like the luckiest man in the world.

LANDING IN FARCLIFF IS ODD. The airport in Farcliff City is familiar, its interior dotted with local chain stores I forgot existed. People are dressed differently—already bundled up for the cooler weather, whereas in Nord, it felt like everyone was trying to soak up as much of the sun as possible before it disappeared for winter.

The passport in my hand says Farcliff, but I feel like a stranger. With Nico by my side, who joined me in Stirling, my feet carry me down an escalator to a row of taxis, and I let the car transport me all the way to my father's offices. No sense delaying the inevitable. The faster I can quit this job, the faster I can go back to Penelope.

When I pull up outside the shiny, window-clad tower with my father's logo branded atop it like a crown, discomfort churns in my gut. How many times have I walked through these halls feeling inadequate? How many times have I dragged an acquisition plan behind me like a trophy, laying it at my father's feet and hoping he'd give me the fatherly approval I so craved?

Too many.

Now, when I step through the rotating doors and stride across the wide lobby, I see just how small it is. Men and women in suits pretending to rush to their offices, feeling important because they have briefcases and titles. For what? To make money for a man who told me I was disgusting?

A veil has been lifted from my eyes, and I see all this for what it is—empty, meaningless, vapid. Carrying my suit jacket over my arm, an elevator whirrs all the way up to the top floor. Only when the doors slide open do nerves finally twist deep in my stomach.

"Are you okay?" They're the first words Nico has spoken to me since we got on the plane. His glasses are slightly crooked, but his eyes are sharp behind them. "You look like you're about to make a bad decision."

"I'm fine," I say. But I'm not fine. I'm about to make a decision, but it's not bad at all. It might be the first good decision I've made in years. Decades.

When we step out of the elevator, my father's receptionist looks up then gestures to the door. "He's waiting for you."

Nodding, I head for the corner office. I knock twice and enter without waiting for an answer, pushing it open and stepping into the inner sanctum of my father's business. The place I dreamed I'd sit behind that polished desk overlooking the city.

Now, it all looks so...small.

"Son," my father says, standing up and extending a hand.

My brows tug together, my gaze drifting from his face to his outstretched hand. *Son?* I clasp his hand in mine and take a seat in the chair across from him.

"I've been waiting for you to get back here and claim your victory."

"My victory?"

"Donovan, Asher. He's ours."

"Oh. Right." My heart tightens slightly at the thought of the merger I'd all but forgotten. I meant to tell Penelope about it, but with everything...

My father leans back, an oily grin sliding across his face. He sighs, intertwining his fingers behind his head as he stares at me from beneath bushy eyebrows. "I have to admit, when you told me you wanted to go to Nord, I didn't think anything would come of it. I thought it would be a waste of time and company funds."

"Thanks for the vote of confidence." My voice is flat. After everything I've done for the man over the years, he still doubted my business savvy?

"You've impressed me, Son." That's twice he's used that word, and it feels as foreign to me as if he were calling me Logan.

I nod. "Thank you, Father." My eyes focus on his desk, tracing the wood grain with my eyes. This is it—this is when I pull the resignation letter out of my suit pocket and slide it over the desk. I tell him thank you for all the opportunities, but I've found something I want more. I wish him the best, shake his hand, then walk away. Forever.

Before I can clear the lump from my throat, though, my father speaks. "You've earned your spot in this office, Asher. I don't even know if I could have done what you did in Nord. Within weeks, you made one of the most lucrative deals we've ever had—and cut Donovan down while you did it. It was sheer brilliance."

And I have Penelope to thank for that. I lift my gaze to my father, nodding. Words don't come.

"You know I've been wanting to retire for some time now," Father says, eyes boring into mine. "I was waiting."

"For what?" I croak.

"For you to step up and show me you could do this."

"You mean for Logan to step up?"

My father waves a hand. "Logan doesn't have half the business brain you do."

His words fall on my ears like stones in a pool. I stare at the aging man before me, knowing in a corner of my brain that this is what I've been waiting for. Decades of my life have been spent aching for my father's approval. I've killed myself to hear him say those words—to acknowledge I'm worthy of this. Of him.

Now that he says it, though, I don't inflate with pride the way I thought I would. I feel...nothing.

My father's eyes sharpen, and he leans his forearms on his desk. His fingers interlace, with a soft clinking of his rings when they touch. "Next week, as soon as the acquisition of Donovan Enterprises is completed, I'm going to announce my retirement, and I'm going to name you as the new director. I've been planning a long holiday with your mother, and I thought we could use it as a trial run. You could take the reins while I'm sitting on the beach sipping cocktails."

"Me?" Finally, my voice works, and all I can manage is that one word.

My father laughs, pleased that I'm shocked. Pleased that he fooled me for years, tortured me when he dangled his affection like a carrot, then used his disgust as a stick.

I fell for it. I did it all—all the dirty work, all the negotiation, all the acquisitions and mergers and deals that needed a strong hand.

I was a fool. An idiot. A coward.

My life comes into sharp focus as I stare at the man who gave me life. The gleam in his eyes dims slightly as I lean forward, reaching into my shirt pocket. I feel the slightly rough edge of the envelope containing my letter of resignation. I pull it out, holding it between my fingers as I lift my eyes to meet my father's.

His gaze sharpens, dropping to the crisp, white envelope. Lips dropping open, I know he's about to say something I won't want to hear.

Before he can speak, though, the door behind me opens. Nico enters, breathless. "Someone leaked it," he says, stumbling toward the desk. "Someone leaked the news of the merger. It's all over the internet."

My father's eyes widen, his gaze shifting to me. Accusing. I shake my head, then turn to Nico. "Who?"

Nico roughs a hand through his hair. "I don't know. Here." He thrusts a tablet into my hand, and headlines scream at me. One after another, after another. All of them talking about a surprise hostile acquisition of Donovan Enterprises by Gerhard, Inc. All of them proclaiming the start of a huge mining conglomerate. Pointing to the new diamond mines in Nord as the final piece of the puzzle.

Handing the tablet to my father, I ignore whatever garbage is coming out of his mouth. Nico stares at me, wide-eyed.

"I know who did this," I say quietly, my voice full of thunder.

"Who?" Nico asks. "Your contact in Nord?"

I snort, shaking my head. "No. Donovan himself."

Donovan—blustery, raging, red-faced as he stormed out of my office. Promising to bury me. Vowing to figure out who told me about the diamond mines.

He's the one who leaked this news, and I know why. Somehow, he put the pieces together. Maybe he heard about my trip to the Summer Palace. He's trying to attack the one thing that means anything to me anymore—my relationship with the Queen.

23

PENELOPE

BACK IN MY office in Stirling, I smile at the stack of paperwork waiting for my signature. My hand drifts over my stomach. I can still hardly believe it. Everything I thought I knew about myself has been smashed, twisted, reflected back to me.

I'm not infertile. I'm not unworthy of love and companionship. I'm not destined to live a lonely life giving everything to my duty as monarch.

I could have it all—I *will* have it all.

My lips still tingle where Asher kissed them this morning, promising to call me as soon as he resigned from his father's business. There was emotion in his eyes, and he'd opened his lips to say something, then just kissed me again, harder, not caring who was watching.

My poor heart doesn't know what hit it. I'm happy and panicked and worried—so emotional I feel like I'm going to puke.

But happiness wins.

Dragging the first bit of paperwork over to me, I grab a pen and cast my eye over the scrambled letters. I can't read. Tears still threaten to spill over my cheeks. With a deep breath, I blink them away and sign my name on the paper—a congratulatory letter to a new school.

My door bangs open and I jump clean out of my chair. Jonah stomps through the door, eyes wild. "Pen," he breathes.

"Jeez, you gave me a fright." My hand rests against my heart, violent pulse thudding through my veins.

"Donovan," Jonah replies, ignoring my words. "Donovan and Gerhard are merging."

Frowning, I tilt my head. "What?"

"They're merging. It was leaked a few minutes ago."

"What do you mean, merging?"

"Donovan is being acquired by Gerhard."

My brother's words still don't make sense. He says them again, then again with slightly different wording. Still, they won't sink in. If Donovan and Gerhard are merging, then they must have been in negotiations for weeks...months. Gerhard is in a position to acquire them, so they must have been sniffing around Donovan Enterprises' business interests.

Business interests in Nord.

Eyes wide, I grab the phone Jonah thrusts at me. He runs his fingers through his hair over and over, worrying at his lip, as if he's scared of what I'll read. *I'm* scared of what I'll read. I hold my brother's gaze for a few moments, then drop my eyes to the article.

Penned by Jacinthe Crawley. What a surprise.

Swallowing back my panic, I read through the article. My heart drops, and drops, and drops.

Asher knew about Donovan Enterprises. He probably followed him to Nord to figure out what Reginald Donovan was planning. Horror ices my veins as my eyes widen.

That day at Gabriel's wedding, I *told* Asher. I said I was supposed to be talking to mining moguls about staying out of Nord. I handed him Donovan's plan right there in the cup of my hand, and I *knew* there was something weird about Asher's reaction.

He told me he came to Nord because he hoped to see me? He told me he was here for *me*? And I fucking *believed* him?

My hand shakes so hard Jonah grabs the phone, coming around my desk to put a hand on my shoulder. "Are you okay, Pen?"

"I...I..." My mouth opens and closes. I try to swallow, but my throat is so tight it's painful. A violent cramp makes me double over, and I reach for the garbage can under my desk just in time. My vomit splashes against the edges as Jonah rubs his hand over my back, saying words I don't hear.

The only thing in my ears is the sound of wind rushing. The sound of my heartbeat. The sound of betrayal.

Asher knew all along. He knew about Donovan. He probably knew about the diamond mines—no wonder he was able to get the application in so quickly.

He *lied*.

How could he wrap his arms around me and tell me he was here for me? How could he tell me he wanted this child —how could he smile at me and tell me he wanted to *marry me*? My hand shakes as I grip the trash can, another body-racking heave making me double over.

"Pen, I'm getting the doctor." Jonah sounds so far away as he rushes around the desk and calls out into the hallway.

It doesn't matter. It doesn't matter that I'm puking. It doesn't matter that I feel like the world is crashing around me.

Asher lied to me. He weaseled his way into my life and made me love him, and all the while he was keeping this news from me. He let me propose this business deal to him, let me think it was my idea. From the beginning, he's been manipulating me. Making me think I was making a good decision for the people of Nord. Allowing me to believe I was saving them from a company like Donovan Enterprises—all the while he was planning this.

He. Was. Planning. This.

Frederick rushes in, then gets on the phone and calls for a doctor. I lean back in my chair, accepting a glass of water from someone. I don't know who. My eyes are unfocused.

I stare at my abdomen, the true horror of my situation settling into my bones.

Asher lied to me, manipulated me, betrayed me—and I'm carrying his child.

In a daze, I answer a doctor's questions. I let him take my blood pressure and check my pulse. I stare at the wall, replaying every interaction I had with Asher over the past few months. Every moment when he could have come clean, could have told me the truth.

That evening, in his hotel room—he made me laugh when he said he wanted to admit he hated fishing. Had he wanted to tell me then? Or when I walked in and told him about my pregnancy—were the words on the tip of his tongue?

Maybe he was happy to keep this information from me forever. Maybe he never intended to tell me the truth at all. Thought I wouldn't find out. Thought he'd weaseled his way into my bed and my heart, and there was nothing I could do to turn him away.

The fucking *nerve* of him.

Ice covers my body and it's hard to think about anything except the caving of my chest. *Betrayal, betrayal, betrayal.* Every lie Asher said over the past few months replays in my mind on a loop, and my stomach sinks down, down, down.

I'm cold. I can barely feel anything, hear anything. I shake the doctor off as I stand up, stalking out of my office. I barely hear the protests from my staff. Barely feel my brother's hand on my arm. I need to be alone. I need to *think*. I need to know if I was really as big a fool as I think I was.

So starved for attention I let that snake into my home. My *bed*. So cold and alone that the first drop of affection made me feel like a new woman.

Pathetic.

I make it to my bedroom, close the door, and crawl under my blankets. Only then, when I'm alone, do I let tears fall from my eyes.

SOME TIME LATER, a knock on my door makes me lift my head. Frederick enters, keeping his eyes cast downward. He holds out a phone. "For you, ma'am."

"Who is it?"

My secretary clears his throat. "It's…Mr. Gerhard, ma'am."

"Tell him to crawl into a hole and die."

"As you wish." Frederick bows and makes to exit the room, but I sit up.

"Wait. Give me the phone."

My secretary's eyes widen ever so slightly, mustache quivering—as much emotion as I've seen on his face in the decades he's worked for me. He gulps, then closes the distance between us and hands me the phone. I wait until he's out of the room before putting it to my ear.

"What." Not a question. A demand. Tell me what the *fuck* I'm supposed to think about all this.

"Pen, I wanted to tell you." Asher's breathless.

"So you knew." My voice sounds like someone else's. It's so cold, emotionless. Under a thick cap of snow and ice, my emotions rage and burn. My anger is muted, somehow, as if it's too deep to unleash. If I let it break, it'll ruin me.

But it's there. My anger is *there*. Simmering, raging.

"Yes, I...I never meant to lie." Asher's voice sounds shredded, unlike I've ever heard it before. He sounds sorry, but I can't...I just can't bring myself to care.

"But you did."

"I know, but you have to understand, Pen—"

"You lost the right to call me that when you lied to me, Mr. Gerhard. Tell me why I should ever speak to you again."

"Our baby—"

"*My* baby." I grip the phone tighter, my eyes narrowing. I wish he could see me right now. I wish he could look at my face and feel my fury. "This child is *mine*. You will never, *ever* see it. Everything we had, Asher, was built on lies. Everything you said to me is blowing in the wind, because I can't trust anything that came out of your mouth. Do you actually care about me? About Nord? About anything other than your daddy's fucking company?"

"I *love* you, Penelope."

"Fuck. You."

"Pen—"

"I'll tell the public I saved some of Xavier's sperm before he died. I'll tell them it's his child, and I'll deny and dismiss any rumors you try to spread."

"Penelope," Asher's voice cracks, and I almost, *almost* feel something. But my whole body feels cold and heavy, and it's hard to move. My anger is slowly freezing my veins, making my blood run cold as my features slide into the old, familiar mask.

"Understand me, Asher," I say quietly. "Whatever happened between us is over. It was over the moment you decided to lie to me at Gabriel's wedding. It was over the moment you lied and told me you came to Nord to see me. It was over the moment you were too much of a coward to tell me the truth and own up to the consequences. Any affection I felt for you has crumbled to dust."

A strangled noise comes over the phone. I ignore it.

"Crawley's article said your father's company was expected to pass to you. Is that what all this was about, Asher? Is that why you came to Nord? Why you used me for information and advancement?"

"I didn't use you, Penelope. Everything we had was real."

I laugh—a cold, humorless sound. "You don't know the meaning of real, Asher. Goodbye."

Holding the phone out for Frederick to take, I stare at the wall. I feel nothing. I'm...empty. My rage is so loud, but it's cold. Like the wind whipping across a frozen lake in the dead of winter. A starless, moonless night that never ends.

I'm alone again. I was always alone—even with Asher.

But my eyes drift down and I slide a hand over my stomach. Not quite alone anymore. Tears flood my eyes and I blink them down my cheeks, sinking down into the pillows. I rub my hand over my abdomen in slow circles, letting tears soak into my pillows.

Not alone anymore. I have a child. I have the one thing I never thought would be possible and no matter what Asher does, or says, or lies about, I'll never forget he gave me a gift. I won't resent my child even if I...even if I hate Asher.

This baby is *mine*. My lifeline. My miracle.

24

ASHER

I HOWL in the lobby of my father's office—an office that will never, *ever* be mine. My letter of resignation is still clutched between white knuckles. I stare at the phone in one hand, letter in the other, and feel the weight of all my mistakes drag me down.

I'm drowning. I'm drowning in my own cowardice, my own lies, in Penelope's righteous anger.

She *should* be mad. Everything she said was true—all of it except the fact that what I feel for her isn't real. My love for Penelope is the only real thing I have to cling to.

"Asher?" My father stands in his doorway, Nico between us approaching with hesitant steps.

I stare at the two of them, shaking my head. "I'm going to talk to Donovan."

"What's the point?" My father shrugs. "He leaked it early, but it's basically just announcing his defeat. The articles weren't negative about the acquisition. Stakeholders will see it as a good thing."

"It's not about stakeholders," I spit. "It's about the fact that this is an attack."

"On what?"

"On *me*."

My father frowns, but I stalk into the elevator and mash the button to close the doors. Nico's face appears in the shrinking opening, but he makes no move to stop the doors and enter the elevator. Maybe he knows, with all his ambition, he's better off staying by my father's side. He sees the shift inside me.

I slip my phone into my pocket and swear when I see the crumpled letter of resignation still in my hand. I should have given it to my father before getting in the elevator, but I can't go back. I need to move forward, to the one person who will take the focus of my pain off Penelope's cold, emotionless voice: Reginald Donovan.

That sniveling, red-faced asshole who took it upon himself to do this.

A strange sort of calm settles over me as I make my way to the Donovan Enterprises building. Sounds are muffled, and I barely hear anything that's spoken to me. I walk straight through the lobby, vaguely aware of the protests of the receptionist. Who cares? She can't stop me. No one can stop me.

I resist the urge to kick down Reggie's door, choosing instead to use my hands. I don't need a dramatic entrance to make him understand how badly I want to throttle him.

Reginald Donovan sits behind his desk with a feline smile on his face. He looks me up and down, taking in my wild eyes, disheveled hair, white knuckles, and lets a slow chuckle slip through his lips. "Asher Gerhard," he croons. "The prodigal son."

"You leaked the news of the merger."

"I thought you'd be happy." His eyebrow arches, and I bristle. "Or was your *contact* in Nord not expecting it?"

"I knew it," I say, shaking my head. "I knew you leaked the news just to get to me."

"As soon as you took that trip to the Summer Palace with the Queen, it all made sense. All made perfect sense." He scoffs, leaning back in his chair. Fat fingers interlace over his generous stomach, and once again I note the sheer determination of his shirt's buttons to do their job.

"You don't know anything."

"I know you whored yourself out to the Queen, of all people, just to get under my skin. Trust you to pull something like that off, Gerhard."

"It had nothing to do with you."

"No? And your father handing his company to you meant nothing either?"

"I don't give a shit about my father's company."

"Could have fooled me." A snort escapes him. "You've been hounding me for months. Attacking my company at every turn and whispering in shareholders' ears. You made this bed, Asher, and now you need to lie in it. Who knows? Maybe the Queen will join you after all. Tell me, is her pussy so sweet you'd throw away your whole future for it?"

It's only after my snarl reaches my ear that I realize I've launched myself across the room. Only when my hands are around his neck that I realize what I'm doing. Only when the two of us hit the ground and his fist connects with my temple that I loosen my grip and roll away.

Reginald huffs, his cheeks red, an evil gleam in his eye. "You actually care about her." He brushes imaginary dust off his shirt as he heaves himself off the ground, shaking his head. "You idiot."

I stare at the man who exposed me to Penelope, and the reality of my situation truly sinks in. Penelope sees me as what I am—what I've always been. The businessman who uses people, who lies and cheats and does whatever needs to be done to make a deal.

I saw another way of living when I was with her, but I didn't realize I can't just walk away from all this. I can't ignore all the actions I've taken that have led me to this point. I can't just walk away from the lies and omissions I've made.

I need to make it right. Somehow. I need to make amends.

My father looks confused when I tell him I'll accept his offer. "You want the company?"

"It would be my honor," I say through a clenched jaw.

"What about"—he waves a hand at the lobby outside his office—"Donovan, the leak, the merger? You didn't seem happy about it."

"I went to see Donovan, and I understand why he did it."

"And why's that?"

"He wanted to control the narrative of the merger. Wanted to make sure it didn't look like a hostile takeover, wanted to assure his shareholders he was still in control. Might work out for the best in the long run. I was..." I clear my throat. "I was angry because I thought he was trying to wriggle out of the deal. He assured me he isn't."

My father nods, his eyebrows arching slightly. "Okay," he finally says, nodding. "Let's proceed. You still want to sit in this chair while I'm away?"

"I'd like nothing more." *Lie*. Another lie. All I want to do is get *out* of that chair. I want to run back to Nord and drop to my knees in front of Penelope, begging for her forgiveness. I want to *stop* lying, never tell another lie as long as I live. I want to be the kind of man Penelope thought I was when she promised her life and child to me.

But there are things I need to do first. I need to prove to

her that I've changed—all I did wasn't to betray her. I'm not the man she thinks I am.

I'm still the man who followed her to Nord, the man who bared himself to her, the man who opened his heart and let himself feel love for the first time in his life. I'm the man she wants me to be. I just need to show her that in a way she understands.

So I sit in front of my father and accept the leadership of the company—however temporary it may be—with a bow of my head, as if he's bestowing some great blessing on me. I ignore the twisting of my gut and I tell myself this is what needs to happen. This is how I atone for my sins, how I shed this skin and become the person I need to be.

25

PENELOPE

THERE'S a hole in my chest the size of the Arctic Ocean. I wander through the Stirling castle gardens, almost offended by the explosion of life and color around me. Summer is supposed to be the best time in Nord. It's what we all live for after long months of cold and snow. This year, it feels stifling to me. Birds flit between trees as I make my way to a bench, lowering myself down to stare at nothing for minutes on end.

Asher lied about...everything.

Two birds sing to each other in call and response from opposite trees. I stare at the dark green branches, wishing it were December instead of August. There'd be no warmth, no greenery, no insects flying around. No delicate melodies from birds trying to woo each other.

There'd just be cold ice as far as the eye can see. Maybe then I'd feel comfortable. If the landscape matched the way I feel in my heart, I'd at least feel at home in my own kingdom. My own home. My own body.

This morning, the doctor told me my due date was the fourth of March. A spring baby, heralding the arrival of new life. A sign of the miracle that happened in my body—something I never thought possible. It's fitting that the baby will arrive with all the other life in Nord, but it still doesn't feel real.

Footsteps make me turn my head to see Silas approaching. Dark smudges mark his under-eyes, and he gives me a wry smile. "Hey, Pen."

"You look rough."

"That makes two of us." Silas snorts, sinking down on the bench beside me. He lets out a long sigh, tilting his head up to soak up the sunlight. "I went to this gnarly party last night."

"Gnarly?" I arch my brows. Is Silas even from the same family as me? The same decade?

He grins. "It was fun."

"Doesn't look fun this morning."

"I'll live."

I wrinkle my nose, saying nothing.

Silas sighs. "Sorry about Gerhard."

Pinching my lips together, I hold back the wave of emotion that threatens to rip me apart. I swallow past the tightness in my throat and shrug. "It was my own fault for getting close to him."

"You know that's not true, Pen."

"Do I? I lost Xavier first, and I was so desperate for affection that I latched onto the first man who made me *feel* something. It's pathetic."

"It's not."

"What do you know about it?"

"I know how hard it is to be alone." My brother's words are so quiet I almost miss the pain in his voice. "You deserve to find someone. Just because you're a queen doesn't mean you have to be on your own."

"I'm not sure I agree with that."

"You don't have to agree for it to be true."

"Maybe I need to be alone in order to be a good leader."

Silas snorts.

I grit my teeth. "Look what happened the first time I tried to be with someone other than Xavier. I got played for a fool, and now I'm waiting for the story to break in the newspapers so the whole kingdom can ridicule me."

"Just because things didn't work out with Asher doesn't mean that's the end of the line for you, Pen."

"So what do you suggest? I go on Tinder? That would go over well with the tabloids." Bitterness soaks every word. Even the birds quiet down. The wind stills, as if the landscape itself wants to show me how it feels to have nothing to keep me company.

"Jonah told me Asher lied about the merger with Donovan. Is he...Is that going ahead? Gerhard is acquiring Donovan Enterprises?"

"When I spoke to him, he didn't deny it. He also didn't deny the fact that he's going to step into his father's role. There's no other way to look at it—he used me to advance his own career. I *let* him use me."

Silas glances at my stomach and clears his throat. "And..."

I pinch my lips. "Yeah. You're going to be an uncle."

He nods, then stretches an arm over my shoulders. "It'll all work out, Penelope."

I don't answer, because I'm not sure it's true. I wrap my arms around my stomach and try to stuff down the worst of my fears—the slithery, quiet voices who whisper to me that my pregnancy won't work out, either. My body will malfunction again. Something will go wrong.

Memories that were buried deep start to surface again. The months and months when I failed to conceive. The heartbreak of fertility procedures. The...*desperation*. The breathless sort of panic that made me feel on edge about everything, all the time. Those years were the worst years of my life. I was lost.

And afterward, resignation.

After years—*years*—of feeling like that, how can I allow myself to hope? In the face of what Asher did, how can I let myself think things will be okay? Even this baby inside me, who's to say my body will work how it's supposed to? All the evidence in my past points to disaster.

Tears burn my eyelids and I pray Silas won't notice. I don't want to have to explain that I'm fighting my own mind and not trusting my own body. How can my brother possibly say that things will work out? He and I have lived different realities. He's the carefree playboy, the party animal who can do no wrong in the eyes of the public.

But me? I'm the villain. Always have been, and I always will be because it's who I need to be in order to rule this kingdom.

Things have never worked out for me. When I dared to think they might—that day in the living room at the Summer Palace—it was Fate's way of playing a cruel joke. I got to see everything I longed for the most. A child. A man to love. A *family*.

Then it was all taken away from me.

Pushing myself off the bench, I straighten my top and give Silas a tight smile. "I should get back. There's lots of work to do."

"Why don't you take time off, Pen? Jonah and I can handle things here. Go back to the Summer Palace and enjoy the last of the warm weeks there. Take a break."

I shake my head. "I can't."

"The baby—"

"Is none of your concern." My voice cuts so harshly Silas flinches. Grinding my teeth together, I turn away and head back to the castle. At least if I'm moving, working, *doing* something, I can't think about the fact that everything inside me is slowly freezing to a big, black lump of ice.

At the beginning of September, nearly a month after Asher left for Farcliff, I read an article about Asher Gerhard accepting the role as director of his father's company. My heart sinks and vaguely, I wonder if I'd held out hope that he would choose me instead of his career. In some small corner of my mind, I must have been wishing he'd arrive at my door and beg for my forgiveness.

A part of me wanted to forgive him.

But as I read the article, the final door shuts, and I realize we'll never be together. I'll raise this child on my own and tell the media his biological father is Xavier. Asher won't exist in my life, and these past few months will be nothing but a dream.

The thought of lying about my child's father makes me feel sick, but I push the feeling down. Above all, I need to maintain stability in the kingdom. Avoid controversy. Be a queen beyond reproach.

Still, denying the child's parentage chips away another piece of my heart, and I dread the day I'll have to announce it to the public.

In addition to lying to me, that's another thing Asher took from me. Bearing my first child—likely my only child—doesn't feel like a joyous occasion. I'm afraid and alone and facing a lifetime of lies. Will I lie to my child, too? Will I deny Asher the right to see his baby?

Those questions weigh heavy on my spirit. It's hard to

move, let alone think about everything facing me in the coming months. After reading the article about Asher's new position at the company, I shuffle to my bedroom, lock the door, and curl into my bed. Alone.

26

ASHER

THE INK IS STILL wet on the acquisition papers when the story breaks in all the major business publications in Farcliff. Donovan Enterprises has been acquired by Gerhard, Inc. I know Penelope will find out—maybe she already has.

This past month has been the most difficult of my life. Not being able to see her, talk to her, reassure her—it makes me feel sick. Every hour that goes by makes my hope dwindle, as if my opportunity to show her my true self is slipping through my fingers.

But I keep going. I watch my father leave for a holiday and take a seat behind his desk. I negotiate with Reginald Donovan and reassure his stakeholders. I have our lawyers draw up the paperwork and forge onward with the acquisition of his company.

I know how it looks from the outside, but I can't let myself stop moving. I can't pause to think about the damage this is doing to my reputation—to my relationship with Penelope. If I think about it too much, I'll lose my nerve.

My father will be away for three weeks. It's the longest holiday he's taken since he started this company, and it's a huge vote of confidence for me. If it had happened three months ago, I'd feel like all my hard work had paid off. I'd feel finally validated for the years of service I did for my father. All the companies I acquired and business deals I brokered.

I'd finally feel seen.

Now, though, it feels empty. Cold.

My fingers drift over the edge of my scar, a whisper of Penelope's touch.

"ARE YOU SURE ABOUT THIS?" Nico glances at me from the other side of my father's desk. He's just emailed me my flight itinerary from Farcliff City to Roston, and he looks... concerned. His brows are drawn together, eyes unusually troubled.

I nod. "Yep."

"Ash, this is..." He clears his throat. "Your father won't be happy."

"I've been letting my father decide my fate my whole life. I think it's time I do something for myself."

"There's no guarantee the Queen will even appreciate what you're doing. She might never speak to you again."

"At least I'll know I tried."

Nico's throat bobs. He takes a deep breath, running fingers through his hair as he searches for the right words. "I have to tell you, Asher, just for my own peace of mind—I don't think this is a good idea."

"Noted."

"You're blowing up your future."

"I'm creating my future."

"You're taking a massive risk."

"Thank you for your input, Nico." My voice is frosty. "That'll be all."

My assistant takes a deep breath, holding it in for a few seconds as if he's trying to decide whether to fight me on this or not. His shoulders deflate, and he nods. "Okay."

"Nico, wait."

He turns, arching a brow.

I gulp. "You don't have to stand beside me for this. If you want to keep working for my father, it's probably best to distance yourself from me. You should stay in Farcliff when I go."

Nico stares at me for a moment, then dips his chin. He agrees. He's choosing his career over me and even though I know it's the best decision for both of us, it stings. The finality of what I'm about to do comes into sharp focus.

I watch my assistant leave and let my eyes drift back to the itinerary. I leave tomorrow to make another landmark deal—one I already know my father won't like.

For once, I don't care what my father thinks. I don't care if he hates me for the rest of his life, because this is the first time I feel like I'm doing the right thing. I'm not motivated by greed or selfish desires for recognition. I'm not chasing validation from someone who forced me to grovel at his feet because of an accident that scarred a third of my body.

I'm doing this for *me*. To prove to myself I can stand up to him. To prove to myself I've changed.

And...I'm doing it for Penelope. I hope she sees what I'm trying to do. I hope she forgives me. Circling at the back of my mind are dark, evil fears. Monsters that keep me up at night, telling me I'll never see my child. Silent fears that echo in my head, telling me I've lost my only chance at love.

If I need to blow up my father's company to prove to her I

love her, so be it. If I need to drag myself through the mud and ruin my own reputation, I'll do it.

Without Penelope, there's nothing. This is my last chance. My only hope.

Maybe I'm a fool, and this will do nothing to prove to her I deserve her. Maybe I'm digging my own grave, and I'll look back on these weeks as the peak of my stupidity. Maybe I'll regret what I'm about to do.

But there's a slim chance I'll reach Penelope. There's a sliver of hope that she'll forgive me, so I have no choice. I have to do it. I'll ruin myself to ask for a second chance.

MICHAEL BURGUNDY IS a tall man—six-foot-four or five, I'd guess. He's heavy-set with sharp, blue eyes. He stares at me above the stack of papers on the conference table, frowning. "I'm not sure I understand, Mr. Gerhard."

"The contract is fairly simple."

"You're selling us the Roston diamond mines for one Nordish dollar?"

"Transferring ownership and the right to all the royalties, yes."

"But...why?"

"Does it matter?"

He puts the contract down and folds his hands on top of it. "With all due respect, Mr. Gerhard, yes, it does matter. We've met a few times now, and our working relationship has been successful thus far. It's no secret that NRG has struggled in the past few years, and we would never have been able to take on this project in Roston without Gerhard's capital. Your proposal...doesn't make sense."

"What doesn't make sense about it?"

"You're losing over eight hundred million dollars in

potential profit." He speaks slowly, never breaking eye contact with me. "Why?"

How can I explain that giving this project back to Nord—back to Penelope—is the only way I can prove to her I don't care about my career? Everything I did here, in Nord, was real? It was for her.

But if I tell Mick that, he'll think I'm insane. Penelope's relationship with me wasn't public knowledge, and I'll sound like I've lost my damn mind. Maybe I have. "I didn't think the hardest part of this would be to get you to agree to a deal that will basically save your company from going under." I lean back in my seat, the long conference table extending on either side of us. Beside me, empty chairs line the conference table. Nico chose to stay in Farcliff.

On the other side of the table, Mick is flanked by two lawyers, a man in his fifties and a woman about a decade younger. They're both staring at me with suspicion in their eyes, keeping a hand on the copies of the contract I provided for them.

Mick inhales. "Mr. Gerhard—"

"Asher."

He nods. "Asher, can you please just explain to me why you'd be making such a blatantly terrible deal for your own company? You've funded the initial mobilization of staff and materials, and basically put together a plan to manage the construction phase of the project. All the outlays so far have been by your side of the joint venture. By pulling out now, you'll see none of the reward. It's an outrageously bad deal for you."

"Rewards aren't only monetary," I answer.

"Stop saying these cryptic, meaningless phrases," Mick snaps. He pinches the bridge of his nose, forcing himself to take a deep breath. I can almost see him counting to ten in his head.

I lean forward, pointing to the stack of papers. "Review the deal with a fine-toothed comb, and you'll see I'm not trying to screw you over. It's...a gift."

"People in our business don't make gifts."

"Maybe I'm trying to get out of this business."

He frowns, but doesn't answer.

I push myself to my feet, nodding to the people across the table. "I'll be in Roston until you make a decision."

As I walk out of the room, a weight starts to lift off my shoulders. It's not completely gone, but I know I'm heading in the right direction. I'm making things right—or at least trying.

27

PENELOPE

FOR ONCE, I don't learn about the biggest development in Nordish business from the news. Mick Burgundy is admitted to my office with a yellow folder in his hand, head bowed, looking almost afraid to speak to me.

I try not to recoil, even though the sight of him reminds me of the biggest mistake of the last ten years of my life. I handed Asher a deal with Mick on a silver platter—handed him exactly what he wanted from me.

But Mick hands me the file and tells me a crazy story about Asher proposing a deal. A deal Asher must be out of his mind to make. A deal that will lose his company millions, if not tens or hundreds of millions. Mick wrings his hands, shrugging. "Our lawyers saw nothing wrong with the contract, Your Majesty. Gerhard really wants to sell us his half of the venture for one dollar."

I blink, then slowly lift my eyes to meet his. Clearing my throat, it takes all my self-control to keep my mask in place. To show no cracks, and to hide the hurricane raging inside me. When I speak, my voice is steady. "When did he approach you with this?"

"Three days ago, ma'am."

"And he's still in Roston?"

"He said he'd stay until we signed the paperwork. I just...I know you were involved in the inception of this joint venture. I thought it was best to bring it to you personally."

"Thank you for that, Mr. Burgundy. Frederick will show you out."

My secretary appears behind the tall CEO, touching his elbow to lead him out. Before they get to the door, though, Mick pauses, glancing over his shoulder. "He said it was a gift," he blurts out.

I frown, cracks appearing in my unbreakable mask. "A gift?"

"That's what he said. I don't know...It makes no sense."

I stand, inclining my head as regally as I can while my heart does its best to burst through my chest. "Thank you, Mr. Burgundy."

As soon as the two men are out of my office, I double over, sucking in a deep breath. Panic squeezes at my chest as confusion rings in my ears.

And, something else...

Bright, silver hope. A thin thread of life that lay buried beneath the ice in my heart, one I was afraid to acknowledge even as it lived on inside me.

A gift...for me.

TIME IS A FUNNY THING. The hours I spend getting to the royal jet and flying to Roston pass in a daze. The blink of an eye. When the plane lands, I hardly even remember who I spoke to or how I got here.

But the seconds that tick by, heartbeat by heartbeat, after I knock on Asher Gerhard's door—those are excruciating. I feel those moments in every nerve ending, every bone, every muscle. I feel them in the warm breeze that ruffles my hair and the sound of leaves rustling in the trees. An eternity passes me by, and still I stand there on Asher's front stoop, waiting for the door to open.

Heartbeat by heartbeat. Thump by thump. Second by never-ending second.

Then, footsteps. The peephole goes dark, and I suffer through another pause that lasts an age. Slowly, as if it's scraping along my very soul, the lock slides open and the door swings inward.

He's...God, how can I put it into words? Asher's there, in front of me, and I can hardly believe he's real. Wearing a white button-down shirt tucked into tight-fitting slacks, he looks like every naughty secretary's wet dream. His shoulders are broader than I remembered, hands flexing and unflexing at his sides. His black belt gleams on his hips, toes wiggling in his dark gray socks. But the man is more than his clothes—he's...everything. I hadn't remembered his features perfectly—hadn't done them justice in my mind, as if the mere thought of Asher's face was too much for my heart to bear. If I'd remembered them as they are, could I have ever walked away from him? Those eyes that seem to see right through me, the lines that bracket his mouth when he's deep in thought, the lips that plagued my dreams for weeks.

He's standing there, staring at me like I'm his whole world. His eyes open wide and his breath catches, and still, the seconds feel like they last forever.

"Penelope." Asher's voice is pure emotion. Pure fire and light, with a raspy edge that sends a tremor shooting down to my toes. His brows tug together ever so slightly, every micro-movement of his face sending jolts of heat through my veins. Without another word, he gulps, steps aside, and lets me in.

I nod to my staff, who remain outside. Asher's arm brushes mine as he closes the door behind me. Asher moves fluidly. Gracefully. And me? I feel like I'll trip over my own shoes if I try to move. My heart is in my throat, thumping so fast I might throw up.

His eyes catch mine, lips opening. My gaze flicks down to his mouth and immediately over to the wall. I need air. A deep breath. Something to clear the hot, dizzying thoughts invading my head.

"You want a drink?" Every word sounds excruciating, as if he has to rip each one from his throat.

I nod, following him down the hallway. The living room is still empty, I note. Walls still bare. Maybe he never meant to stay here after all. Blood turns sluggish in my veins at the thought, and I focus on the movement of my legs. One foot in front of the other.

My eyes drift up Asher's long legs, snagging on his ass. Damn those pants. I blink two or three times as if it'll help to clear the lust clouding my vision. It doesn't.

Asher mumbles something about tea, coffee, and a vague excuse about lack of options. I croak, "Water." A glass lands on the table in front of me, and I force myself to crawl my gaze up to his.

"You're here."

"Mick Burgundy came to see me."

Asher gulps, his throat bobbing. He turns his back to me, grabbing a glass of his own, then slides into the chair across from mine. My eyes drift behind him, to the kitchen island where I...where we...

"Did you see the contract?" The rough edge to Asher's voice is the only indication he's feeling even a fraction of what I feel.

Forcing myself to meet his gaze, I nod. "Yes. It's not a very fair proposal." I touch the base of my water glass. "To you, I mean. You'll lose millions."

"I don't care."

His words find every weakness in my heart's armor and try to pry it open. I sit up straighter, staring at a bead of condensation on my glass. "You cared about nothing except business for years—lied to me to get yourself ahead—and now you're telling me you don't care."

Pause. Then he whispers, "Yes."

"Why?"

I feel more than I hear the way Asher's breath stays stuck in his throat. I watch the hurt ripple over his face, tensing every feature as he stares at the table that separates us.

"Why would you do that, Asher? And you told Mick it was a gift? Is this some sort of joke?"

"No," he nearly shouts, flicking his gaze up to mine. "It's not a joke. It's...it's the first good thing I've ever done. The first thing that felt right."

"You're giving this mine to NRG."

"I'm giving this mine to *you*, Penelope. The mines mean nothing to me. My career means nothing. I don't want any of it. I know my father will fire me. I know I'm ruining my career. I know everyone will remember me for this, and not the hundreds of successful negotiations I did before. I know this will be my legacy, and no one will understand why. Not one person in this world will understand how I could do this, but I hoped..." He sucks in a trembling breath, curling his hands into fists. "I hoped you might."

Those cracks in my armor are wider now. Blood starts welling at the openings, ready to flow free. I grind my teeth together to stop my lip from trembling, forcing myself to stare at this man. To try to understand him.

"Penelope," he gasps, as if he can hardly breathe. "I'm so

sorry. I should have told you about the merger when I first came to Nord. I should have told you before that, at Gabriel's wedding! I should have been honest with you from the start, but I was a coward. You walked into my life all elegance and beauty and strength, and I felt so small. I felt weak and unworthy of you, and I was so fucking terrified you'd see me for what I was. Every time you looked at me, I thought you'd finally see the broken, burned boy I am inside. But you never did—you kept giving me your smiles and laughter and you gave me *life*, Pen. Lying to you is the only thing I've ever regretted. In all the shitty things I've done in my life, hurting you...it broke me. Tore me to shreds. And I know that's no excuse, but, Pen, I feel like I can't breathe without you."

With a breath, Asher fists his hands through his hair. He stares at his glass of water, as if he's afraid to meet my gaze. "I was a coward to lie to you. A coward to hide the truth from you. A coward to run here to do my father's bidding when I should have seen this for what it is." He lifts his eyes to mine, endless pain swimming in their depths. "I'm in love with you, Penelope. Desperately, foolishly in love with you. But you're a queen, and who am I? How can I ever be worthy of you? I thought if I gave you all the diamonds in Nord, it might make a dent in the absolute train wreck I've created. I thought if I blew up my own career and everything I used to care about, maybe I could prove to you—to myself—that it doesn't matter. Nothing matters at all...except...you."

His last word is nothing more than a whisper, but it echoes through my soul, waking up every part of me that I thought died long ago. I blink a river of tears down my cheeks, letting the armor around my heart fall away.

My voice is nothing more than a rasp when I finally speak. "You're no more a coward than me, Asher. I've loved you since you let me slap you across the face and asked for more. Maybe before that, when you saved me from Gabriel's wedding and showed me what it felt like to live again. From the very first moment you stood beside those roses because I *knew*, I just had this feeling you were thinking of me when you touched them... But I was too scared to admit it to myself, to you, to anyone." My bottom lip trembles so hard it's difficult to speak. I close my eyes just to save myself from the assault of his gaze, breathing deep to say the words I've tried to ignore for weeks. Months. "I love you, Asher. I could never deny it, and I could never let this child grow up without knowing its father. Without knowing you."

Asher's beside me in an instant, yanking me out of my chair and crushing his lips to mine. His kiss is violent, needy, and everything that's been missing from my life. His lips brand mine with a vow. An oath. A promise to never let me go again. I cling onto his broad shoulders to show him I feel the same, melting into his body as if it's the only safe place that's ever existed.

He scrapes his teeth along my lip and shoves his tongue into my mouth, using rough hands to pull me closer. I thread my fingers through his hair and tug and pull him closer because all I want is more, more, more. I can finally *breathe*. I feel alive for the first time in years.

Asher pulls away, wiping the endless tears from my cheeks. He presses his lips to my cheeks and licks my tears away, swallowing them down like they belong to him. "Forgive me, Pen. Forgive me for being such an idiot. For lying and keeping things from you and for not being brave enough to face what I feel for you."

I let out a long breath, leaning my cheek against his chest. "There's nothing to forgive," I whisper.

"But there is, Penelope. Please, I need to hear it."

I pull away to see the last traces of agony written in his

features. With my fingers, I trace his eyebrows, cheeks, lips. My touch drifts to the edge of his scar, the bumpy skin familiar beneath my fingertips. Asher shivers, closing his eyes when I touch it. Letting out a sigh, I nod. "I forgive you, Asher. But please, no more lies."

"No more lies," he promises. "I don't think I could survive anything like this again."

A grin tugs at my lips. "And there are only so many diamond mines in Nord available for you to pledge your love to me. I'm not sure how much bigger than this you can go."

Asher chuckles, a deep, warm sound that rumbles through his chest and into mine. He touches his nose to mine, eyes crinkling as he smiles. "The only thing I could give my Queen was a slice of her own country back before I pledge my life at her feet. I'm not planning on screwing up like this again."

"What will your father say?"

"I don't care." The words slide out of his lips so surely that I know he's telling the truth.

Whatever happens after today—after the Roston diamond mines are signed over to Nord's national resource group—it won't change the simple fact that has changed the course of my life forever. "I love you," I say, tilting my head toward his to ask for another kiss.

"You have no idea how much I love hearing those words, Pen."

"So say them back." I grin.

Asher's lips brush mine. "I love you." He lays a soft kiss on my lips. "I'm *in* love with you." Another kiss. "And I'll never stop loving you." A third kiss to seal that vow I thought I'd never hear. Asher drops to his knees and lays a soft kiss on my stomach, letting out a shaky sigh. "And you, baby, I'll devote my life to making you happy. I'll do anything for you, anything for your mother, anything to make sure the two of you have everything you need. I promise."

I thread my fingers through Asher's dark hair, sighing out the last of the chill inside me. He's the boy who walked through fire and lived—and the man who broke through the layer of ice around my heart.

My one, my only, my everything. My Asher.

EPILOGUE
PENELOPE

ASHER and I get married on a cool September afternoon, about six weeks after our conversation in Roston. We do it at the Summer Palace, where we can have privacy. It's quiet, with only family and a few close friends in attendance—but it's perfect. Asher looks dapper in his navy suit, his eyes shining when he watches me walk down the aisle.

I struggle not to cry the whole ceremony, which is a feeling I'm still not accustomed to. I've spent the past decade feeling cold distance from my emotions, but I can't say I mind. Feeling all my emotions without restraint is intense, but it's worth it. It means I can open myself up to love and let myself believe good things are coming.

After the ceremony, when we make it to the main ballroom of the Summer Palace, I lean my head on Asher's shoulder. Beside me, my husband stiffens. I follow his gaze to the corner of the room, where his brother Logan stands by the wall. Over the past few weeks, Asher's told me about Logan—about how inadequate he felt next to him when they grew up. How Logan and he were pitted against each other, and how he wishes things had been different between them.

Asher invited his whole family to the wedding and expected none of them to show up, but I guess he was wrong about that.

His brother is handsome, in a prettier way than Asher. He doesn't have the ruggedness that I love in my husband. Logan pushes himself off the wall and walks up to us, chin down. He glances at me, bowing. "Your Majesty."

I squeeze Asher's hand, inclining my head at his brother.

My husband clears his throat. "I didn't think you'd come."

"To your wedding? I wouldn't miss it." Logan's eyes shine, his throat bobbing as he swallows. "I just wanted to say... congratulations. You deserve happiness."

Redness flushes over Asher's cheeks, and he drops his head. I can tell he's struggling for words. My brave, selfless man, who gave everything up to prove his love for me, is surprised that his brother made the trip up here. Surprised to hear a kind word from him.

I extend my arms toward Logan, wrapping him in a quick hug. "Thank you for coming."

Asher does the same, clearing his throat as he pulls away. He looks dangerously close to crying. He extends a hand toward his brother and they shake, holding each other's gaze.

Emotion chokes me—even more than when I walked down the aisle. Asher's parents might not be here, but his brother's presence means a lot. It means there might be a chance for reconciliation with his own family. It means, maybe, he didn't give everything up to be with me.

Music starts, a waiter appears with drinks of champagne and sparkling grape juice for me, and I welcome Logan to my palace, my kingdom, my life.

Wolfe and Rowan appear at my side, along with Silas and Jonah. I'm surrounded by all the people I love, celebrating a union I thought would never happen. Little Wren dances and dances until he collapses into a heap and starts snoring. I smile, looking at my nephew as I sweep my hand over my stomach.

The sight of Wren no longer fills me with fear and resentment. I look at my nephew with nothing but love, and I finally understand how Wolfe felt all those months ago. Love hits you right in the gut—and love for a child? Forget it. Mine isn't even born yet, but I already feel overwhelmed.

"Have I ever told you how gorgeous you are?" Asher nuzzles his face into my neck, dropping a soft kiss behind my ear.

I smile, sliding my hand around his waist. Tonight, I'm not a queen. My responsibilities are shoved aside for a few blissful hours, and I just enjoy basking in the light of my new life. My new love.

When the dancing winds down, I stand up and slip my hand into Asher's. Silas grins, wrapping me in a big bear hug, then Jonah does the same.

Finally, Wolfe comes to stand in front of me and drops a soft kiss on both my cheeks. "I'm happy for you, Penelope. I haven't seen you smile this much since we were kids."

Leaning my head on Asher's shoulder, we walk toward the exit. No one protests or asks us to stay longer. They let us leave and we let them dance and drink long into the night. I'd much rather be alone with Asher, anyway.

Our wedding night is tender. Slow and passionate, then intense. Asher worships my body and makes me feel his love from head to toe. I do the same for him and when it's over, we're sweaty and tangled in each other's arms, smiling as a blanket of happiness covers us both.

"How do you think the public will react to the news about the baby?" Asher slides his hand over my stomach.

"Well, when we announced our engagement, the reaction

was supportive. They might not expect it to happen this fast, but any controversy will blow over. It has to."

"They want you to be happy, you know." Asher kisses my temple.

His words ring through me, and I let them sink in—the true meaning of them. The people of Nord want *me* to be happy. There was no outrage when Asher and I announced our engagement. Not talk of corruption and controversy. There was only...celebration. Happiness that I had finally found someone after Xavier.

The articles and editorials shocked me, if I'm honest. We broke the news about a month ago, and the positive reaction was another reminder that my isolation and my coldness were a defense mechanism that only hurt myself. I can only imagine the celebration in the kingdom when we announce the pregnancy.

Asher tightens his arms around me, letting out a long sigh. "I love you, Penelope."

Warmth floods me from head to toe. "I love you, too, Asher. More than you know."

OUR BABY GIRL is born at the beginning of March, healthy and screaming her little lungs out. Asher and I cry—a lot. My love for my daughter is overwhelming. It drags me under, and I let it.

Of course people do the math. They know it's only six months between the end of September and the beginning of March, and rumors fly. It's not exactly what I'd like as the Queen of Nord, but if I'm honest, it's hard to care.

I have a *daughter*. I bore a child of my own body.

The words of a few people in the kingdom? Whispers and gossip?

Meaningless. My daughter is a princess, and anyone who denies it isn't worthy of my attention.

The negative whispers about my affair with Asher soon fade, though, and when we release the first pictures of Princess Neva, there's nothing but rejoicing. The whole kingdom celebrates our daughter as the miracle she is—the heir no one thought would exist.

ASHER'S FATHER doesn't speak to him for a full year. We send pictures of our baby girl and try to reach out every couple of months, but silence answers back. Mr. Gerhard is angry with his son, which is understandable. Asher sold off a huge chunk of the company without remorse, then handed in his resignation. He basically launched a grenade at his relationship with his father and was ready to accept the consequences.

Even though Asher assures me it was worth it—and every time I see him with Neva, I believe him—it still pains me to think he can't have a relationship with his father. Every time we hear nothing back from Farcliff, I know it hurts Asher, but he brushes off his pain and gives me a soft smile. My brave man, ready to face anything for the sake of our love.

Finally, before Neva turns one, we receive a letter in the mail. Asher opens it, jaw clenched, then lets out a long sigh. His shoulders drop, and it looks like some of the pain he's been carrying is finally easing. "He wants to meet her," he says, lifting his eyes to mine. "My father wants to meet his granddaughter."

I smile, nodding. "Let's invite him to Nord."

And so, another relationship begins to mend. It started with Asher and me, mending our own hearts. Then that healing extended to our families, to our kingdom, to everyone who had called me cold and heartless and barren. The love we have for each other permeated every nook and cranny in Nord, and it healed all the bitterness it touched.

His father might never fully forgive Asher, but at least the conversation is starting. That frost can melt, just like the ice that used to encase my own heart. Love has the power to do that. Asher's love, my love, Neva's love—it blankets everything in warmth and goodness and makes me forget what it felt like to be alone.

With Asher by my side and Neva in my arms, I'm not turning my back on my duty. I'm a better queen than I was before, because I have them. I have their love and support—and I can give it back tenfold to my people.

I thought my coldness made me strong, but I was wrong.

Asher's love makes me stronger. Unbreakable.

He makes me, quite simply, *happy*.

~

EXTENDED EPILOGUE

ASHER

A SINGLE CANDLE flickers on Neva's three-tiered birthday cake as the last few notes of the Happy Birthday Song ring out. Why a one-year-old needs a multi-tiered cake, I'll never understand—but then again, a lot of my life as a royal has been new to me. I grew up in a wealthy family, but living in a castle and having a personal butler and a chef...that's not something I'm used to.

Having an army of servants following me around, having people *bow* to me and call me titles I can hardly remember for myself—it can be an exercise in patience sometimes.

Not that I mind. The benefits far outweigh the few moments when I want to disappear.

Penelope smiles at me from the other side of the table, her hands clutched at her breast. Tears shine in her eyes as she shifts her gaze from me down to our daughter in my arms. Love soaks through her stare, and a beautiful warmth spreads through my chest.

Family.

That's what we are. For the first time in my life, I feel like I have a real family. I nuzzle my face next to Neva's face as she points her finger toward the white cake. It has delicate, multi-colored flowers piped all over its sides, with big swirls of frosting piped all along the top.

Outrageous for a one-year-old? Yes. But not surprising.

Silas lifts a glass of wine toward my daughter and me. "*And many more...*" he sings, grinning. The room full of family and friends waits in hushed silence for my daughter to huff out the candle.

"Blow it out, Neva," I say to my daughter, inching her forward. "Ready? One, two, three..." I take a deep breath and blow out the candle for her as she lets spittle fly from her mouth. Everyone claps. I laugh, looking up to meet Penelope's gaze.

My eyes snag on hers, joy filling me up from head to toe. I feel so light I might float up to the ceiling. In this room, with Silas, Wolfe, Jonah, Rowan, and Logan, we have all our siblings together. My eyes shift from Logan to the man and woman beside him, and I can't help but let my smile widen.

My mother and father stand there, looking slightly uncomfortable but happy, nonetheless. My relationship with my father is still tense, but having him here means a lot to me.

We're celebrating the birthday of Nord's heir, my daughter. *Daughter.* I never thought I'd have a wife, let alone a child. I thought I'd fill my life with work until I died. I thought I'd end up alone, because I never thought I could have true happiness.

But I'm here. I have it. All contained in Penelope's eyes...

...which I stare at for a few moments too long. Neva obviously gets impatient staring at the tower of sugar and deliciousness in front of her and tips her face forward.

Damn, this kid is strong for someone who was in the womb a year ago.

Her body pitches toward the cake, slipping out of my grasp. It happens in seconds, but it almost feels like I watch everything happen in slow motion. Neva's body leans forward as my hand slides over her front to try to catch her. Her little hands grab at the white cake in front of her, a gleeful, mischievous expression on her giggling face.

She gets it from her mother. I remember that exact face from our time in boarding school.

And my daughter's beautiful, cute, photo-ready, trouble-finding face?

It lands right on the top tier of the cake. Her hands smash into the second tier before I can pull her away. The kid is still freaking giggling. She leans her head back against my shoulder and stares at me, laughing. Her hairline is caked in frosting. Bits of cake cling to her forehead, her chubby little cheeks, her lips, her *eyelashes*.

My daughter, the future Queen of Nord, is covered in cake. She reaches for me, smearing cake all over my shirt and *still*, the girl is laughing.

And so is everyone else. Silas shouts, raising his glass, and everyone drinks to my daughter's cake-covered face.

"Neva." I sigh, reaching to wipe a glob of frosting and cake crumbs from her eyes.

Penelope appears beside me with a cloth, cleaning our daughter's face in moments. She purses her lips as she moves to the hands, flicking her eyes up to mine.

"What?" My voice rises a few octaves. "You're looking at me like this is my fault."

"Say cheese!" We both turn to see Wolfe with a phone in his hand pointed at us, grinning from ear to ear. He looks at the screen, tilting it toward Silas as they both burst out laughing. Penelope makes an exasperated noise, and Wolfe glances at her. "You'll be laughing about this your whole life, Pen. I'm just making sure you remember it."

"This cake was gifted to us by one of the local bakeries. What are we supposed to tell them?"

I shrug, licking frosting off my finger. "Tell them Neva loved it."

Finally, Penelope's lips tug ever so slightly into a smile. She flicks her eyes from me to Neva to continue cleaning the cake remnants off our daughter's face, but I catch her smile widening.

One of the castle staff members moves to the cake and starts cutting it, and another waiter refills everyone's glasses. I hold Neva still as Penelope does the last of the cleanup, then I lean over and catch my wife's lips in mine.

She softens against me, then smiles against my lips. "You're insufferable, Asher."

"Me?"

"Yes, you."

"I think you secretly love these moments. When you've slipped back into queen mode for too long, you need something like this to pull you out of it."

"Queen mode?" Penelope pops a brow.

My heart expands. Even when she's looking at me like she can't stand me, there's always a glimmer in her eye. I love this woman so much. I see her lead her country with determination and strength, then stand by my side and tell me *I'm* strong. She has no idea how much I admire her. "My queen," I answer, nuzzling my nose against hers.

Neva leans over and plants a sloppy kiss on her mother's cheek, softening the last of the ice from Penelope's features. Penelope takes Neva from my arms and snuggles our daughter close, taking a deep breath. "I can't believe you're one already, baby girl."

"Best year of my life." I reach over to tuck a strand of Penelope's golden hair behind her ear, leaning my forehead against hers. "Let's eat cake."

AFTER THE PARTY DIES DOWN, I find myself staring out one of the palace windows at the lawns surrounding us. A thick blanket of snow still covers everything here in March, but it's starting to melt. The days are getting longer, and I know my second winter in Nord will soon melt into spring.

It's...*home*. Even in the dead of winter, when we only had a couple of hours of daylight. Even when it was so cold outside my lungs felt like they were freezing solid, I still haven't felt the desire to go home.

Someone clears their throat behind me, and I turn to see my father in the doorway. He lifts up a glass of alcohol toward me and I nod, accepting it.

"Congratulations, Son. Neva's beautiful."

Son.

I let my lips slide into a smile. "Light of my life."

My father takes a sip of his drink, shifting his gaze to the window. The sun has sunk below the horizon, and the last few rays of light will soon fade. He turns to face me and holds out his hand for me to shake. "It's good to see you happy, Asher."

A lump lodges itself in my throat. I nod, shaking my father's hand, then try to wash down my emotion with a sip of alcohol—whiskey. Penelope's choice. Turns out she's right. I had terrible taste in whiskey.

"Dad," I start, my voice nothing more than a croak. "I wanted to say I'm sorry about everything that happened. Selling the mine in Roston..."

"It's okay," he says, surprising me. My father snorts,

shaking his head. "I asked you to close the merger with Donovan. I didn't ask you to start a new branch of the business." He shakes his head. "The things we do for love, huh? Did you know your grandfather didn't want me to marry your mother? He didn't speak to me from the day we got married to the day he died. It...it hurt your mother. I didn't want to put your wife through something similar."

"I didn't know," I rasp.

"It was before you were born." He looks in my eyes and nods. "You deserve to be happy."

Such simple words, but they shake me to my core. I'd always looked at my father as a businessman before anything else, as ruthless as I'd aspired to be. I never thought of him as anything more. I'd never thought of him as a man who might *feel.*

He shakes his head. "The older I get, the more I realize I might have been stupid to spend so much time at work. I'm nearly seventy now, watching you and Logan grow up and move away, and it makes me think maybe I got everything all wrong."

"Dad..."

"Asher, just promise me you'll give that little girl all your time. You won't forget that she's the most important thing in your life." His eyes shine as he meets my gaze, lips pursing as if he's trying to contain a torrent of emotions.

I put my glass down on a side table and wrap my father in a hug. It's unfamiliar—I'm not sure I've hugged him since I was a child—but after a few seconds he wraps his arms around me and pats my back. We pull away, both clearing our throats, and my father finishes his drink and nods. He walks away without another word, and I let out a long sigh.

Penelope enters the room a few moments later, tilting her head. "Everything okay?"

I smile, opening my arms for her to come to me. She nuzzles against my chest, head over my scarred skin, and wraps her arms around my waist.

"Everything's fine," I finally answer, resting my chin on her head. "I think my father might actually agree with my decision to stay here."

"It's Neva," Penelope says, pulling away to smile at me. "He couldn't resist her. Next thing he'll be spoiling her rotten."

I laugh, shaking my head. "I'm not sure he's the spoiling type."

"Just wait, Asher. Babies have power over grumpy, old men."

I grunt, smiling. "And you have power over me."

She laughs, rising up onto her toes to lay a soft kiss on my lips. "Let's go to bed, husband. I want to show you how much I love you."

My wife—my queen, the love of my life—takes me by the hand and leads me through the silent castle halls to our bedroom.

She doesn't get the chance to show me anything, though, because I lay her down and show her just what she means to me again, and again, and again.

Maybe I'm hoping for another baby, or maybe I just can't get enough of Penelope. Either way, I'll die happy if I get to prove my love to her every night for the rest of my life.

~

Keep reading for a preview of Book 9: Rogue Prince!

ROGUE PRINCE

ROYALLY UNEXPECTED: BOOK NINE

JAZZ

ADJUSTING the pink pig's snout strapped to my nose, I throw a sideways glance at my best friend. "Was this really the only Halloween costume left?"

Rhea's lips tug into a shit-eating grin. "You flaked on me at the last minute to go shopping, so I guess you'll never know the answer to that question."

"I was *working*. You know I leave for the royal tour next week." I touch the snout again, pulling the elastic digging into my cheeks as it holds the snout in place. "I'm the youngest journalist on tour, Rhea, and the only one who's come out openly against monarchy in Nord. I need to be prepared for everything. I'm not expecting Prince Wolfe to be friendly with me when we get on that plane."

"Yes, Jazzypants, I know. How could I forget that my best friend is the badass known as Jacinthe Crawley? The journalist who takes no prisoners and says exactly what she wants with no fear of retribution." Rhea reaches over to pinch my bony hip. "The woman who somehow *forgets to eat*, which is entirely beyond my ability to comprehend."

I dodge her hand and swat it away. "I eat plenty. Maybe I

forget to have lunch once in a while when I'm busy with work." I stare pointedly at my friend. "Like when I'm preparing for the biggest assignment of my career, for example, and don't have time to go costume shopping for a party I never even wanted to go to in the first place."

"Sounds horrible. All the more reason to take an evening off and come out with me. You'll be gone for three whole months. How will I cope?" My best friend pouts at me in the mirror, putting a hand on her wide hip. No boniness there, only lush, womanly curves.

Rhea's been by my side since we were college roommates at eighteen, and every Halloween she seems to somehow convince me to dress like an idiot. I turn back to the mirror hanging by my front door, checking how my black, slinky dress looks in the back, then grimacing when I see the way my spine protrudes, every vertebrae clearly visible all the way up to my neck. Maybe Rhea's right—I need to work less and eat more. I shift my cheap, synthetic wig so it falls in shiny yellow curls halfway down my back. At least that'll hide the worst of the boniness. Huffing, I scratch my scalp. "This wig is itchy. I don't think I'm meant to be a blonde."

"Do you ever stop complaining?" Rhea laughs, adjusting her bra to make sure her generous chest is on full display. Dressed as a sexy version of the Queen of Hearts, Rhea is a total knockout. Her tight leather miniskirt hugs her in all the right places, complemented by the strategically placed playing cards glued to her bodice.

At least I know I'll be able to follow the trail of male drool to find her if I get lost at this dumb party.

"Ironic that I'm the Queen of Hearts when you're the one who keeps screaming, 'Off with their heads.'" Rhea's eyes twinkle as she meets my gaze. "I saw your article online today. You made the homepage of the *Stirling Times* website."

I wave a hand. "The monarchy is an outdated institution, and I'll never stop talking about how it should be abolished." Letting my gaze drift from her costume to mine, I frown. "I find it hard to believe there was no sexy Alice costume to match yours."

"I find it hard to believe you would disrespect Miss Piggy by being so upset about representing her," Rhea counters. She arches an eyebrow, light twinkling off her glittery red eyeshadow. "Who knows? Maybe you'll find your Kermit tonight."

I snort, the sound more pig-like than I intended. "Doubtful."

"With that attitude, it is." Rhea hooks her arm through mine, laughing. "Come on. No more grumpiness. You're done working for the day. Leave all your stress at the office, Jazz. It's Halloween! We're dressed up, on our way to the wildest party in Nord. You can hook up with a man dressed up like a Smurf and wake up covered in blue body paint, then go back to work on Monday and pretend it never happened. You can *live* tonight."

I grumble in response, but a hint of a grin tugs at my lips.

Rhea doesn't miss the half-smile. She laughs, nudging me with her shoulder. "See? I knew you needed a night out. You can go back to being the serious journalist when you get on that royal jet for the tour. Your boss has been too hard on you lately."

"He's just doing his job."

"He's treating you like a robot instead of a person. You've written more articles about abolishing the monarchy in the past six weeks than any other journalist has in their whole life. I think it's affecting the way you look at this country. You think it's all going to fall apart just because our head of state is the Queen."

"If we were a republic, we could govern ourselves."

"Ugh, forget I said anything." Rhea flicks the tip of my pig's snout. "Tonight, we focus on finding you a man with a very large, thick, throbbing—"

"Rhea!"

My best friend laughs as a car honks outside. "Cab's here," she says, tugging my hand toward the door. "You'll thank me tomorrow."

"For what?"

"For pulling you away from your computer, for once."

I let Rhea lead me outside, knowing what she's actually doing when she's dragging me to this Halloween party. This weekend is the anniversary of my father's death, and every year I bury myself in work to forget how much it hurts. Somehow, Rhea always manages to pierce through my shell. This year, it was the promise of a massive Halloween party and weeks—*weeks*—of pestering me to go with her.

As we step outside, a blast of cold air makes me hug my jacket tighter. I exhale sharply and shuffle to the waiting taxi. The weather has already turned in Nord, and soon the whole kingdom will be covered in snow.

Nord is an arctic country, north of Canada. Winters are long here, but they're beautiful. There's something special about the silence of a land smothered in snow for months at a time, the life that thrives in a place as inhospitable as this.

Right now, my existence feels less like thriving and more like *clinging on for dear life.*

We slide into the cab and I touch the ring on the middle finger of my right hand. My father's ring. It's always been loose, and twisting it around my finger brings me comfort. I know I should get it resized, but the thought of handing it over to a jeweler makes my stomach knot. I keep meaning to

buy a chain for it so I can wear it around my neck, but I just...
I haven't gotten around to it.

So, slightly oversized and not exactly my taste, but it's on
my finger—always. A little gold ball sits on the band,
surrounded by twelve tiny diamonds. Running my finger over
the band, then the ball, then each of the diamonds, I stare out
the window. I twist the ring around my finger once, then do it
all over again. Band, ball, diamonds, twist. Band, ball,
diamonds, twist.

It's soothing.

My father received the ring for thirty years of service at
Lord Birchal's manor. Thirty years tending Birchal's gardens
and maintaining the huge mansion. My father managed the
house and land for a man who called him the wrong name
for every one of those thirty years—every time Birchal said
Mr. Crawford instead of *Mr. Crawley*, I wanted to scream, but
Dad said nothing. He stood there, head bowed, answering to
the wrong name.

All those decades, he toiled while Birchal and his family
sat on their plush cushions and waited for their breakfasts to
be delivered in bed. My father worked himself to the bone,
waking up at dawn every single day, never taking a day off—
and for what?

For a ring? For a man who was supposedly noble but
couldn't find his way out of a bathtub without the help of a
servant?

The fact that my father prized this ring above everything
else infuriated me. He never realized that this ring was
nothing but a symbol of our servitude. It was a shackle
around his finger, chaining him to his lord.

When my father gave me the ring on his deathbed, I
wanted to hurl it at Lord Birchal's face, or shove it down his
son's throat. Sniveling, lying Liam Birchal, who promised me

the world then pretended he'd never said a word. I don't know if my hatred for the monarchy started with my father's treatment by Lord Birchal or after what happened between me and his son.

But Dad had stared at me, his withering body too weak to do anything but wheeze. He patted my hand with cold fingers and forced his lips into a smile. "Take care of your mother, Jazz. She only has you, now."

I'd nodded, holding back the river of tears threatening to spill onto my cheeks. I would have promised anything.

Watching my father die with no one but me beside him, I wanted to wring the Queen's neck for letting this happen. I wanted to set the capital city on fire and show all those monarchist assholes what they'd done to him. *They* did this. *They* worked him too hard. *They* made him forget to take care of himself and stole all the years we could have had together.

They didn't even come to the hospital to pay their respects.

Yes, I wanted to kill them all. But all I did was take the ring and cry—then I wiped my cheeks and started writing about abolishing the monarchy.

Band, ball, diamonds, twist.

"Hey," Rhea says, sliding her hand over mine to stop the movement of my fingers. "You okay?"

Pinching my lips into a smile, I nod. "Yeah. Fine." I slip my hands under my thighs to stop fidgeting.

"I was thinking tomorrow we could go up to the ridge on Treo Mountain to that spot where we scattered your dad's ashes. I bought candles and flowers this morning—we could have a little memorial." She looks at me, eyes soft.

My heart thumps as emotion wells up inside me. Rhea planned that for me? She remembered the exact day of my father's passing and went out of her way to do something? I...

I don't deserve her as a friend. She's too good. She puts up with me working all the time and giving her scraps of my attention, then goes and does something like this for me.

Rhea's lips curl as she arches her eyebrows. "Plus, the hike up to the ridge will help with the hangover."

"I'm not planning on being hungover tomorrow."

"That makes one of us."

I laugh, leaning over to lay my head on her shoulder. Rhea rests her cheek on top of my head, and a tiny bit of tension is released from my body. The space between my shoulder blades eases ever so slightly, and I let myself actually see the landscape passing us by.

I love my country. My family has lived in Nord for hundreds of years, and I feel the pulse of this place in my veins. We're in the outskirts of the city, where suburbs yield to pine trees and the wilderness starts to stake its claim on the land.

"Where is this party, again?"

"The old Velly watermill," Rhea replies. "They've refurbished it."

"Who?"

"Whoever planned this party," Rhea laughs, shrugging. "All I know is I got an invite, and it's supposed to be insane."

"I don't know why I let you drag me to these kinds of things."

"It's because you secretly-not-so-secretly love it, and you love me, and you love being dragged out of your boring, lame existence. You pretend you enjoy writing all those depressing revolutionary articles, but a big part of you just wants to say *fuck it* and actually live a little."

"Wow. Don't hold back, Rhea." I pretend to roll my eyes, and I can't help but laugh. "Savage."

"I only speak the truth."

"Mm." I sit up just as the taxi turns off the main road onto a narrow gravel laneway. Tall pine trees stand straight in thick bunches on either side of the road, with a few deciduous trees sprinkled in between.

My chest tightens as music thumps in the distance, and Rhea lets out an excited giggle. "This is going to be fun."

I don't answer. The taxi pulls up to a large timber building. The huge waterwheel pokes over the back of it, light spilling from every window. Plastic skeletons and jack-o-lanterns litter the front lawn, with scarecrows sitting on either side of the entrance like guards.

Rhea hands the driver a few bills as we exit the car, then comes around the back of the taxi to stand beside me. "Are you excited?"

I force a smile. "Very."

It's... mostly true. I haven't been to a party in a long time. Last year, Rhea convinced me to go to a bar for Halloween and I stayed for all of one hour. A party like this? It's been *years*. I'm not one for crowds, to start, and this particular weekend is always difficult. But Rhea is here, and she's right. I need to loosen up.

So, I touch the tip of my pink snout, smooth my hands over the top of my wig, and let Rhea lead me to the front door.

A bouncer dressed in all black stands next to the porch stairs, holding out a hand. Rhea produces her phone, taps on it a few times, and spins it toward him. Our invitations are displayed on the screen for the bouncer to check. He nods, then steps aside.

Music blares when we open the door, a crush of bodies visible just beyond the threshold to the next room. To our left, a bar is set up with bartenders wearing nothing but black pants and bow ties. The female bartenders have tight black miniskirts on, complete with black cat ears on their heads.

I sweep my gaze toward the crowd on the dance floor. A Sasquatch and his sexy park ranger girlfriend grind their bodies together on the dance floor. A man in a skeleton costume with his mask pushed up over his head tips a brown bottle toward his lips. A group of women dressed as various animals—well, they're wearing headbands with ears—make their way to the middle of the dance floor amidst screams and laughter.

It's...gosh, I don't even know. It feels like college again. At twenty-eight, I think I might be too old for this. Rhea takes my hand and drags me to the left. She takes my jacket off and hands it to a woman running the coat check line, then pulls me toward the bar.

"Two vodka sodas please, gorgeous." Rhea smiles at the tall, sandy-haired man behind the bar. He nods, pouring us our drinks within seconds.

Another man—tall, dark-skinned, and dressed like Zorro—slides over to Rhea with a troublemaking grin on his face. "Didn't think I'd see you here, Rhea." He takes her hand in his and lays a soft kiss on her fingers. "Looking delicious as usual."

Rhea throws me a glance over her shoulder, winks, and leads the man to the dance floor. I'm left standing there, drink in hand, with music pounding in my ears.

The dance floor looks...busy. I shudder. Instead of heading across the foyer toward it, I walk along the bar and deeper into the building, poking my head into various rooms. The whole place is decorated with cobwebs, spooky lighting, skeletons leaning against corners. A woman in a witch's costume falls out of a broom closet, arms wrapped around a guy in a wig. I don't know what his costume is supposed to be, because he's mostly not wearing anything at all.

Swerving out of the way, I spill my drink down my front. "*Shit.*" I brush my hand over the wet patch on my dress. My steps lead me to a door at the back of the building, and when I spill out into the cool air, I let out a long breath.

That's better.

I look over my shoulder through a window to see a second dance room set up at the back of the building. The people inside move as one mass, grinding and flailing to the loud music. Gulping down half my drink, I turn to look at the countryside in front of me.

It's quiet here, apart from the raging party behind me. I take a few steps, feet crunching on dry leaves. A wooden deck extends toward the edge of the building, with a handrail blocking access to the creek running along the side of the exterior wall. I lean on the handrail, putting my drink on its flat surface, and let my eyes drift over the huge, stationary waterwheel to my right. My eyes follow the line of the creek below the deck. The water level is low, with tall rushes lining the bank on either side.

Band, ball, diamonds, twist. I'm definitely too old to be here. Maybe there are people my age in there, but their souls are younger than mine. They don't carry the kind of burdens I do.

I let out a long breath, letting my thoughts drift to my father.

I miss him. Dad was my favorite person in the whole world. He was my own personal superhero, able to fix anything he laid his hands on. He made my world brighter. His laugh was big and unrestrained, and his hugs felt like a warm, cozy blanket on a cold winter's day.

He took care of Mom after her diagnosis, his movements

quiet and soft whenever he had to go near her. The love he had for her made my heart ache. My father's strength took many forms, none stronger than the way he cared for my mother.

But when his head was bowed in front of Lord Birchal or another member of the supposed elite, he looked small. He didn't see himself as worthy of their presence, which I never understood. Dad was worth a thousand Birchals.

A messy lump of emotion lodges itself in my throat. My eyes mist, vision blurs. The music is still loud, thumping in my ear to the beat of my heart. I lift one hand to wipe my eyes, letting the other hand dangle over the edge of the handrail.

Thoughts rage inside me so loud that I barely feel the whisper of the ring as it slides down my middle finger. Barely realize it slips off until it touches the tip of my finger, disappearing into the darkness below.

Gone.

Just as my grief for my father starts to overwhelm me, the last piece I have of him drops from my hand. A cry escapes my lips as I brush my palms over my eyes, panic welling up inside my throat. My hands are covered in black smears from my makeup, but I don't care. Fingers wrap around the handrail as I struggle to clear my blurry vision. Breaths are short, sharp.

I can't lose it. Can't let it leave me forever. I *can't*.

That ring represents my father. It's the last thing I have. It's the only piece of jewelry I wear. The only thing I always have. *Always*.

As my vision clears, tears falling to the darkness below, I look over the edge of the handrail as panic winds around my chest. I need to find it. Need to see a little glimmer of gold in the rushes. *Need*.

I knew I shouldn't have come to this stupid party. I should have spent the weekend at the office or buried under my blankets with a tub of ice cream to keep me company.

Not here—not in some part of the countryside I don't know, where my father's ring will be gone forever. My chest feels tight. My breaths are staggered, and it's hard for me to piece my thoughts together. Panic blares in my blood, pumping ice-cold through my body.

I can't even move. My eyes try to focus on the rushes below for a glimpse of gold, but...when did it get so hard to breathe?

Finally, piercing through the fear gripping my body, a voice sounds behind me. Deep, masculine, with a hint of amusement. "Didn't think I'd find you here, Miss Piggy."

Turning to see the source of the voice, I almost cackle. I'm unhinged. I *want* to laugh, if only to release some of the tension winding around my throat. Rhea would. Did she set this up? I wouldn't put it past her.

Standing on the edge of the wooden platform overlooking the creek is none other than Kermit the Frog.

Well, it would be Kermit if Kermit were drop-dead gorgeous.

He's wearing a crisp green tuxedo jacket with a mask covering his face. The jacket is cut in a way so the lapels look like Kermit's collar, and there's no mistaking the particular shade of green. Dark hair curls around the edges of the mask, and his eyes—

For just a second, I forget about my panic. I forget about my ring, about everything wrong with this weekend. I forget about the fact that I'm going to have to spend three months away from home, away from my mother, away from everything that feels familiar.

Deep, piercing blue, this man's eyes look like they'd

promise me the world, and I'd believe them. He takes a step toward me, each movement purposeful. Powerful. Lethal.

The man is wearing a green tux and a frog mask, yet everything inside me tightens. It's... It must be the panic making me feel this way. I'm emotional. It's not him. My lips part, but my mouth is too dry to say anything.

He closes the distance between us, saying nothing, then reaches up and wipes his thumb over my cheek. It comes away black with smudged mascara. Tilting his head, he searches my face. "What's wrong, princess?"

That voice... I've heard that voice before. I know it. It sends an echo deep into my soul as an ache pulses between my legs. He's familiar in a way I've never felt before. I *know* him.

I can't think straight.

I close my eyes, dropping my head. I shake it as I gather myself, willing my voice to work. "I'm fine." It's a squeaky croak, sounding more like Miss Piggy than I could if I tried.

There it is again—his finger. The pad of his thumb swipes across my other cheek and I find myself exhaling as I tilt my head up toward him. Opening my eyes, I stare at the man.

"I'll ask you again," he says quietly, the noise of the music fading into nothing. There's no one here but us. Everything seems to melt away except the feeling of his hand cupping my face, his body so close to mine. He smells like...what is it? Like *man*. Like sweet, spicy musk. I can't think of anything except how good it feels to have him this close to me. He dips his head closer, lips just an inch from mine. "What's wrong, princess?"

Get Rogue Prince on www.lilianmonroe.com

ALSO BY LILIAN MONROE

For all books, visit:

www.lilianmonroe.com

Brother's Best Friend Romance

Shouldn't Want You

Can't Have You

Don't Need You

Won't Miss You

Military Romance

His Vow

His Oath

His Word

The Complete Protector Series

Enemies to Lovers Romance

Hate at First Sight

Loathe at First Sight

Despise at First Sight

The Complete Love/Hate Series

Secret Baby/Accidental Pregnancy Romance:

Knocked Up by the CEO

Knocked Up by the Single Dad

Knocked Up…Again!

Knocked Up by the Billionaire's Son

The Complete Unexpected Series

Yours for Christmas

Bad Prince

Heartless Prince

Cruel Prince

Broken Prince

Wicked Prince

Wrong Prince

Lone Prince

Ice Queen

Rogue Prince

Fake Engagement/ Fake Marriage Romance:

Engaged to Mr. Right

Engaged to Mr. Wrong

Engaged to Mr. Perfect

Mr Right: The Complete Fake Engagement Series

Mountain Man Romance:

Lie to Me

Swear to Me

Run to Me

The Complete Clarke Brothers Series

Extra-Steamy Rock Star Romance:

Garrett

Maddox

Carter

The Complete Rock Hard Series

<u>Sexy Doctors:</u>

Doctor O

Doctor D

Doctor L

The Complete Doctor's Orders Series

<u>Time Travel Romance:</u>

The Cause

<u>A little something different:</u>

Second Chance: A Rockstar Romance in North Korea